LEE COUNTY LIBRARY
107 Hawkins Ave.
Sanford, N. C. 27330

A SLOW SUICIDE

Books by William Jovanovich

Now, Barabbas
Madmen Must
The Money Trail
The World's Last Night
A Slow Suicide

A SLOW SUICIDE

·

WILLIAM JOVANOVICH

LEE COUNTY LIBRARY
107 Hawkins Ave.
Sanford, N. C. 27330

Harcourt Brace Jovanovich, Publishers

SAN DIEGO   NEW YORK   LONDON

HBJ

Copyright © 1991 by William Jovanovich

All rights reserved. No part of this publication
may be reproduced or transmitted in any form or
by any means, electronic or mechanical, including
photocopy, recording, or any information storage
and retrieval system, without permission in
writing from the publisher.

Requests for permission to make copies of any
part of the work should be mailed to:
Permissions Department, Harcourt Brace Jovanovich, Publishers,
Orlando, Florida 32887.

Library of Congress Cataloging-in-Publication Data
Jovanovich, William.
A slow suicide/William Jovanovich.—1st ed.
p.   cm.
ISBN 0-15-183095-9
I. Title.
PS3560.084S5   1991
813'.54—dc20   90-40056

Designed by Trina Stahl

Printed in the United States of America

First edition

A B C D E

A SLOW
SUICIDE

CHAPTER ONE

T HE STORY OF MARK PETRIE BEGINS WITH A MAN HE NEVER met, a small-time grifter, a man who took an enormous leap but didn't land. After serving three years in Dannemora Prison for auto theft, Terry Dunn reported to a parole officer in his hometown of Yonkers, New York; and at the station house there met a police sergeant who, after observing Terry over several months, decided to trust him to take part in a few heists the sergeant had meticulously laid out. One of these jobs especially impressed Terry, who was teamed up with two men whose true names he never knew—the sergeant was canny enough not to form a team that could proceed without him. From a mansion in nearby Pelham, the three of them loaded rugs, silver, jewelry, and TVs and stereos into a truck that was itself stolen, and the truck and contents were together delivered to a Puerto Rican fence in the Bronx, in a continuous transaction that took but three hours door to door.

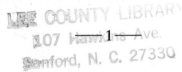
LEE COUNTY LIBRARY
107 Hawkins Ave.
Sanford, N. C. 27330

1

His parole up, Terry left for Durham, North Carolina, to live with his married sister and there met a trucker who showed him how to carry to North Jersey loads of contraband cigarettes—packs not bearing the federal and state tax stamps that constitute 80 percent of the wholesale cost of a smoke. The large gross revenue surprised Terry, but so did the expenses: to rent an eighteen-wheel trailer truck for three days cost twelve thousand dollars. If the two of them could put only twenty-five thousand down on a secondhand rig, they could own it within a year. What Terry needed was a large score. It was like any other business where you need a loan to get going.

One day the sergeant phoned Terry long-distance—out of the blue. "Call me from a pay phone at this number in an hour," he told him. Once they were both talking from public booths, the sergeant continued:"I hear you want to own a rig."

"Somebody from Yonkers is down here?"

"I hear all kinds of things, there and here, and one is about a job that pays twenty-five Gs to you and twenty-five to me."

"You're kidding! Nobody pays that much. Not even to ice a guy."

"You got it. It's a hit, an easy one. An old man in a hospital."

"Jesus! I don't even carry a piece. You told me not to. From the start, you told me."

"You don't need a piece. All you need is a pillow. There's one on his bed. Fifty Gs. Your own rig. Twenty-five Gs to you."

Terry looked down at the veins bulging in his wrist from his tight grip on the receiver. Killing was altogether another matter and, to his mind, had nothing to do with business— only with insults, feuds, and war. His voice cracked as he objected. "Man, this is heavy. I don't know. I got to think."

"Let me tell you how it is with thinking." The sergeant

was serious here, generalizing from long experience. "On big things, you make up your mind fast. On little things, like buying a mattress or car cover, you take your time."

Terry was astonished to hear himself confess, "Jesus, I'm only a thief."

"I know who you are. This is a promotion. Yes or no?"

Terry swallowed. He finally said, "Yes."

"Here's a number. Call it and a man will tell you where to meet him. Friday morning is when you call, in New York, at exactly nine o'clock. I'll send him your photo."

"No. Just tell him what I look like. I don't want my picture ending up in a New York City police file."

The sergeant was impressed: the kid had picked up some smarts while down south. "He needs to know it's you for sure."

"Then give him a code word."

"That's kid stuff."

"So? Tell him I'll say Dannemora."

The sergeant laughed. "That's a name you're not likely to forget. Now, listen up. Don't fly. Don't leave any name on a computer. And when you drive, use four wheels, not eighteen. You get my drift?"

It *was* possible to undertake shady business with someone without obtaining an obvious or positive identification of him. In fact, the cop in Yonkers had exchanged a couple of favors with Roger Fredson yet had never met him. One time, when the cop had stopped a car that on a cursory search turned out to hold a lot of cash, the driver, before he was booked, had asked the sergeant to make the legally mandated single telephone call for him. On the other end of the line was Fredson. After both car and driver were immediately released, ten thousand dollars in used twenties was mailed in a shoe box to the sergeant's home address. A year later, Fredson telephoned him in aid of another attorney whose client in New York had been charged with murder one. The sergeant had researched the "open files" in Yonkers and found an armed robbery that had occurred on the same day as the murder; and after bribing a local hood to testify, he had put through an arrest warrant. The attorney seized on the coincidence of dates and succeeded in having a Westchester County court try the defendant, who was convicted of robbery and sentenced to ten years at Attica, eligible for parole in five. Fifteen thousand dollars came in the mail early on, another ten thousand when the Attica doors closed.

Now, Fredson wanted a lot and was willing to pay a lot. It was proposed that fifteen thousand, plus a thousand for expenses, be paid to Dunn when he showed up. The remaining thirty-five thousand would go to Yonkers when the job was done. The sergeant was willing to accept these terms because he didn't want Terry to quibble over his advance. But, having urged Terry to think fast on big things, he'd unwittingly found a convert. The advance was enough, Terry decided, only if the deal went through. What if, on arriving in New York, he was told that the victim had gone home or died? He could hardly strong-arm the middleman over the telephone! So it was that Terry decided to truck a load of cigarettes to Newark as insurance.

All went well until, at the highway weigh station near Trenton, the scale showed four hundred pounds more than the manifest. Terry's truck registration, driver's license, and liability insurance were all in order; and, as usual, the cigarette packs in the top rows of cartons near the rear doors carried the required number of stamps. But the weight discrepancy made the station officers curious; and a search revealed that Terry was the victim of a scam quite apart from his own. Somebody had loaded among the cartons two-pound cans of coffee heavily laced with high-grade hashish—coffee aroma ostensibly throws off police dogs trained to sniff out dope. Terry had unwittingly been the "mule" for drug dealers. And of course the stampless cartons were also discovered in the search.

It was a possible narcotics rap that sent Terry into panic. He could stand a federal charge on transporting contraband— legal goods except for the lack of stamps—but narcotics carried big sentences, up to twenty years in the joint. He stammered and wept and finally begged the agent in the Trenton FBI office to allow him to trade information for the promise of a reduced sentence. Mostly, he wanted to stay out of the dread hands of the narcs, the DEA. Given encouragement but no guarantees, he confessed that he'd been told of a hit and a telephone number in Manhattan he was to call. He refused to say how he had been commissioned. When asked if a photograph had been furnished, he was proud to say that a description of himself was all that had been furnished, but in his self-congratulation forgot to mention the password.

The FBI ran the telephone number through its Washington equipment and found, as expected, that it was a "black box" relay that sent the originally dialed number to terminate silently at four different receivers before it rang at the fifth. For this number, the name of Roger Fredson was extracted from the computer for identification purposes. That ran up a red flag: "Call Commission. Do not log. Erase this inquiry." Within an hour, an inspector from the Commission took charge of Terry. But he was not booked. The Commission carried a very big stick branded "The White House."

In Southeast Washington at its headquarters in Anacostia, when the Commission received the information on Terry Dunn, Tannenbaum, the Chief of Operations, was immediately struck by Terry's physical similarity, in size and coloring and facial features, to a commission inspector—a CI—named Mark Petrie. It was a fateful serendipity, so unusual and so timely that Tannenbaum took it to the Commissioner himself.

As for Terry Dunn, his biography was of no further interest to anyone but himself. Yet it must have struck the God of Thieves that it was a pity of sorts that a man who had been adjured to think big was never to know he had stumbled into a caper so huge that it soon moved nations and changed history.

For a mere moment, Mark Petrie didn't recognize his own boss, the Commission's Chief of Operations. Petrie nervously recalled a joke about a man in a theater who starts up the aisle at intermission and sees ahead someone entirely familiar but whose name escapes him. Embarrassed, he decides to brass it out. "How are you? You staying in town or traveling again?" The second man says, "Don't be silly. I'm your dentist." Petrie had never before seen Tannenbaum standing up and thus had only guessed at his height; and he'd never seen the Chief's bald head covered by a hat. On all previous occasions when Tannenbaum had personally briefed him, they had driven about Washington or Silver Spring, Maryland. Now, walking on Fifty-seventh Street in Manhattan, they were able to converse unobtrusively by staying four feet apart and not keeping stride. Tannenbaum was Petrie's height, six feet three, but thin and stooped.

"For Shurtz, it's new, isn't it, using violence?" Petrie said. "I read the file. His connection to the Mafia isn't much for them, a side dish, really. Shurtz has apparently never even carried a gun."

"He's getting old and can't abide the prospect of spending twenty years in prison. He's got to silence Hentleman, his bookkeeper, whose records show the payments to those six customs officials we identified who looked the other way when

Shurtz smuggled in those anabolic steroids and Pentamidine, among other drugs."

"The steroids crossed the border at San Diego?"

"He was buying from a plant in Tijuana once owned by the Panamanian boss, Noriega. Pentamidine he gets from the U.K. It's the antipneumonia drug for AIDS patients."

Petrie was wearing a cheap leather jacket, a baseball cap, chinos, a plaid shirt, thick-soled Thom McAn shoes, and a day's beard. His impersonation was superficial; all depended on whether Fredson saw in his face and body a likeness to Terry Dunn.

His hands were in the jacket pockets and his head down when he asked, "What's the point of my impersonation?"

"Hentleman wants more money to testify. If we simulate the hit, his grown sons and his brother will surely force him to give in straight away."

"Will his relatives be in the room?"

"No, just the patient and another CI. He'll disarm you. The relatives will be summoned from the solarium. The CI will have an extra twenty-two automatic that he'll later say was taken from you. It's safer that way."

"Safer for whom?"

Petrie had never before been so relentless in asking about an assignment. But then, never before had the Chief come into the field, in fact right onto the street.

"Hentleman is dying," Petrie said. It was not a question.

A whole block was traversed. The silence oppressed Tannenbaum and caused him to reveal more than he would normally have been inclined to. "Shurtz may be smart enough to fear a deathbed confession. When I taught law"—Petrie almost stopped suddenly on hearing this from an executive of an organization devoted to anonymity and secrecy—"I told my students that in canon law a dying man is held to be truthful because he seeks grace, whereas in civil law it's presumed that he has nothing to gain from lying with his last breath."

This commentary put between them a distance of the sort that separates teacher from pupil. Petrie accepted that Tannenbaum would say no more right now. They parted.

On Forty-seventh Street just off Fifth, Petrie entered a building that was a narrow stack of floors serviced by a tiny elevator. When at nine o'clock he had called the number furnished by the real Dunn, he had been told the address and instructed to push the blank elevator button above "6." He emerged from the elevator into a small entry whose only other exit was an office door. It opened before he could press the buzzer. Before him stood a slender man of about forty-five wearing a Turnbull and Asser shirt and a three-piece suit. Beyond, Petrie saw that the room was sparsely furnished, containing only four armchairs facing a lacquered table and, against one wall, an old-fashioned cocktail bar. Fredson shut the door and picked up from the table a small cassette player, turning up the volume to create "white noise," making conversation comprehensible but not reproducible. For what seemed a whole minute Fredson looked away, as if preparing to make a momentous remark. He coughed, cleared his throat, and adjusted the already perfect knot of his tie.

"I get it," Petrie said. "We wait long enough for the guy to die of old age. You never ordered a hit before, right?"

"Give me the code word."

"Are you kidding?" Petrie said quickly, caught on the blind side. "You want me to ice some guy in a hospital but first we play word games? Cut the shit. I want twenty up front, plus the thousand for expenses."

"Twenty? Your boss in Yonkers said fifteen."

"Well, I'm not in Yonkers. I'm here. And this place looks to me rented by the hour."

Petrie was relieved to be arguing about money because it was getting them past the tricky parts, the code word and the "boss in Yonkers" of which he knew nothing. It wasn't like the Commission to have slipped up this way. Of course, it wasn't like the Commission to playact a murder, either. Today was unique.

Fredson frowned, turning over Petrie's last comment like a silver dealer looking for a sterling mark. Then he resumed on what he hoped was a less contentious note. "It's Harkness Pavilion, Room 901. That's the private wing of Columbia Presbyterian Hospital. The man is a patient, name of Hentleman."

"What? A *private* hospital? That means it's small! Shit. No way. Too many security eyes."

"Now don't get funny. I've been there and the Pavilion is like an airport, with lots of people around."

"Twenty. That's it. You pay up or get yourself another boy."

Fredson, looking at Petrie's cheap pants and dirty fingernails and ashamed to be bargaining over a man's life, wanted the transaction to conclude. He rose and walked to the cocktail sideboard, reached inside to pluck out sheaves of hundred-dollar bills, holding these by the edges, leaving no prints. His client, Shurtz, had prudently expected that Fredson might be pressed for more money.

"It's twenty. Count it somewhere else. Two things, Dunn. I never saw you. This office is used by three professional persons and not one of them has ever been served with anything—not even a parking ticket. The people hiring you want it done within the next six hours. And if you fail, these people will make you pay back more than the money."

"That's four things."

The ride down in the tiny elevator caused Petrie to recall his days working at Pooley, an engineering company whose offices on Madison Avenue were in a building owned by the late and still legendary real-estate tycoon, William Zeckendorf. One night a junior officer had given him a tour of Zeckendorf's office and they had ascended in a four-passenger elevator rounded and shiny like the inside of a beer can. A huge desk dominated a circular room and under the desktop were buttons that controlled floodlights shining down from the ceiling. The tour guide had said slyly that when Zeckendorf was selling, he turned on red-hued lights to excite the buyer, but when he was buying released a flood of depressing blue. How come, Petrie had asked, playing it straight, the great man wasn't himself affected by the lights? The answer was ready: "He's a very tolerant guy. Color makes no difference to him."

That had been long ago, and now was no time for the romance of business. He stood in a phone booth saying, "Mrs. Alberts, this is me again. I was to call at three." The sequence depended on the number of calls made within a twenty-four-hour period. Thirty seconds elapsed while his voice, recorded, was compared with a voice print on file. "I'll be on Thirty-fourth Street, walking east from Sixth. Forty minutes."

"Fredson is in a great hurry. He didn't argue when I demanded twenty," he reported to Tannenbaum as they resumed walking. "What if Hentleman dies before I appear?"

"Hentleman's relatives will be just as shocked by a late attempt as by one made on time."

"Do *they* know where he's hidden his records?"

"I'm sure they do. A bookkeeper wouldn't be careless about files."

"It seems elaborate, Chief."

"That could be. But then, gaining evidence against corrupt officials isn't simply one, two, three. Crooks in public office learn to disguise the trails of their graft. Ours is not a simple profession. We guard against the guardians. You heard me give the original Latin, no doubt, when I lectured to your class of recruits. Ten years ago, was it?"

Petrie couldn't think of a countering argument. Simulating the murder of a man wasn't day-to-day work, after all. He'd never before heard of such during his ten years as a CI. He'd never made an arrest—U.S. marshals were called in to do that, usually—and had fired his automatic for real but twice.

At Second Avenue, Tannenbaum turned aside and halfway down the block entered a dark sedan. Petrie saw the Chief bend his figure as if he were in prayer or pain, but of course he was only minding his head—and the hat.

CHAPTER TWO

F ROM THE TRUNK OF A RENTED HERTZ CAR PETRIE TOOK A
suitcase. Then, crouched in the backseat, he changed into a
white shirt, plain tie, and blue-striped suit. He hadn't told
Tannenbaum he was planning to change clothes and was
doing so only to give himself better odds of not being accosted
when he entered Harkness Pavilion from the Fort Washington
Avenue entrance.

Eleven years earlier he had himself been a patient here. An
old nurse had told him that little had changed since the 1930s.
Those days, she would see the relatives and legatees of the sick
and dying alight from their LaSalles and Pierce Arrows under
the splendid bronze portico. No such sights occurred nowadays. An intern who happened also to be a gifted musician had
been killed by a mugger within sight of the portico. Now, security guards were everywhere and ID tags required of visitors.

Petrie entered through a side door used by employees and

stepped around a huge woman with a wig like a beaver hat who was arguing with a clerk seated behind a glass booth. He passed unnoticed into a corridor where signs pointed one way to "Radiology" and, opposite, to "Service Elevator." He took the elevator to the eighth floor to verify the typical layout of rooms and hallways and exits that he recalled that time when he was a patient. The floor plan was a cross, on the left a few rooms and a nurses' kiosk, on the right six rooms, and straight ahead a long corridor with rooms on both sides that ended at a solarium. His recollections confirmed, he took the passenger elevator to nine.

Hairs tickled his wrist. Why was it so quiet? No one was in sight. Was this merely a pause in hospital routine? True, at noon the rooms had already been mopped but lunch was not yet being served. Also, since operations and X rays and other tests were mostly performed in the morning, no trolleys or wheelchairs were in view. But he wanted something to concentrate his attention, to obtrude.

It did. A man of middle height, blond-haired, no older than thirty, stepped around the nurses' kiosk. He wore a suit with a jacket loose enough to accommodate a shoulder holster. He nodded his head in the direction of the floor's right arm. In a flash it occurred to Petrie that this man, no doubt a CI like himself, had come out to satisfy himself that it was Petrie. He had not expected someone wearing a suit.

Petrie pushed through the door of Room 901. A single glance at the man in the bed to his left made him drop to his knees next to the L-shaped wall of the bathroom. Then he arose only slightly and risked taking low Groucho Marx steps around the corner of the L. He dove through the open bathroom door, hearing popping sounds as he fell. Reversing his position on the bathroom floor, while rubbing the shoulder that had struck the base of the toilet, he saw that the room's windowpanes were splintered at the top by sunbursts. The popping sounds, he recognized, had been made by a .22 fitted with a silencer. The aim had been too high. Were these warning shots only? A warning against what?

The man in the bed called out. "You *are* trapped, you know. You can't ring for a nurse. Come out. I won't shoot if I see your hands high." The pretender lying in the bed was the sole person in the room. Petrie had grasped that the moment he dropped to the floor.

He rushed out the bathroom door with both hands ready. He let fly a nickeled bedpan with his left hand while keeping low and then dove onto the bed and swung a urinal like a pendulum, forward knocking the .22 pistol out of the shooter's right hand, backward slapping his jawbone. The man slumped unconscious. As Petrie climbed off the bed and retrieved the gun from the linoleum floor, a sound from the hall gave him barely enough time to stand next to the dusty linen folds of a bed screen on the blind side of the door. The blond man he had seen in the corridor entered, his gun hand leading. Petrie slammed the barrel of the .22 against the nape of his neck. A blow to the vertebral arteries was numbing but rarely fatal—that he'd learned at the Commission boot camp.

Breathing hard, his fingers twitching, Petrie slid the .22 under the bed and stepped outside. In the hallway a bulky man in a brown suit approached, clearly another backup, his right hand in his coat pocket. Petrie had the advantage simply because he was not expected. He drove his fist into the man's chest, straight over his heart, causing him to drop in place like a stone block. Petrie then turned into the long corridor and a few steps along it found the door to the fire stairs, which he took down to the basement, where he knew he could cross over from Harkness to the main building. On reaching the parking area facing Broadway, next to the emergency ambulance entrance, he walked slowly down the street to find the Hertz car.

Driving across the George Washington Bridge, he could derive nothing sensible from the bizarre sequence of events. There was, here, no mistaken identity—despite his having worn a suit. What had made him drop to his knees? It was the gun. Yes. He'd seen the gun first thing! But had he expected *both* backups? Perhaps he had regarded a single unexpected circumstance as not being conclusive—unlike the mountain climber who escapes a falling rock and shouts with joy, only to trigger a snowslide.

But such self-congratulation did nothing to dispel the shock of realizing that the Commission, his own organization, had tried under threat of a gun to detain him, at the least, and maybe to wound or kill him. Pumping the steering wheel, rhythmically grasping and releasing it, he tried to put some quality into the events at Harkness—and was oddly embarrassed that nothing came to mind. Once long ago, on returning from the first of his two trips to the Soviet Union while working for Pooley, he had stopped in Copenhagen. His business done, he'd sought out the little park where stood the statue of Kierkegaard. He'd stared into the stone face of the father of existentialism for ten minutes or more. He had found he couldn't ponder anything meaningful—or, ironically, meaningless. It was like that now.

Petrie pulled off the turnpike onto a paved plaza, parked, and removed the key from the ignition, although no one was in sight. He collected his Terry Dunn clothes and dropped them into a large trash bin. Then, in a phone booth, he assembled coins while listening to the gasp of cars speeding by. A voice different from the earlier one answered. Mrs. Alberts was like the Betty Crocker of the ads, a personage, not always the same person.

"This is Petrie. Don't bother running through the numbers or checking the voice print. I want Matthews. I know I'm violating regulations, using names on the line. Get him!"

"Where are you, sir?"

Well done, Mrs. Alberts. Find out where a man is before asking what he's about. When Matthews came on, Petrie said, "I just found out my life doesn't conform to actuarial tables. Matthews, do you believe in actuaries?"

"Come in. There was a mix-up, that's all. It will be clear."

"What will be clear? Why would you set up a big chessboard and go through all the moves just to reach a simple endgame—capturing or killing me?"

"Come in. We'll talk it out."

"I don't have time and neither do you, apparently. Who set the timetable, Matthews?"

Roger Fredson picked up the telephone in his office in the World Trade Center and heard Nick Calvino snorting like a boxer holding one glove to his nose while jabbing with the other. "Goddamn. Goddamn. Your man dint do it."

"Where is he?"

"Who, for cry sakes? The fuckin' witness? He's dead."

Only because Shurtz paid him handsomely did Fredson suffer the humiliation of listening to a thug like Calvino, ostensibly Gunther Shurtz's bodyguard. Indeed, Fredson's regular law practice paid the rent only for his World Trade Center office, not for his eight-room Manhattan apartment. Told now that Shurtz wanted to see him, Fredson immediately called an FBI agent who lived in Queens, a man who had five kids and a mortgage and who'd once said he could "live with it," his informing, so long as the information he sold didn't physically harm any other law enforcement officer. Two hours later, both using street pay telephones, the FBI informer reported to Fredson that Dunn had been picked up in Trenton in his eighteen-wheeler carrying contraband cigarettes—also dope he claimed was not his. He'd been in somebody's custody since late yesterday. Whose custody? That was a mystery. He had not been booked by any local or state or federal agencies. Not so far.

Awaiting Shurtz at the office on Forty-seventh Street, Fredson stood at the sideboard trying to compose himself by drinking Pernod from a fluted champagne glass. His fondness for the Parisian workingman's morning pick-me-up, he liked to tell women, was his sole "perversity." An hour later, Shurtz arrived with Calvino, as usual chain-smoking his Players cigarettes. The Players were a familiar sight for an Englishman, but the handkerchief Shurtz tucked up the left sleeve of his suit jacket was a mannerism seen years ago only in the City or in Mayfair, never in the grimy East End of London where Shurtz had grown up. Later, when he lived in South Africa, Shurtz had once been told by a Cape Colored how disgusting it was of westerners to "carry excrement in your purses, pockets, and sleeves." Shurtz hadn't grasped that the man was talking about handkerchiefs.

"Now, dear boy," he said to Fredson, speaking against the white noise of the cassette player. "Our man in Yonkers, what does he say?"

"I described Dunn in full detail. The cop says it was close but not him. And he hasn't heard from Dunn."

"Now, why would a ringer show up?"

"Gunther, God intervened. You're safe. You said Hentleman is dead." Actually, it was Calvino who had said so, when he recklessly called on the office telephone.

"Why would the feds send in a fake Dunn, Roger my boy? The penny hasn't dropped. There were *two* fakes. The other one was waiting inside the hospital room, in the bed. That nurse we bribed said that this man left two more blokes unconscious before he got free."

"*You're* free, Gunther."

"Where's the real Dunn? You called our man? What does the FBI say?"

"Gunther," Fredson said reluctantly, because he didn't want to fuel Shurtz's fantasy, "nobody knows who took the real Dunn into custody. Some unknown feds took over."

Fredson was astonished that Shurtz was allowing Calvino to hear all this informative dialogue, because the thug would then tell the Las Vegas Mafia who gave Shurtz protection. Yet Shurtz's native wit was not doubted by Fredson, any more than it had been by the colony of East End Jews who had suffered the shame that their rabbi's own son was a "wide boy," a petty crook who fenced stolen goods and forged documents. Fortunately for them, one day in 1958 two sergeants from Scotland Yard had escorted young Gunther to Easthampton to put him on a ship bound for South Africa—to give another country a taste.

"No witness, no case," Fredson continued. "Even Hentleman's records can't convict. Nobody can attest when he made a notation or to what end."

"Roger has missed something, hasn't he, Nick?"

Calvino was startled. He bunched his beefy hands, causing Fredson to notice once more his manicured nails. It was no wonder so many mobsters were shot in barbershops.

"Gee, Gunner, ya know. I'm no good wit something deep, ya know, like now."

"Okay, Nick, don't get shirty. Let me tell you."

As Shurtz ground out another Players in the ashtray on the lacquered table and bent his head with its close-cropped gray hair and fleshy nose and jowls, Fredson noticed, not for the first time, that the hair protruding from Shurtz's nostrils and ears was like gristle.

"There's something here worth a packet. To set up a fed agent while he was setting me up, now that takes a packet of time and money. It had to be worth it. Why did they surprise one of their own blokes like that? He's running now! What's he got? A document, like those Pentagon Papers from years ago? A formula? Computer plans? Bank account numbers? Roger my boy, alive he must be worth a fortune."

Calvino looked at Fredson triumphantly and said, "God-damn. Right, Gunner. We'll get back the twenty bills."

"More, far more, Nick. But how do we find him? What we need is eyes and ears. I've a fancy, Nick, it may be time to call on your uncles, the worthy gentlemen in Las Vegas."

After they left, Fredson went to the sideboard and downed a Pernod without pausing for any epicurean reflections. Of all people, Shurtz knew the Mafia were never beholden, and as partners never equal. Shurtz was able to stay in business with them simply because they didn't find his scam profitable enough to take it over. Calvino's uncles never saw the eight-page color ads in medical magazines for a *single* drug. Nor did they know that a single drug could be worth up to half a *billion* dollars to its manufacturer in annual sales. Early on, Shurtz had imported from Great Britain the heart drug Inderal, which at the time was banned in the United States by the Food and Drug Administration. Once approved, it became the second best selling drug in America. Indeed, Shurtz's recent troubles had arisen from his peculiar brand of do-gooding. His bookkeeper, Hentleman, had believed, or half-believed, that his boss helped sick people. When his own wife fell ill and was not improving under her doctor's care, Shurtz had provided a concentrate made of a "miracle" protein. She had died within hours of being injected. Hentleman had proceeded to suffer a heart attack and, weakened and remorseful, had turned against his employer.

Fredson shuddered and poured another Pernod.

In Washington, Matthews studied the man seated before him and thought it surprising that white people were never said to be colored, yet here was Connors with his red hair and brown freckles and, now, a blue chin.

"No doubt your mother taught you, as mine did, not to complain, not to explain."

God in heaven, Connors thought, do I have to keep playing straight man to guys like this? Their heartiness was self-administered and self-satisfying—like masturbation.

"I've read the debriefing," Matthews continued. "The Commission has no complaint about your part in what transpired."

Connors stared. Was he being exculpated? One day, just once, he'd like to make the climactic speech in a play never to be enacted. *Do you know, Matthews, why so many of us Catholic Irish enlist and persist and die for the intelligence services? It's because our mothers and our bonny, blarney priests drill into us an unqestioning faith in authority. We are sold into the service.* Instead, he said, "The hit man wasn't armed. Now, why would he come in clean? Why would he be unprepared for guards watching over the patient?"

"*You* were armed, Connors."

"I was also given incomplete instructions. He was wearing a suit. If he was a street wise guy, a hitter, how come he knew just where to hide—in the bathroom? And how come he came out shooting with urinals and bedpans?"

Matthews ignored the sarcasm and said, "You've got three weeks of R and R coming to you. Put your feet up, Connors. And thanks."

That's the ticket. Hearty lad that he was, he could hoist a few boilermakers with his buddies at a local bar. Well, Matthews old boy, I'm off to Cape Cod to play a few rounds on true links—golf on the seaside—where on one hole you can play a seven iron in the morning, wind with, and on the same hole in the afternoon use a four wood, wind against.

Haagstrom, the Commissioner, was placatory when he came in after having listened in on Connors. Such eavesdropping was possible whenever Matthews switched on his intercom. There were times it was useful. This was one.

"He can hardly be expected to make sense of something that was as rare and complicated as this—like a triple play."

Matthews shot his eyebrows, the bushy ends turning up, and said with a touch of irony, "Rare things *do* happen. In fact, I once saw a pitcher make one by himself, catching a fly near third, bases full, touching the bag and then tagging the runner retreating to second."

Haagstrom winced. His deputy was trivializing a desperate condition. "My mistake was to be prompted by the coincidence that Petrie and Dunn looked somewhat alike." He paused in a spasm of pain. "We were going against our nature. The Commission exposes secrets, but now the President has ordered us to guard a secret. It is an unusual charge. And unusual charges call for unusual means. We've never before sought to detain a CI, let alone hunt one."

"Commissioner, we agreed on this plan, Tannenbaum and I. You were not alone in this."

Haagstrom leaned back, careful not to rub his temples despite an incipient attack of his arteritis, that horrible yet untreatable inflammation of the arteries in his temples and forehead. Physicians at Bethesda did not suspect the ailment and could not report it because its symptoms were unapparent to the observer—and irregular.

"Our main threat," Matthews continued, "is the press. Petrie may go to them."

"No. He will try to find someone to help him search his memory. But he *will* be outraged." The Commissioner looked at his deputy closely. "He may try right off to avenge himself man to man."

"You mean pick us off one by one? Like the Count of Monte Cristo? Commissioner, why do I get the notion that you admire him?"

Watching the eyebrows shoot as Matthews's mood changed to scorn, the Commissioner spoke firmly. "I know we sent CIs to Denver to watch his house in Littleton. If he doesn't go there—as I expect he won't—then we have a decision to make. Half of our forty CIs are already committed to the surveillance of the scientists who have worked with the USSR on the discovery. If we use the other half to search for Petrie, then our usual work will stop. Matt, you and the Chief see me later this afternoon on whether or not I should ask the President to bring in the FBI."

"I hate the notion that we can't handle this ourselves. Commissioner, he's our man. We know his tendencies. He knows ours. You're right about his not going to the press—if we keep it in the family. If you do agree to keep it inside the Commission, what story do we give the CIs on the hunt?"

"God knows, there is a lot we can use. We can give them his real name, Pyotorov, the fact that he speaks fluent Russian, his two trips to the Soviet Union, his Princeton degree in engineering."

He rose to return to his own office and turned back only to say, "No, Matt, it's not that I admire him. Today, I don't admire us."

Alone, Matthews considered the fact that the Commission didn't have a safe house, but it could afford to create one, perhaps could rent a cabin in the Catoctin Mountains west of Washington, near Camp David in fact, and keep Petrie under guard. After the discovery was made known worldwide, Petrie could be financially compensated. When Matthews had at the start proposed simply calling Petrie in to seize him, Haagstrom and Tannenbaum, both lawyers and the Commissioner a former judge, had recoiled from so obvious a violation of habeas corpus and due process. The Deputy could not see the distinction between one kind of detention and another. Take the plan as it was supposed to have unfolded. Connors was supposed to have kept Petrie inside the hospital room under gunpoint until Bizuski and Donato, stationed outside, came in. Then they'd lead Petrie away, he himself all the while presuming this was being done for the benefit of Hentleman's relatives. Once they were all outside the hospital, it was presumed that Tannenbaum would ask Petrie to volunteer to go into seclusion. If he refused, then they'd compel him. The notion had been to *begin* Petrie's detention with an operation within a detailed context suitable to the Commission's regular duties.

"This way," the Chief had explained, "we have a point of reference. That is, should the matter come under review later, we can readily claim that in the course of an operation, Petrie became physically or psychologically impaired and needed treatment and convalescence. The fact is that there will be a legitimate operation. Even unclear and incomplete, there will be *some* records."

"To hang a man with," the Deputy had said glumly.

Matthews had been outvoted. There were only three votes because no one else in the Commission knew the discovery existed.

What had not been explained aloud was something all three were aware of, namely, that Congress could become involved because Petrie, a man who seemed to have few friends, was a boyhood chum and at Princeton had been the confidant of Nicholas Miroset, now a congressman from Fairbanks, Alaska. Miroset, a former football player for Princeton and later the Cleveland Browns, was known to be genial among his peers in the House, but he could be stubborn. If Petrie were hurt in the absence of "extenuating circumstances," even the President might not be able to keep Miroset quiet. Even so, Matthews had been troubled by a nagging sense, like a rock in the shoe, that somehow the Commissioner for his own reasons had welcomed complications.

Matthews had been elated when the Commission was given the stupendous task of guarding the great secret—the joint discovery of the United States and the Soviet Union—and when CIs were assigned the job of watching the scientists who knew the secret and had pledged to keep it safe. Not until two months later had it occurred to Matthews that Petrie—because of his knowledge and early associations before he joined the Commission in 1980—was possibly himself a candidate for surveillance. Petrie had studied at Princeton, the center for American experiments in fusion; and in Moscow he'd come to know well the famous Professor Turcheff while traveling for his former employer, Pooley.

As he lit a cigar, seated at the desk with its splendid appointments but no paperwork showing, Matthews was troubled over the word he'd introduced into his own thoughts just now. Complications. But he had no doubts about one thing: he was opposed to bringing in the FBI just because the Commission had so many fewer agents. This operation was first class and world class all the way. It called for an elite force.

CHAPTER THREE

————— • —————

I T WAS IN 1978 THAT PETRIE HAD MET TURCHEFF THE FIRST
time. Petrie had stood in one of the great halls of GUM eating ice cream, the best buy in that vast department store,
along with Armenian wines. The meeting ostensibly occurred
by mere chance. The woman who was Petrie's companion turned
and smiled at a man of about fifty-five, short in stature, broad
of face, with brown eyes and a thick gray mustache.

"My dear Professor," Ludmilla Yetsin said. "You are no
doubt observing a timing phenomenon, demand outrunning an
ever-increasing supply." She was tall, with a figure quite trim
for a Russian woman over thirty, small waist, delicately inclined neck, full breasts and calves. She was blond and, so far,
had been spared the miserable Russian hennas and peroxides
that made so many women in Moscow look old and hard tem-
pered.

"It is wicked to burden an American visitor with such formulations. He walks like John Wayne." Accidentally, the Professor was still speaking in Russian when he asked, "Are you a cowboy?"

Petrie laughed and hitched his belt. He replied, in Russian, "I *do* come from the old West. From Colorado."

"You speak excellent Russian? Good. I am Viktor Ivanovich Turcheff, formerly this young woman's instructor in chemistry at the University and now—thank God for her promotion—her colleague."

"I am honored, Professor. I am Alexandr Vladimirovich Pyotorov." (Petrie was the name he would gain two years later on joining the Commission.) "I work for an American construction company called Pooley that builds and services equipment for fuel plants."

Ludmilla explained, "We met this morning at a conference at the National Technological Exhibition."

"I am spared such torture these days. The only thing worse than being talked about is to be talked at. Well. It's nearly five o'clock. Will you be my guests for tea? Ludmilla Androvna?"

"I'm expected within a quarter hour at another meeting. Go with him, Pyotorov. He knows everything. I learned over his knee." This last she said in English.

The Professor replied, in English, "I believe Americans learn *at* the knee. Naughty girls are spanked *over* it."

For a second Pyotorov thought she was peeved. But as she said abruptly, "Good-bye then," he recognized the usual stiff etiquette of Eastern Europeans. She took Turcheff's hand in a single chopping motion and then extended the hand to Pyotorov, who kissed it in the continental style, nose to the wrist, lips barely touching the skin. Ludmilla was slightly flustered and departed hurriedly.

"She's married, you know." Turcheff spoke in Russian, as he did steadily thereafter.

"I'm sorry to hear it," Pyotorov replied. "I was about to lay seige to that woman tonight. She's beautiful."

"Tonight, her husband, poor devil, will pay for your most un-American hand kissing."

They had walked out of Red Square and turned into Gorky Street, where goods were more plentiful than in shops elsewhere but the window displays no more imaginative. Luring buyers was hardly at issue. The fact that the boxes on display, for spices, powders, dried foods, were empty was itself damning: the stores couldn't spare any part of their inventory for show. As the two of them paused at a corner of the ring road that has the Kremlin as its center, Turcheff began asking about American shopping centers, making small talk in a stilted scholarly manner.

"GUM is our Crystal Palace. The English destroyed theirs, just as the French tore down Les Halles. Its original name was *Torgovuije Ryadi,* 'trading rows.' A name ought to describe function—you saw the rows or bays inside."

They moved on, Turcheff hunched in his coat, his stiff gray hair barricading his neck where the fur hat didn't reach. He moved briskly, silently. Pyotorov was used to this. Russians don't talk much as they move: they must pause to make a point. Soon, two squares off the street called Novoslobodskaya, they arrived at a nineteenth-century building with a deeply scored egg-and-dart motif over the lintels.

Pyotorov said quickly, while they were still on the street, "I hope you are not offended, Professor, if I say that I know our meeting in GUM was hardly accidental. Ludmilla led me to you. You were waiting. I am not an American agent. Also, I doubt that you are a Russian agent. You spoke Russian to me before Ludmilla had a chance to tell you I understand the language. Professor, I *really* am here on engineering business. To make money if possible, not to cause trouble."

"Ah, that makes you candid and me incompetent, is that it? Well, I myself hold no confidences, and if you don't, we are together unburdened."

As the first week passed, they fell into the habit of meeting for a walk most days at about five o'clock, after Turcheff returned from the University and Pyotorov was finished with his business meetings at various bureaus and factories. Pyotorov was sometimes away from Moscow calling on the bureaus that managed mines, docks, and dams. He took overnight trains to Minsk, to Leningrad, and to Kiev, and once he flew to Baku. In Moscow, he stayed at the Hotel Rossiya and entertained Turcheff at dinner there, as well as at the Café Czechoslovakia, where only foreigners and trade officials could afford to eat.

Turcheff lived alone—his wife had died three years earlier and they'd been childless. Because of his status as an eminent scientist, he'd been able to keep his four-room apartment despite the rule that allotted nine square meters for each Soviet citizen. During the second week, when on several nights Pyotorov was invited to a late tea in Turcheff's flat, the Professor was surprised by Pyotorov's confession that he was occupied with one or another young woman—occupied all night, that is. Naively, Turcheff regarded Pyotorov's quick connection with women as evidence supporting his general theory that Russians and Americans both suffer a certain loneliness that comes of inhabiting vast spaces. He remarked to Pyotorov that a Russian, like an American, will tell his life story to the stranger on the bench opposite even before the train has left the station.

"What's worse," Pyotorov said, "is that he tells the truth!"

"Do you suppose people tell their biographies to give a purpose to their lives?"

"Who can tell what the climax of his life is as he lives it? Isn't it what Chekhov says in his plays? His characters keep looking for the point—and it eludes them. There's a lot to be said for living uncritically from day to day."

Turcheff was sitting with his back to the apartment windows overlooking the street. Outside it was dim and cold, the air gray from frost. He looked at the younger man with a certain amusement, his eyes signaling a riposte.

"Day to day, you say, do you? It is the prescription for a sensualist. Are you a sensualist, Alexandr Vladimirovich?"

"Only when it comes to women," he replied, causing Turcheff to laugh as he had not in months.

When Alexandr Vladimirovich Pyotorov told *his* story to the Professor, he did not begin with his parents' immigration into the United States from Quebec. Nor did he mention their living in a coal camp near Frederick, Colorado, after his birth in 1954. He began his account with 1960, when the Pyotorov family lived on California Street in Denver, on the downstairs floor of a rooming house his mother managed. The roomers were Serbs and Poles and Russians who came to Denver mostly in the summer when they were laid off from the coal mines of northern Colorado, or else were packinghouse stiffs who, like Alexandr's father, worked at the Swift or Armour plants in Globeville. When his mother fell ill, the family moved to the second floor of the rooming house and became tenants, no longer managers. She didn't live long after that, a victim of esophageal cancer, a disease whose symptoms appear late, when its ravages are already advanced. On the very day following her burial, at the Orthodox cemetery near Globeville, his father left for the southern Colorado coalfields near Trinidad. He hadn't told Alexandr he was going. He'd spoken only to Nikolai Miroset's father, to whom he gave nine hundred dollars for Alexandr's room and board—at the rate of fifty dollars a month, enough to carry him through the two nine-month terms of his junior and senior years of high school. The Miroset family mirrored the Pyotorovs: immigrant Russian parents with a single child, Nikolai (Americanized to Nicholas when he first went to school), who was Alexandr's age. It was the Mirosets who managed the rooming house after the Pyotorovs moved upstairs. As it turned out, Alexandr's father showed up in Denver only once more, the August before his son left for Princeton. He gave Alexandr a hundred dollars and said he'd write, but never did. The son returned a year later to bury his father and was shocked to find he had died of alcoholism. Alexandr had never seen him drunk.

"How was it possible that you knew so little of your father's grief?" Turcheff asked sympathetically, if also pointedly.

"We were like three people waiting in a bus station."

"What a terrible thing to say! Did you suffer a lack of feeling? I cannot believe you did, considering that you are now a generous, uncritical, and reliable man. Perhaps you suffer some deep reservation whenever you are made intimate. It's possible. Loyalty to persons is harder than a larger loyalty."

Turcheff was shocked in part because he had always presumed and expected families to be a reliable consolation, in dire moments at least. He'd had no such consolation himself because both his parents had died by the time he left Volvograd at nineteen to go to the University. Of his few remaining aunts and uncles and cousins, some had come only twice to Moscow. His wife's family had been early settlers in Siberia, three thousand miles eastward, and he'd never met any of them, not even when he and his wife were married in Moscow. Nonetheless, he shared with all Russians, of upper ranks and lower depths, a sentimental regard for the wholeness of families and the closeness of relatives.

"How is it that in your American literature the families fade away? There are so many solitary heroes in Melville,

Hemingway, Whitman, Faulkner. In your plays, the families torture each other—in O'Neill and Tennessee Williams."

"I am impressed! When on earth did you find time to read all that?"

"I cannot pretend I was a great reader except for chemistry and physics. I am not. Most of what I know about literature and history comes of attending lectures. But then, how did you come to speak Russian so well?"

"The Mirosets spoke a more educated Russian than my parents did, and they also made me attend classes at the Orthodox church. I also studied it at Princeton."

Now Turcheff painfully related his impoverishment during his years of schooling. He was grateful to the state for his opportunities, he said, and somewhat defensively reminded his young friend that science thrived in the Soviet Union because it was a meritocracy that rewarded scholarship.

"We should not be judged by simple appearances," he warned Pyotorov. "Take those million-odd women physicians who practice neighborhood medicine. They are little better than midwives. Yet our endocrinologists and immunologists win Nobel prizes. Our advancement in particle physics as well as in conductivity by chemical means is perhaps ahead of that of the Americans."

"I surrender!" Pyotorov exclaimed. Then he unwittingly stumbled into the very area that Soviet officialdom had hoped he might enter once the Professor had been ordered to put himself in the way of this young American whose technical background and competency in Russian gave the KGB grounds to suspect that he was a CIA agent.

"Where did you begin your research in chemistry?" Pyotorov asked.

"In redefining certain properties of elements, especially in respect of finding what was possible in fusion. Nothing new, really."

"And afterward?"

"I worked on polymers, the giant molecules, looking for bonding agents."

"For your space probes?"

Turcheff turned aside this innocent but dangerous venturing by asking Pyotorov how he began his own studies. Wasn't the great university of Princeton very expensive to attend?

"It was and is. Let me tell you something that will seem to you odd, Viktor Ivanovich—no, not odd, just American pragmatism. Nikolai Miroset and I made ourselves into a trading or bargaining package. We were both football players, although he was quicker and stronger. I was a straight-A student but Nikolai was not a top scholar. When an affluent Denver lawyer who was a graduate of Princeton came to our high school to recruit athletes, offering tuition and room and board, Nikolai said he and I would go together or not at all. As it turned out, Nikolai played football all four years at Princeton, but I was cut from the team after a year. By then, my instructors— rather than the football coaches—had become my advocates. I kept my scholarship but lost my room and board."

"Surely your examination scores were determining. You make university sound like a bazaar!"

"Our bargaining was over how to pay some of the costs. Princeton is a private university, supported by its students and alumni—the old students who become rich and sentimental."

"I know now what has become of you. And what became of Nikolai?"

"He played professional football in Cleveland and then went to Fairbanks, Alaska. He's now a congressman."

"Quite incredible! You Americans move about at will, fall

in and out of luck, and somehow land on your feet—and start running."

"We aren't supermen, Viktor Ivanovich. We're people who let everything run to its end. That's the ultimate liberty, don't you think?"

This remark, Pyotorov found, suddenly seemed to strike Turcheff as momentous. He stopped speaking and nervously stroked his mustache, as if it needed straightening in order to oversee his remarks.

"Letting things run to their end is not generally harmless, Alexandr Vladimirovich. No. It can be dire, even lethal. Letting things run to their end can become the ultimate tyranny for a person in a state without internal limits."

Several days later, Turcheff himself reintroduced the subject by asking, "How can you be expected to divine the depths of our situation? When I was a member of the Committee on Science as Applied to the Economy, my academic colleagues and I could barely stand to look at the report in front of us. The five-year plan had called for a three-percent increase in coal. We failed sixfold. In chemicals, my specialty, the goal was ten and three-tenths percent. We achieved three. Our failure was ignored the way one might avert one's eyes from an insane person undressing in public as he speaks. I remember that I kept asking myself: who is watching our struggle? Who keeps score of our failures? The Marxists have a stock answer—history. The Christians say it's God."

"What torments you, Viktor Ivanovich? Is it that people live in vain?"

Turcheff replied, "In vain? Yes. History wants sacrifices. So does the Hebrew God. As for the Christians, they have collectivized their sacrifices by saying that Christ died for us all."

Turcheff returned to the discussion two days later. His discourse was always open-ended, marked by dashes and semi-colons.

"Let me tell you how awful it becomes. Once I went to Tbilisi in Georgia, to a conference on fusion, along with physicists and chemical researchers and engineers. We were allowed to stay in the new hotel, just completed, where it was hoped foreigners with hard currency would come, Tbilisi being a picturesque place, Stalin's hometown, and the Georgians a fine, friendly, hearty people. But the place was humiliating for me. The doors would not close. The toilet had water but not the bathtub. I had to bribe the floor concierge to get me a blanket. All this in a new hotel designed for tourists! It was Easter and I insisted on going to mass. But I was not allowed to go alone to the cathedral. The car that took me included a state militiaman, who followed me inside. On the floor of the church were old women. And drunken men. Prostitutes. Beggars. Above them on the stage, the altar, were priests dressed like the seventeenth-century boyars, in black robes with broad brown belts. Behind them were the acolytes, like doves, thin young men with beards that could have been penciled on. I wept for them, for myself, for my country. My God, had we fought and worked and starved to arrive here? And why was I being guarded by a militiaman? Against faith? No. It was against the plain sight of the subversion of energy and hope in all those broken people!"

Just before Pyotorov departed from Denmark and Great Britain at the end of his first trip, which had lasted five weeks, Turcheff began to feel a certain loss or incompleteness. They had talked almost intimately about enormous, dreadful issues but had said little of themselves. Accordingly, on one occasion he decided to become the symbolic Russian on the train.

"You are what now? Twenty-five years old? You were born too late to fight in Vietnam. How is it you aren't married?"

"Viktor Ivanovich, people are supposed to marry for love, not sex. So far, I've found no love. But I've found many generous women."

"I won't ask more." Turcheff laughed then. "Of course I shall."

"You recall that I lost my room and board money at Princeton, although Nikolai Miroset kept his? At Princeton there is a tradition of undergraduates running their own businesses while they are in school—laundry service, delivering food at night, selling newspapers. I decided to make cheap air sweeteners to sell in a town called Camden, not far from Princeton."

"Let me guess. You put petrol into bottles along with a scent to kill the petrol odor."

"Right!"

"And how did you manage the spray mechanism?"

"Spraying was too costly. I put dense nylon sponges in the bottles. When the bottles were uncapped, they gave off the scent slowly as the petrol evaporated."

"Ah," Turcheff exclaimed, laughing. "You are telling me about petrol, not love. There will be no gossip, then, only capitalist propaganda about how you owned a factory."

"No, no. Wait! I found a young Cuban woman whose relatives were out of work. I gave a couple of them the job of doing the bottling. And I gave myself the Cuban lady."

"Did she teach you Spanish?"

"I knew the rudiments. She filled in the spaces, as it were."

"Rudiments! This is better than a French novel." Turcheff smiled. "I've never read a French novel."

"You are baiting me now. Anyway, I'll confess more. Each summer, Nikolai and I managed to find jobs and save some money for school. Once, Nikolai found out that a movie was being made in Mexico, on the coast of the Gulf of California. The producers were building an airstrip, houses, towers—a whole set—on the beach. It was a satire on World War II, about the Battle of Salerno, I think. Nikolai and I hitchhiked through Colorado and New Mexico and then rode a Mexican bus to Guaymas, the nearest town. We spent only four dollars apiece for transportation."

"You became actors?"

"No, we helped build the sets, along with Mexicans."

"Including Mexican women?"

"Right."

"More of your moving about. More of your landing on your feet. More American fantasy."

"But, Viktor, what's wrong with more?"

"You Americans have your own devil. If scarcity is the shame of my country, then abundance is yours, your material excesses."

"It's not that simple!"

"You recall, Alexandr Vladimirovich, I chided you once about unbridled liberty. But let me admit that when a people must deny the obvious, *that* becomes their oppression. Scarcity makes liars of us all. Scarcity makes us ashamed."

"There is a reverse, Viktor Ivanovich. It's pride. One summer before I left for college I worked in the same packinghouse where my father used to work. It was donkey labor. I carried sides of beef weighing a hundred pounds in and out of coolers kept at forty degrees—enough to inflict instant arthritis! You say people are made ashamed by scarcity. Well, they can also become too proud of having worked hard. At Princeton, amid my moneyed classmates, I had to guard against wearing my poor beginnings and hard labor like a badge of honor."

Turcheff was curious. It had not occurred to him until now that Pyotorov was probably a man with few friends.

"Did you ever introduce the Cuban lady in Camden to your moneyed classmates?"

"No, I didn't."

"No doubt that was because you were moving up, moving away?"

"*Touché*. Well, I did leave her the bottling business."

"Of course. Alexandr Vladimirovich, it is presumptuous of me, but I refer you to the attraction of low life, what the French call a longing for the mud, *nostalgie de la boue*."

Pyotorov smarted under this criticism. Had he sought out the lowborn? It was true that his inclination was to seek women for the pleasure they afforded, especially everyday women, while he sought out men for their company and good opinion. It was quite the opposite of what was said to be typical of homosexuals. He thanked God for small mercies.

CHAPTER FOUR

———— • ————

T PHILADELPHIA'S INTERNATIONAL AIRPORT, PETRIE LEFT THE Hertz car in a long-stay lot and took from the trunk a suit- case in which he had earlier put his automatic pistol and all but two thousand of the cash. He bought a ticket and checked the suitcase to Omaha—a destination that was no more than five hundred miles from Denver to which there was the earliest nonstop flight. In Omaha, he rented an Avis car, showing a different driver's license than the one he had used in New York. He drove out to Route 80 and followed it southwest along the Platte. After an hour he switched to secondary roads, Route 183 going south, then Route 6 westward into Colorado. About six o'clock in the morning, he drove into Denver on the four- lane Interstate 70, which was elevated in the area where it passed Globeville, a workingmen's suburb. From the interstate he saw the meager frame houses and the streets that, now cut off by the highway, were dead ends. Only one of the several packinghouses and smelter stacks emitted fumes: here, clean air meant less work. He saw the onion dome of the Russian Orthodox church and, beyond, the rose cottonwoods guarding the graveyard where his mother and father now lay.

He didn't dare risk going to his apartment in Littleton because it was surely being staked out by the Commission. Lying south of Denver below the breaks and draws of the Rockies, Littleton had once been a small town of ranchers and railroad workers. It had grown into a suburb of prosperous commuters as Denver's east side increasingly turned black and Hispanic and Oriental in population, while in the north and west sides near to downtown the small, neat brick houses continued to be occupied by the middle class and by blue-collar workers. South Denver already held the university, some large estates, and Cherry Hills Country Club. Petrie's Littleton apartment, on the seventh floor of a relatively new building, was his official residence and was so recorded in the confidential records in the Deputy's office. Yet he kept only a few changes of clothes there. His valuables he'd moved elsewhere two years earlier: two hundred and twenty thousand dollars in cash, his father's gold watch and chain and the fob that was a cruciform, and an eight-inch-square wooden icon, a true antique, which his mother had kept always above her bed.

Although he was sure he hadn't been followed by any CIs from Philadelphia to Omaha to Denver, he hadn't considered the possibility that someone else might be keeping him in view.

In fact, the Mortella family of Las Vegas was doing just that. Shurtz had called Mario Mortella in Las Vegas within minutes of hearing about the fiasco in the hospital from the nurse he'd bribed. He had told Mario he'd pay unlimited expense money for "eyes" to watch Newark Airport and Philadelphia International, giving a description of the so-called Dunn. He said that it was a matter of great importance involving a man the feds wanted who could be worth a lot. Shurtz said he was certain the man was crossing the George Washington Bridge. Mario was skeptical but took the plunge. If Shurtz offered money, he was serious. Gunther Shurtz was not a spender and rarely a gambler.

Petrie parked his car near downtown, on Curtis Street, where a construction project was under way on a lot covered with the detritus of red bricks. The earthmovers and mechanical hoes still stood motionless this early in the morning. It was a place where he knew his Avis rental from Omaha would not be stolen or damaged over the period of a day and a night. It was important to keep this car safe because he couldn't risk going to a car-rental office again when he left Denver.

On his walk to Alcarita's apartment he stopped to deposit the suitcase, now empty, in a locker at the bus station on Eighteenth Street and then threw the locker key down a street drain. Also, on the way, he reflected that the Commission must be under an enormous restraint. How had he managed to travel two thousand miles by car, by air, without being recognized and detained? It must be because the Commission had not called in *any* outside help, not U.S. marshals, not the FBI, not the Secret Service. There was here a great paradox: Petrie was a threat, but for the Commission to make that fact known to outsiders was possibly a still bigger threat.

God! He wanted to hold Cara overnight, to forget all these paradoxes that had the look of fatalities. He had lived with Alcarita Obregon for two years. Before that, no woman had ever stayed with him at the Littleton apartment—none for longer than a single night. Before he joined the Commission and after, for eleven years, he'd lived on Park Avenue in Manhattan in a two-bedroom rent-controlled apartment. There, a girl he had first met at Princeton had come to stay with him three years after they graduated. She was in residence, so to speak, for

almost two years but left when she became convinced that he
wasn't going to marry her. Another time, he had persuaded a
secretary from Pooley's accounting department to move in, an
Irish girl with thick red hair and fair skin and a deep laugh
that was like water bubbling. She had been a high-school
dropout at sixteen and was only eighteen when she moved in.
She expected nothing "permanent," she said; and one day announced she had found a man who would marry her. Petrie
had congratulated her and she'd burst into tears. If he was
always truthful, he was too often unfeeling—more than one
woman had found it so. There was a waitress, then a UN
Spanish translator, then a graduate student at NYU. After he
joined the Commission in 1980, he had kept the apartment
until 1987, when he had asked to be transferred to Denver.
The CI who had been his predecessor, he was told, had died
of a massive infarction—on the sidewalk. Soon after he arrived in Denver, he had found Alcarita Obregon.

The door had hardly clicked shut behind him when Carita
reached up to grip his neck with her long red nails and run her
tongue over the inside rind of his lips. When he beckoned her
to step outside, she drew back, puzzled and affronted, but he
urged her out and across the sidewalk to the Chevrolet he'd
bought her nine months earlier. He was reasonably sure that
the Commission did not know about Alcarita Obregon, yet
how could he be certain? He could hardly explain to Cara that
tiny transmitters might now be nestling in light fixtures or wall
moldings. For her, it was quite enough physics to realize that
the wind can carry the wail of approaching police cars.

In the Commission files, along with the Littleton address,
was written his true name, Alexander (Anglicized) Pyotorov,
in the hand of the Chief of Section One himself. The names of
all the Commission's field investigators were lodged in a file
cabinet that could be opened only by the Chief of Operations,

the Deputy, and Haagstrom, the Commissioner. All CIs were given pseudonyms when they entered the organization. Pyotorov had become Mark Petrie, the name he called himself at all times while on duty. Like the other CIs, he used his own name off duty and where he lived—although Alcarita Obregon knew him as Alex Hoffman. The professional anonymity of the CIs was made still more secure by the documents they carried identifying them as representatives of the Interior Department authorized to monitor government contracts for equipment and services. This helped to explain both their frequent travels and their repeated presence in Washington. Further, so that a CI could more easily maintain his professional anonymity, he was never assigned to a region where he might have lived as a working adult. Petrie had been eligible to return to Denver because he was unmarried, had no relatives in the city or suburbs, and had left the area twenty years earlier. All these Commission restrictions were not foolproof, yet the fact was that in ten years Petrie had never known another CI's true name or professional background.

He looked at Carita leaning against the locked passenger door with one leg doubled under, showing a silky thigh. Her blouse was too small and molded her nipples. Driving to Denver he'd made a Rorschach test of her body, divining its features from rain spots on the pavement or windshield—like the minister in *Rain* who, dreaming, saw the breasts of Sadie Thompson as sand hills in his native Nebraska. Carita's near nudity made him agitated, much as he had once felt when he refused a whore in Tijuana. Under the yellow-white arc lights of a street near the border station, the whore had raised her dress to show her pubic hair and the flecked aureoles of her breasts, then had turned to reveal the cleavage of her tight buttocks. *"No se equivoque, señor. Soy toda mujer, por detras y por delante.* Don't be confused, mister. I am a woman front

and back." He had given her fifty dollars and replied, *"Es verdad eres toda mujer. Solamente el tiempo me ditiente de ti.*
Truly you are a woman. Only time keeps me from you."

Now, he told Carita that he must leave Denver the next
day—not unusual because he regularly came and went. But
for the first time he also asked her to leave Denver temporar-
ily. Her eyes narrowed, her lips pursed, then she leaned across
and kissed his lips to stop them.

Two years earlier, she had been walking toward Arapahoe
Street, where her parents lived with her brother, Tony, and his
wife and two children, and had stopped at Stout Street waiting
for the traffic to pass. On the far curb stood a tall man wearing a suit. A car went by, then another. She stood as if on a
precipice, steadying herself; then he came across the chasm
and put his huge hands on her waist. It had seemed so genteel
in the twilight when he asked, Will you have dinner with me?
He spoke in Spanish, which was unexpected and wonderful.
I'm not dressed correctly, she replied. It is sad, he said. No one
had ever spoken to her before of sadness except as the face of
terror—a sickness or accident or betrayal of love. I am, she
said then, a decent person, but I invite you to my house for
coffee. In her apartment, he had sat in the overstuffed chair
with lace doilies pinned to the back and arms as she began
telling her story—against inborn caution.

With her mother and father and Tony and her sister, Teresita, she had walked across the border near Nogales, crossing
an arroyo and squeezing through a wire fence. It was desert
on both sides of the border, but over generations her family
had got used to heat, working in cotton and sugarcane fields
and in the copper mines of northern Sonora. Her mother had
carried money in her underpants and cradled in her arms the
family's photographs and medicines. The others had carried
simple tools, pots, dry wood, Sterno cans, but no weapons. In

Colorado, they'd worked together pulling beets in Longmont. Then Teresita had left home to marry a man who worked in a steel mill in Pueblo, and Tony had got a job at a refinery in Brighton, near Denver, and had soon married and become the father of two children, taking his parents to live with him. Alcarita had married a boy of nineteen while on a visit to her sister in Pueblo. Within three months he had died in a knife fight in Walsenburg, leaving her a widow at eighteen. She had returned to Denver with a man twice her age who promised her a church wedding. By the time she found out he was already married and regularly saw his wife, she had quit her job at a box factory under the Broadway Viaduct. Now she was jobless.

The tall man sitting in her overstuffed chair had got up and come over to tell her she was brave, kissing her lightly on the lips. He had left then—to her astonishment.

That first time he saw Alcarita, he'd been on a sentimental journey to see the rooming house on California Street where he'd lived with his parents and later the Mirosets. As he'd stood on the sidewalk, he hadn't been able to think of anything—like that time in Copenhagen. He later realized that his approaching Alcarita that same day, as she was headed toward her brother Tony's house, had been a longing for something personal, something involving, to happen to him at that moment, in that place. He had in fact passed the building where Alcarita now lived every day from the age of six to eleven while attending Ebert Elementary School.

None of Alcarita's family had asked about his origins or his trade. Alcarita's father credited him with being, at the very least, a prosperous trader, perhaps a dealer in gems or silver who had Latin connections. That would explain his fluency in Spanish and his carrying a lot of cash but little luggage. Carita had not been perturbed by such speculations. Everyone had secrets, didn't they? You didn't tell others everything, because you were ashamed to. Her parents could not write their own names, in Spanish or English, but no stranger knew that—not even her lover, Alex.

The next morning he sat at the kitchen table in front of a small electric range over which hung a precipitant steam from bacon and taco and chickory. Petrie cleared his plate because for Carita a man's appetite was a litmus to test his ardor.

"I want you to visit your sister in Pueblo. Tony can drive you with his family, can't he? He's not working, what with the strike at the Brighton plant. It's only three hours' drive. Take your mother and father. They would like the trip."

"You worked it out," she said, her back to him as she stood at the sink. "Tony can drive. My folks can leave. Just like that." Then she whirled around and immediately her figure became the foretelling of her loss—shoulders down, the magnificent breasts pendant, her hand holding a fork like a straight razor. "You got plans of your own, right? Well, I've got some too. I'll wait here, as usual."

"Cara, will you listen! Some men will come looking for me and they might hurt you. Listen, they will think you know things in my life. It will be a mistake, yet it could happen. You can be hurt by mistake. Will you listen?"

"Listen, yourself. You don't have to tell me over and over, like I'm a kid. I'm not a kid."

"Carita," he said, pouring a third cup of coffee. "We don't have much time."

"I hear the sound of your leaving. Is that how love sounds? I am ignorant. Tell me." Then, "If they find me, I'll be with my family."

He comprehended. "Yes, Cara, protect your family first of

all. Don't let them suffer because of me." He stood, after placing forty fifty-dollar bills on the table. "I want you to be patient. I don't want you to worry. There's a difference."

"There is not."

As he drove out of Denver that morning in the Avis car
he'd reclaimed from the building site, he told himself he now
had the time to conduct a patient reconnoitering of his memory. Yet from the moment he had entered Room 901 at the
hospital his shock and rage had not kept him from analyzing
in sequence what had occurred and, by means of analog, accepting or discarding possibilities on their face, yes or no. At
one point he had assumed he was guilty: everyone is guilty
according to the Old Testament, or, if one prefers, Freud.

When the Chief had told him that he'd be apprehended—
after playacting the hit for the benefit of Hentleman and his
relatives—Petrie had assumed that U.S. marshals would be his
temporary captors. The CIs by law could gather information,
interview witnesses, study documents, and collect other legally
admissible evidence, such as videotapes and audiotapes. Although they were trained to shoot expertly and were allowed
to carry handguns in order to protect themselves or, rarely, a
witness, it was their usual practice to call in the marshals to
arrest suspects once the Commission had built a case that would
stand up in court. Any district judge, on application, could
alert federal marshals to carry out the court's orders. In a sense,
marshals were an ad hoc police force. They were not an elite
unit, having no continuous tradition that defined their role or,
worse, could tempt them at times to exceed their authority.

Petrie had undertaken a large number of assignments over
the period of his ten years with the Commission. After gradu-
ation from its boot camp near Liberal, Kansas, he had been

sent to Seattle to study Air Force contracts and with two other CIs had found evidence of kickbacks and payments for non-existent parts. Air Force officers, Defense Department purchasing agents, and even some Government Accounting Office staff members were in due course arrested. Later, at Madison, Wisconsin, he had single-handed caught some FBI agents who used computer hackers at the university to siphon off money from certain accounts in Miami. On one mission he and other CIs became involved in illegal arms dealing—not to gather evidence against the dealers but to flush out U.S. bank examiners who allowed certain banks to "launder" the dirty money by their issuing cashier's checks for cash and not reporting such transactions, as required by federal law, above ten thousand dollars.

But no mission, no operation was comparable to the grand assignment the President now gave to the Commission, one unknown to Petrie by even the merest inference because he was not one of the CIs assigned. Twenty inspectors, half the Commission field force, were sent to keep watch over laboratory sites as well as individual scientists who were involved in a great event, the discovery and application of an astonishing new technology. They were told not much of the nature of the discovery, only its importance. Of course, Petrie wasn't aware that he was not included. Tannenbaum had at first argued for his inclusion in this corps, but the Soviet authorities had objected that he'd become too close to Professor Turcheff during his visits to Moscow in 1978 and 1979. At the time—this was in October of 1990—not one of the three Commission officials believed that Petrie knew of the discovery or even that he could surmise some of its properties. Later, they took another tack.

Turcheff, by coincidence, had once spoken to Pyotorov

about intelligence agencies. But of course Turcheff knew nothing about the Commission in 1978 and 1979, any more than Pyotorov himself did.

"Intelligence people are uniquely insensitive," Turcheff had said, "because like fish in a tank they can't perceive their own environment—it's all water and always water. It's the reason they tend to share secrets with others. They want to make sure of something *else*, to prove themselves real. Unless secrets are shared, they're not much different from symptoms of paranoia."

Petrie was fairly sure he wasn't being followed as he drove north out of Denver. He made U-turns in Longmont and again in Cheyenne, Wyoming, to check whether another car was following or leading him. When he reached Laramie, he ditched the rented car in a small parking lot, wiped off his prints with a pocket handkerchief, and threw the ignition key onto the roof of a one-story building. Then he proceeded to a second-hand-car lot where he bought a four-year-old Ford LTD, after bargaining a bit with the owner to show he was in no hurry. A block away from the lot, he sat in the Ford waiting. No one arrived to talk with the dealer; and when the windowless shack was closed for the day and padlocked and the light bulbs that looped the perimeter turned on, Petrie headed off toward the Wasatch range in Utah. He planned to drive all night without stopping, out of Wyoming and across Utah into Nevada as far as Winnemucca—or maybe even Reno, if he made good time. Crossing the desert, he paid small attention to car lights ahead or behind because there was no point. In the desert the tracks are so few and narrow you can't hide even if you can run. As the sunrise rimmed the desert flats, he reflected on his being alone. Traveling light, with only a small suitcase taken from Alcarita's apartment and a dispatch case in the back seat, ought to help him now. *But being alone did not.* He badly needed someone to talk to who could outwit his memory and so cause oddments to rise between the cracks of his consciousness.

At about the time Petrie was entering Reno, Nick Calvino was sitting with his uncle Mario in a casino two hundred miles south, staring at the girls dancing on the stage above the bar in their tiny top hats and lacquered blond wigs and rhinestone G-strings so narrow they disappeared between powdered buttocks. Goddamn. He really liked Las Vegas. Somebody had told him that this place even had real schools and churches, not to speak of a college. Nick hadn't seen these because all three times he'd been here he had gone from the airport straight to the Playmall Hotel on the Strip. Other than hotels and casinos, he'd seen only the Convention Center, which struck him as cheap looking for such a big noise as Las Vegas. His uncle Renato had explained it by saying that nobody invested much in carpets and chandeliers without slots and card tables.

Uncle Mario was speaking now, at a normal pitch, yet Nick could hardly hear him over the sound of the new Gavotte Rock, which hit heavy on every third note. "If we can't hear each other, kid, neither can the feds." Mario laughed in short bursts, like a car honking, whenever he told a joke. "Tell that Shurtz your uncles ain't going into this thing just because some sick guy died a day early."

Try as he might, Nick couldn't keep his eyes from straying to the girls, so tall and tight skinned. He sure would like a woman who was wound tight and would scream with pleasure when he broke in! His wife Angie just sighed, like a tire losing air. Uncle Renato, who had paid for their honeymoon to Bermuda, had later consoled him. Be patient, he had said, because a woman gets better as she ages. But for cry sakes, who wanted the mother of teenage children to become a horny bitch?

"Gunner," Nick repeated, "says there's a lot of money in

this." He had earlier recounted the events in New York, having practiced on the flight to Las Vegas to get all the details straight.

"You let the Jew think we want the money. We'll use anything that's here to trade for our hostages the narcs hold. You never tell him what I just said!" Mario leaned over and slapped Nick's face in a jovial avuncular gesture that hurt like hell.

"Gunner will be pissed off if there's no money for him."

"He can piss all the way to his heaven. What's wrong with you, Nick? You think he's got a big scam? Shit, it's nothing like what Renato was selling when they had those my-cin drugs after the war in 1945. Now, *that* was big. Fuck Shurtz. Some day you come here to work for Renato."

"Is he here? I kinna like to pay my respects. Like, ya know."

"Kid, he loves you like a son since your papa died, but he's tied up. You have a good time tonight at the tables and tomorrow morning you catch a nonstop so you can have supper with Angie at home. It's later in the East—they're backward out there." He honked. Nick smiled tentatively. Was it a joke? "Here's ten Cs. Play some cards or dice. It's on the house—the White House. And, Nick, tell the Jew that finding this guy is like looking for a needle in a haystack. And you and I know that if you want a needle, you go to a tailor, right?"

After he left, Mario reflected that Nick Calvino was every bit as dim as his father, who had married into the Mortella family. Old Sergio Mortella had commanded his three sons, Mario, Renato, and Roberto, to support the Calvinos. Renato's having made Nick the bodyguard of Gunther Shurtz was a double joke, what the old man, his father, used to call *ironia*. After all, if Nick was hopeless as a bodyguard, he could nonetheless be a witness. Nick couldn't guard a cat but he might be able to tell you where it slept. About *ironia*, a very high-class kind of humor, their father had first heard of it from

Aldo Tuzzi, a Venetian aristocrat turned educator who kept nagging the government in Rome to help the poor and sick of Sicily. Tuzzi was a saint, Don Mortella had told his sons, and twice had given him fifty thousand dollars to help the orphans of Palermo. Tuzzi had once told Mortella that it would be true *ironia* if the Mafia were ever legally elected to office—they could hardly bribe themselves.

Walking around the hotel pool to reach his own cottage, Mario was convinced that Renato had been right not to allow Nick to know of Shurtz's first telephone call, which had alerted them to pick up the scent of the fed in Philadelphia and trace him all the way to Denver. Moreover, they had tailed him out of Denver by using three cars, two alternating behind and one leading. They had watched him buy the LTD and were on him now, as he seemed to be heading toward San Francisco. Renato wanted to see where he put down before they made a move on him. As Mario unlocked his cottage door, he thought that, while there *might* be something in this chase, it didn't make it any easier with Nick on hand. Jesus! The kid was stupid. He really should be stomping grapes in the old country. No, he'd drown. Mario honked as he went inside.

CHAPTER FIVE

———— • ————

HAAGSTROM SPOKE INTO THE RECEIVER OF THE BLUE TELE-
phone that bore neither buttons nor a slot for a coded card
and was activated only when picked up in the White House
by the Chief of Staff. Soon, the President himself was on the
line, alone.

"Yes, Mr. President, we can buy information and thereby
keep it exclusive. Expression of information is property and
can legally be transacted." He listened. "Of course, sir. I'm
still convinced he doesn't realize what it is he knows." A pause.
"Thank you, Mr. President."

He put down the receiver, placed his elbows on the desk
to press his palms hard against both temples. The pain! His
arteritis was making metronome swings between the ganglia,
left, right, right, left. He gasped, holding his breath, though it
never worked, this reducing of the oxygen in his arteries, the
turning down of the blood jets. The disease was so relentless

that he was no longer surprised by the pain—not even when he awoke at night to find himself gripping the sides of the bed as if on a ledge. Over the years Haagstrom had come to conceive of his suffering as the exquisite punishment of a Clever God who struck a man precisely where he kept his pride, who struck over and over to remind him that someone who tries to prefigure the defeat of his own devisings—a man who comprehends that hopefulness is not a principal quality of intelligence—should logically become the victim of his own mentation.

Over the years, the Commission's work had largely been that of rooting out corruption among federal agents, like those customs officials Shurtz had bribed. The Commission's employees could not operate outside the United States, and so in only a few instances had the Commission dealt with foreign matters; one was Iran-Contra in its domestic aspects, and on two occasions certain Interior officials had compromised the United States in dealings with Japanese manufacturers. Now, all the splendid past work of the Commission seemed about to be blotted out in a single moment—like a hand held high can obliterate the whole sun.

In the second year of President Bush's first term, a discovery had been confirmed, a scientific breakthrough achieved by the U.S. and the USSR. Several months before the attempt against Petrie, the Commissioner had been summoned to the White House and told by the President, who sat alone in the Oval Office, that the United States and the Soviet Union had for a period of eight years, over scratchy times and good times, exchanged data and through repeated trials had finally confirmed—with a joy that had made some Soviet leaders actually weep—that they had created a scientific device to create almost limitless energy. Now, the Commission was being recruited to make sure that this secret, its theory and its technology, was not lost to other nations. The risk of leaks was stupendous. Quite apart from the monetary value, which could be counted in *trillions,* there was the peculiar stress that keepers of confidences undergo. Had Turcheff known of this discovery, his views on the "environment" of keepers of secrets might apply here.

But there was more. In statehood, as in politics or crime, there is always more. The two powers had made a deal called the Protocol. In the Commission the deal was known only to Haagstrom. He was not allowed to tell his Deputy or the Chief of Operations of this diplomatic accord, although all three of them knew the outlines of the technology itself. The deal made sense, seen one way; seen another, it showed a severe lack of sensibility. The two powers had agreed that the bounty of the discovery—not its actual technology but its products—should be given immediately to poor countries in Eastern Europe, Asia, Africa, and South America, with some political exceptions. Moreover, each of the two powers had agreed that if it was to gain an economic head start, it must keep the technology secret, for a time at least, from Great Britain, France, Germany, China, Japan, South Korea, Australia, and all other nations. It was the Soviet Union that had demanded a head start. It managed to convince the United States that three years would be long enough for the USSR to rebuild its industry, renew its agriculture, and thus become competitive with other rich countries. The United States agreed, mostly because it had internal problems that could be solved more easily if international competition were not to begin on Day One.

So far, so good. Then the USSR astounded President Bush by insisting on making the technology, not just goods but the secret discovery itself, available to Poland. Bush knew the Russians and Poles had a long history of mutual hatred, beginning with the two partitions of Poland in the eighteenth century and intensified by forty-five years of domination by the Russians after World War II. Their differences, furthermore, were many: the Russians regarded the Poles as romantics or *naifs*, while the Poles saw the Russians as bullies and boors. And on and on. Yet despite it all there remained the stark facts of geography and economics. Hitler and Stalin, like Napoleon, were aware that between Paris and Moscow lies a flat plain with no intervening hills, let alone mountains. Now a reunited Germany dominated that plain. If the Soviets were given a boundless supply of energy and at the same time included in their partnership Poland—the largest Eastern European nation and one that bordered on Germany—the USSR would present to the world a defensible expanse from the Pacific to the middle of Europe. And since a deal is a deal and fair is fair, the Americans had one nation they could choose: Canada. Had Great Britain not agreed to join Europe in '92, there might have been a toss-up between the two. But not now: not only were the United States and Canada best trading partners, but Canada was also the first line of defense, over the Arctic Circle, against the largest Asiatic powers, the USSR, Japan, and China. Although Bush didn't put much faith in *that* argument, he allowed it to be made. It was far tougher to decide which nations would be denied goods and services. The Soviet Union didn't want to help Pakistan. The United States was unwilling to see Vietnam receive enough goods to threaten its neighbors. In the end it was agreed that, for three years only, no products of the technology would go to the rogue nations that owned dangerous technology for war: Iraq, Libya, and North Korea. President Bush was additionally relieved that these three nations had small populations and no known starvation.

"You understand, Commissioner," the President had said to Haagstrom, "the goods and services we will dispense are huge. Let me lay this on you. Twenty trillion dollars. That's twenty thousand million dollars! The figure is a bit exaggerated; after all, the poor countries will contribute to their own welfare—their soil and forests and minerals and of course the work of their people."

"Sir," the Commissioner had replied. "Three years is a long time in any event. But if such a secret can be preserved, it's a *very* long time. Why do *we* need a head start?"

"We don't, in absolute terms. But since we have an agreement, we might as well make use of it. I've got in mind a huge program to aid two segments of our population: the homeless poor, including of course members of minority groups and migrant workers and illegals and the drug addicts. With this technology, we can enlarge some small cities in the Midwest, the South, the West, each of, say, forty thousand people—all in aid of these damaged people."

"Sir, I hope I am not impertinent in anticipating that if the United States creates zones or small cities, as you say, where addicts can recover and the homeless be given shelter and the illegal immigrants given education and useful work, some liberals are sure to complain that we will be imitating, in reverse, the old Soviet gulags."

"Commissioner, I've got to admit that I hadn't asked myself that question. A couple of economists at the Hoover Institution did, however, and the answer is that we give those *categories* of people a priority to own houses and take jobs within such cities and zones. Only that—first choice. We won't force anyone. Maybe such a plan will not be needed if the workers in Detroit, Chicago, Pittsburgh, Buffalo—you name it—are creating better shelter for themselves and are hired to renew the infrastructure, the roads, bridges, all the rest."

The President was hoping the talk was over. Haagstrom was visibly disturbed. It was natural to worry about the political repercussions of the diplomatic agreement, but Bush wondered if there was more. The Commissioner had for a long time served as a judge. He was looking now at the issue of equity, at what was fair—precisely the question that was hardest for a politician to answer. What is fair tomorrow? What is fair in the eye of eternity?

"Mr. President, how can we be sure that the leaders of poor countries won't give our bounty only to their supporters and starve their opponents?"

"That's covered too. Any country receiving the benefits of the discovery has to agree to on-site inspection by joint Soviet-U.S. military forces—as in Ethiopia or Cambodia."

"Sir," Haagstrom persisted. "Wouldn't that become an inducement for rebels to overthrow the present governments?"

"Commissioner," the President replied, "that possibility bothers me enormously. But the Soviets will never agree to give up the technology before they are economically stronger. So, right now, it's a three-year plan of a four-nation monopoly."

And so it happened that the Commissioner was given charge of keeping secure the largest secret in the history of nations. The Commission had been chosen by its four Regents—the President, the Speaker of the House, and the majority and minority leaders of the Senate—because it bore no conflict of interest. It had no espionage network in place.

"Commissioner? May I come up for a moment?" It was Tannenbaum. When he was seated, his spare body folded into an armchair as if by hinged sections, he said, "I'm terribly sorry over the mess. It's my fault."

Tannenbaum still smarted from the hypocrisy of his replies to Petrie's skepticism during those two fateful strolls in New York City. When the Chief had reached Harkness to check on the condition of Connors and Bizuski and Donato, the three CIs who had been incapacitated by Petrie, he himself was nearly numb. He couldn't help wondering, bitterly, what the Russians would think of an intelligence organization that could not contain a single person—and, worse, one of its own employees.

"We were presuming that Turcheff had told Petrie enough for him to guess. That wasn't much to go on," he told Haagstrom. "I realize that now. But Turcheff *did* run."

"Chief, the Russians made a mistake. There was no need for their Deputy to the President to have interrogated the Professor over Petrie's visits in 1978 and 1979. Turcheff knew Petrie was not a government agent of any sort. I guess it was the Marxist penchant for dialectics. One, Turcheff understands the technology. Two, since Petrie was not an agent for the United States when he saw Turcheff, then the Professor could have talked freely with him on scientific matters. Three, realizing what he'd done, Turcheff has fled Moscow."

Tannenbaum was astonished at the bad luck and incompetence that had marked the whole awful train of events. It didn't help that it was the Soviets who had made the first mistake.

Haagstrom put the heels of his palms to his head only briefly, resuming, "Chief, look at it this way. Turcheff is a sophisticated man. When the Deputy came, he began to ask himself: what's the issue here? With the Cold War ended, what *could* be at issue? Probably, he started generically, by asking what general differences or likenesses exist among nations. War, that's one. Dogma, that's another. Nationality. And finally economics—groceries for everyone."

"And," said Tannenbaum, now feeling more at ease in taking part in this homegrown dialectic, "the Soviet Union has abandoned dogma as an instrument of state policy. The United States is satisfied that in most parts of the world nationalities are having their day. We didn't go to war over Eastern Europe for the past forty-five years, so why assume we would do so today? The war is over. Gorbachev had, you recall, even asked for *joint* maneuvers! So, Commissioner, Turcheff says to himself, it must be groceries!"

"He does that. And since the study of economics cannot of itself become a state secret, it alone could hardly bring the Deputy to Turcheff's flat."

The Chief added, "So, to Turcheff it had to be an enormous discovery that creates groceries for everyone, big enough so that you can't risk anyone's knowing about it unofficially— even if he's a patriot like Professor Turcheff."

In the adjoining office, as the Commissioner talked with Tannenbaum, Matthews sat contentedly puffing on a Cuban cigar. His secretary always removed the bands from these illegal Havanas as a concession to the letter of the law. It was of more significance that even if Matthews bought cigars made in Tampa he'd not be permitted to fit them with bands bearing a Commission logo or seal. There was no logo.

In 1974 President Ford had created a Commission on Monitoring Government Bureaus and Agencies. Contrary to the habit of government, the Commission had never gained an acronym. (CMGBA was, for one thing, just too close to KGB.) By 1990 the Commission was spending just over two hundred million dollars a year despite its relatively small staff. In the field were the forty CIs, and in the headquarters building in the Anacostia section of the capital were about seventy other employees. This building originally had been a Masonic temple and its marble-faced corridors and the six-foot-thick exterior walls were an accidental bonus to security. On the top floor were Haagstrom and Matthews, the Deputy for Administration. Next below was Tannenbaum's Operations, Section Three. Below him was Section Two, Records and Research. In the basement was Four, Communications. On the ground floor was a twenty-foot-high space with stacks holding books; and on its open mezzanine above stood desks for the ostensible use of scholars. Admission to this library was said to be gained by submission of written application. In truth, few persons applied and none was accepted. The building was listed in Washington directories as the National Institute of Information Theory.

Keeping an even ash by a most delicate inspiration, Matthews recalled that he'd first conceived his dislike for Petrie when he'd told the young CI that in the good old days cigars were especially fine because the women in the factories in Cuba rolled the leaves against the soft skin of their inner thighs. Petrie had spoiled the occasion by saying that Batista, the former sergeant who had ruled Cuba before Castro, had once told someone, *"Es un cuento maravilloso pero no es verdad.* It's a wonderful story but, alas, untrue."

This Petrie had said in English. Neither Matthews nor anyone else in the Commission realized he spoke Spanish—it being an aspect of his formal knowledge that Petrie had not declared when he was recruited and accepted because he hadn't wanted by chance to reveal his old involvement with his Cuban lady. Matthews, irritated, had brought away from that occasion the shrewd notion that Petrie's flaw was his erudition: knowledge, like material possessions, sooner or later demands to be displayed.

As for display, the Commission was forbidden the use of "seals, logos, marks, crests, emblems, and mottoes." That wording was part of the Charter, which held the Commission's duty to be: "It will monitor all federal agencies including but not restricted to the Secret Service and Internal Revenue Service and Government Accounting Office and Central Intelligence Agency and Federal Bureau of Investigation and Drug

Enforcement Agency and customs and immigration and all banking and trade and transport bureaus or divisions including those both military and civilian whose employees or collaborators of employees are deemed whether acting singly or jointly to have committed a crime under any and all current and future pertaining laws of the United States."

Matthews had once complained that this primary definition was not properly punctuated: it used no commas or semicolons. But the Commissioner, who had been successively an attorney and a judge before his appointment, knew that whereas punctuation can clarify, it also can qualify and limit. President Ford had wanted the Commission not to be limited in its power to investigate any part of government, as he had told Haagstrom when he was installed as the Commissioner in 1974. Vietnam and Watergate, one the continuing specter of Democrats, the other of Republicans, had come to be seen as actions that were in part authorized by no more than mere inferences. It was in the nature of things that plans can grow from fantasies and be allowed to persist if not subjected to the bite of reality and the rasp of specificity. It all followed Vietnam, really. Watergate was bad—although Europeans could never quite comprehend how "official lying" was so reprehensible that it brought down a President—but Vietnam, counting deaths, was fifty-five thousand times worse. Men had died there from deliberately distorted intelligence, from a confusion of causes and results—so distorted that Tet, an American victory, was reported in the home press as a defeat; and General Giap was considered by the Americans a shrewd commander when in fact his strategy after 1954 was generally bad.

So it was, President Ford had reasoned, himself a Yale lawyer, that "limited actions" and "punitive situations," as they were called by members of Kennedy's and Johnson's National Security Councils, had turned into a full-scale war. The Commission was created to warn its Regents, in time, should any federal agencies allow "contingency plans" to be tested in the field and "strategic games" to be played out to the point that they became real through inadvertence or miscalculation or malfeasance. The assassination of Diem, carried out by President Kennedy, and the Gulf of Tonkin Resolution, pushed through Congress by President Johnson, stood as examples of this kind of official hypocrisy and duplicity.

It was the second of the four Regents of the Commission, the Speaker of the House, who, on the occasion of Haagstrom's installation in a private ceremony in the White House, had said, "We can't allow you to have a motto, as the President told you. That's more than whim. But if there were a motto, it ought to be *Sed quis custodiet ipsos custodes?* Who is to guard the guardians themselves?" Unlike Matthews, Haagstrom had never regretted the President's injunction against insignia: give a man a flag, and he will call others to it.

CHAPTER SIX

M ATTHEWS LOOKED NONPLUSSED, FOR HIM AN UNCOMFORT-
able expression. Watching him closely, Tannenbaum fully
expected a contentious commentary to ensue. Still, Matthews had a right. The Commission's pursuit of Petrie was
surely the least skillful exercise in its sixteen-year history. The
Commissioner had refused to relent when Tannenbaum asked
for help from the FBI and the Treasury Department's Secret
Service because, he argued, there weren't enough CIs to sustain
a fast chase. The Commissioner had been adamant. Matthews
concurred with him. Now Tannenbaum waited.

"Why would you assume," Matthews asked the Chief, "that
he might be staying somewhere else in Denver after avoiding
his place in Littleton? You're not saying it's like that story of
Poe 'The Purloined Letter'? That he's staying in the obvious
place because we will dismiss it as being too obvious?"

Tannenbaum looked at him steadily as he replied. "Matt,

for a couple of years he has used the Littleton place hardly at all. He pays the rent by mail and keeps a downtown P.O. box. I think he's got a second place or is living with someone. He's been a traveler all his life and he's unmarried. If one place is home to him, it's Denver. He once must have felt safe there—as a child."

Home. Home is where, at the very least, you were on one occasion celebrated. One Sunday in February of 1954, following mass, an infant had been presented to God cleansed and blessed, held high in the hands of a Russian Orthodox priest who faced the iconostasis first to the left, next to the right. This was immediately after the tall Serb coal miner who was his godfather had held Alexandr, both with their backs against the altar, and three times had spit out the Devil. The infant emerged from the ceremony as Alexandr Vladimirovich Pyotorov, following the Russian patronymic custom of carrying his father's first name as his second. As for the Pyotorov name, it had survived several passages. Before his birth, his parents had entered America through Canada. Earlier, his father had undergone the mixed fate of being a Soviet soldier captured by the Germans and then being sent to a work camp in occupied France. Once liberated, he had obtained a passport and visa to enter Quebec and there he had married a second-generation Russian woman. Claiming her brother, who was a U.S. citizen, they were allowed to enter from Montreal. Although they had been married three years, his father had convinced his mother that their children should be born in America: after his travail in Europe, Canada seemed only a second prize. But there were not children, only a single child.

Alexandr Vladimirovich felt no reminiscent affection for any house in Denver—in any event, he'd lived in a rooming house—and he hadn't been a communicant of the church in

Globeville. So what were the ties that bind? Denver was his youth, his boyhood, the place where he'd been for the last time happily vulnerable. His triumphs in school as a scholar and on the playing field were irreplaceable.

Tannenbaum was not off the mark. He now told Matthews he'd need at least eight CIs to sweep the city.

"Go ahead," Matthews instructed him, rolling a new cigar in one hand and tapping it flutelike to listen for the dread sound of dryness. "We have the edge, Chief. It always being easier to follow than to lead, harder to back down than climb up."

And so the Commission broke its ironclad rule without, of course, its own inspectors knowing it. Tannenbaum told the CIs to look for Alexander Pyotorov, born in Frederick, Colorado, in 1954, moved to Denver in 1959, attended Ebert Elementary School, Cole Junior High School, and Manual Training High School. Later he attended Princeton on a football scholarship and earned a degree in engineering, and then for four years worked for Pooley, Inc.

The Mirosets alone should have made it easy to track Pyotorov, but not as the parents of Congressman Nicholas Miroset from Fairbanks, Alaska. The CIs were told not to pursue anything relating to the Mirosets. Pyotorov's picture was shown to families living near the packinghouses in Globeville and to the priest at the Serbian and Russian Orthodox Church of the Transfiguration, who proved to be too young to have known the Pyotorovs. None of his parishioners had heard anything of Alexandr since his father was buried in 1973. Then the CIs concentrated their search on the downtown area, beginning at California Street and sweeping eastward toward Ebert Elementary and St. Luke's Hospital. They hit paydirt when a girl of ten remarked that the man in the photograph was rich. How so? He gave her five dollars to buy an ice-cream bar when everyone knows they cost only a dollar. Where does the rich man live? With Alcarita Obregon, of course, "but he's not like us." Not a Chicano? Right.

Tannenbaum arrived at six the next morning. Richard Ortiz, a CI born in El Paso of Mexican parents, was suitably disguised in a thin corduroy jumpsuit with flared trousers and a tight-fitting velveteen shirt buttoned like an Eisenhower jacket when he went to the row terrace and explained to a neighbor, whose suspicions he overcame by flattery, that Alcarita had bought a number that had won eight hundred dollars. The neighbor urged him to leave the prize money because Alcarita had gone only briefly to visit her sister in Pueblo. Ortiz gave her three authentic numbers he'd bought downtown from a street hawker. He kissed her fat lips and left.

When the CIs gathered in Pueblo that afternoon, among them was Jesus Martinez, another janissary, a Mexican-American like Ortiz. It was his notion to crowd the Commission men along with Alcarita and her sister and Teresita's husband and her parents into the kitchen of the small frame house in Pueblo—making the victims feed on each other's fears in close quarters, as happens in a jail holding tank. It was pathetically typical, Ortiz thought, that Alcarita should accept the authority of these strangers without even asking to see identification. Why did his people always *accept*? In Western movies you could always recognize the *federales* by their mustaches, bad teeth, and ill-fitting chalk-colored uniforms. Did Alcarita presume that Anglo officials were so confident, or so endowed, that they need not dress alike in order to act together?

"It doesn't seem right," the Chief said, "that this man betrayed your family."

"He warned me. He said you would be chasing him. He got away. He didn't just leave." It was, Martinez thought, a nice distinction.

"Did he say who we were?"

"Why? Don't you know?"

"Tell her that her family is in trouble." A senior CI addressed Martinez.

"Let her talk first," Ortiz interrupted in Spanish.

"These people are illegals," Martinez challenged him, also in Spanish.

Tannenbaum motioned Ortiz to proceed. *"Tu hombre se ha metido en un problema serio. Lo buscaron por mucho tiempo. Es un criminal. Pero, sele hace difícil. No lo culpes.* Your man is in serious trouble. He's a big criminal. Still, it's hard on him. Don't blame him."

"I do not blame him," Carita retorted in English, denying any affinity with her inquisitor. "He did nothing bad to me. I don't care"—she pointed to Tannenbaum—"what he did to him."

"But, Señora," Ortiz said softly, "he *did* harm you. He told you to come to Pueblo, right? Then, he finished some business in Denver without your being in the way. Finally, he gained a two-day head start on us by giving out where you could be found. He *did* use you."

She cried as if branded, her large brown eyes glistening. As she pushed her shoulders back to gain air, she noticed with contempt how the strangers became aware of her rising breasts.

Ortiz persisted. "You know his handwriting? Of course you do. Then, Señora, please read." The forgery was a much-folded note bearing her name, the Denver address, Tony's place of work, and, more, her sister's married name.

Martinez said, "He's clever. It took three days for this letter to reach Washington and two days for us to find you here. I am sorry for you, Señora."

Her family and the CIs watched as she stared helplessly at the paper. What no one, not even Teresita, could guess was that out of the chaos of impressions Alcarita was beginning to form the consoling notion that her lover's crime was not one of property, not of theft, but one of politics. If he had betrayed her—which she did not yet accept—it was allowable if he was following a cause greater than mere mortal love. That notion freed her in a particular way. Now she must trade something with these business-suited *federales* to protect her family. She began slowly to tell them that "Alex Hoffman" had been in and out of Denver over the past two years. She knew nothing of his business except that he was prosperous and generous. What she finally gave them, in a concrete exchange for safety for her family, was to relate that once she had accused him of infidelity when she found a card in his suit pocket bearing a woman's name. He had assuaged her by saying it was only someone who sold real estate in a California town. Which town? She remembered, she said, because it sounded Spanish but wasn't. Petaluma.

Then it was settled. A young Chicano lawyer in Pueblo in due course—after many wheels moved in Washington—obtained for the adults of the family the documents that allowed them to stay forever in the United States.

As he drove through the city, Petrie reflected that San Francisco was besotted by its own glamour, a sensation that was cheaply renewed by the passing admiration of the tourist trade—much as a wino gets a slight buzz from plain water. He crossed over the Golden Gate Bridge and passed the turn-off to Mill Valley, a town where migration lawyers and psychiatrists and other Yuppies had managed to drive up rents and unwittingly had forced out some of the writers and artists whose company they had originally valued. A few of those bohemian refugees had moved to the stark headlands northward. Two years before, Petrie had found a lodge of two rooms situated near the water, one not visible from secondary roads, let alone from the main north-south freeway, Route 101, some distance away. He had bought it from a real-estate dealer in Petaluma, using Alfred Porter as the name on the deed and title. For a recluse, the place was perfect. Huge boulders sectioned off the beach into defiles of cold water. The road to the lodge had become, through calculated neglect, two tracks overgrown with Russian thistle and needle grass. His closest neighbors, who on rare occasions walked over the headlands from houses similarly placed, were two young men who fashioned silver whenever they could afford the cost of the metal and a woman of about thirty who worked a loom inside her house. His neighbors knew him only as Al and believed he owned a used-car dealership, was divorced and childless, and had come to this isolated place to mull things over and write a novel. His cover was plausible: he wore suits, drove automobiles of different makes and license plates, invited no guests, and kept on the table next to a typewriter sheaves of manuscript, which, as a matter of fact, was the text of a thirties novel of no renown and small merit.

Now, as he reached a point between two hillocks short of the tracks to the lodge, he parked the car he had bought in Laramie. He removed the license plates and put them in the trunk and proceeded along the roadway until, startled, he saw a thin twist of smoke emerging from the large stone chimney of the lodge. He crouched below the crest of the bluff overlooking the ocean. He could see that the insubstantial lock on the box on the porch was still unforced. It held rubber boots, old sweaters, cans of Sterno, as well as some cans of cling peaches—a motley appeasement intended to keep intruders from rifling the house itself. Outside the double window in the main room, facing north, the open metal shutters banged loosely against the wall from the wind. Petrie tightened his raincoat against the rasping cold and settled down to watch. Soon, the lodge's only door was opened and then slammed shut from the force of the wind. A boy of sixteen or so stood on the edge of the small porch. He wore a sweatshirt and heavy jeans. A few minutes later, a girl with blond braids came out and stood next to him, hugging herself with her arms in a cable-stitched sweater. After they returned inside, Petrie started to work his way down, clutching branches of the sturdy Sargent cypresses to keep from slipping. He walked past the bedroom, where the shutters were closed, to the front and pushed open the door as he announced loudly, "It's called breaking and entering."

The woman jumped up and held a fist to her mouth. The boy spoke rapidly. "The door was open. We didn't take anything."

From a distance he had misjudged the girl. The boy was no more than sixteen; but she was a woman in her mid-thirties. She was either the boy's mother or his stepmother, or maybe an aunt, he figured. Both were blond, fine featured, lithe.

"We just forced a window," the boy said too quickly.

"Kid, the shutters swing from interior hasps and even a crowbar can't force them. You came down that oversized chimney like a squirrel after you tore away the netting I put there to keep squirrels out. You've got scratches and soot stains on your hands and arms."

"We didn't trash you!" the woman declaimed angrily. "We opened your canned spaghetti and sat in your chairs like the three bears—only there are just two of us."

"There's always a third bear," Petrie told her as he moved farther into the room. "Where are you from?"

"We won't say. It's a constitutional right," she retorted. She was serious, he noted with some surprise.

"I give you that. But I'm still going to frisk your constitutions."

"Don't linger."

The boy frowned, disapproving more of her than of him, Petrie thought. He motioned them to face the wall next to the unshuttered window and went through a duffel and two back-packs, finding no weapons, not even a flare. Then he ran his hands, ladderlike, over their bodies and confirmed his first impression that she was blessed with a narrow waist and slim thighs. The braids, the headband, and her jeans were a little out of fashion, like her idiom, "trash." As he stepped back he was stricken by a desire that they not leave right away. Out-side, it was closing time, the sun setting, the bluffs purpled into gloom. He wanted company. Hoping to detain them, he or-dered the boy to bring in more wood from the metal cradle on the porch.

"Mom? Joanie?"

"It's okay, Scott. He's not dangerous. Just horny."

Petrie swung the iron grill from a slot in the fireplace, then went into the bedroom and without bothering to disguise his hidey-hole under the linoleum brought from the cellar an arm-ful of powdered eggs, pancake batter, smoked sausage, and hard-crusted bread.

"Who are you?" she taunted him. "There are no names anywhere. The cans are stripped of labels. How do you know what to eat? Zounds, even the Three-in-One oil is in a plastic bottle. You must be the Ultimate Consumer. Go crazy, do you, seeing name brands? I don't wonder your name isn't on that typing. What a dull book you're writing—or typewriting."

Petrie didn't reply. A tincture of gorge rose in his throat like acid in a test tube. He resisted his own anger by asking the boy, who had returned with the logs, "Are you on the road?" It was also a term out of fashion.

Scott replied earnestly, "We weren't bumming. My mother and I were visiting some guys who make silver things near here, and we left our car above their house. When we tried to walk along the beach, I fell in. Your place was the only one close by where I could get dry. My mother walked up the roadway but couldn't find anyone at the other house near here."

His mother laughed, her voice deep but not unpleasant. "Scott, give him our passport and Swiss bank account numbers while you're at it." Then she looked at Petrie, squinting. "I know who you are! You're the 'old gringo,' Ambrose Bierce, come back to life from Mexico. Or maybe you're just Neal Cassady, who didn't die in Mexico after all."

Petrie astonished himself by saying, "Cassady and I come from the same town." It was not only unnecessary; it was dangerous, giving out some biography.

"Who was Cassady?" the boy asked.

"He was somebody who was famous for being famous. He was like a black hole in the universe—a lot of gravity with small matter."

"That's wild!" Scott looked at him admiringly.

"We're leaving," his mother declared angrily, kicking one of the backpacks toward Scott.

Petrie felt a surge through his arteries and strode from the fireplace to seize her arms. Unaware, he squeezed harder and harder until she was wet eyed from pain, her cheeks reddening. She managed to look past him to see her son raising the backpack to throw it at Petrie.

"No, Scott! No! I'm all right. Really."

"I'm sorry. I know there isn't a third bear. I really am sorry. You can go."

"Why can't we stay and eat, Mom?"

"He didn't *invite* us. He's not used to people. I know what that's like, but it doesn't change things."

She tucked her braids of blond hair into the front of her sweater, Indian style, picked up the duffel and her backpack, and led her son from the lodge. Petrie watched them climb the roadway until they were high enough to double back on the bluff and head southward. He opened the bedroom shutters to watch, but soon they were lost to the fog. Then, listening to the wind rise as he sat at the window, he saw nothing but the glistening tracery of a nearby buckeye tree. Closing the shutters, he decided not to eat and threw water on the flames. He lay on the floor. When he heard the knock on the door a couple of hours later, he knew who it was—but he didn't feel proud.

CHAPTER SEVEN

———— • ————

DON'T WANT TO EXPLAIN," SHE TOLD PETRIE. HER HAIR WAS flattened from the light rain, her cheeks and forehead stippled. He didn't ask anything except the whereabouts and safety of her son.

"Where's Scott?"

"He's driving to his father's house in Berkeley. He ran down and told the silver boys that I was waiting in the car to drive him home. The car belongs to my ex. Scott is staying with him for a couple of weeks. God, why am I explaining?"

She was relieved that he didn't appear to be triumphant or even content. On the way back she had decided that he wasn't mean spirited, despite the arm wrestling. He had looked to her self-isolated and angry. She'd seen those qualities in herself, one summoning the other. Bizarrely, it occurred to her that she hadn't danced on a proper ballroom floor since she was in prep school. Without a word, she went into the bedroom, shed her jeans and sweater and shirt, kicked off the Adidas shoes, and slid, shuddering, between the cold sheets.

She awoke, alone in bed, to the aroma of coffee. Raising her head, propped on both elbows, she realized the house had become a cocoon and she was reminded of her childhood days at her family's place in Sea Ranch, on the coast a hundred miles north of San Francisco. There she used to marvel how at night the fog magically allowed the sea to disappear and made the bluffs behind their house rise up like waves—turning a person around in defiance of the gyroscope in the inner ear. After she used the bathroom and dressed, she opened the bedroom door and saw him cooking last night's food as this morning's breakfast. On the floor lay a pallet where he'd spent the night.

They sat at opposite ends of the bench, as on a teeter-totter. She told him, the hot coffee making her lisp, about Sea Ranch.

"Once I saw a play set in a steambath," he said. "The porter was a Puerto Rican—like a New York apartment house super—who went about his duties in a calm and knowing manner. He was the Angel Gabriel. The people in the mist of Purgatory kept complaining they were lost, but he assured them they were simply not found."

"You're not found, either. You're hidden here. Aren't you?"

"No, Joan, it's just not home to me. Does Scott live with you?"

"During school days, yes. What's your name?"

"Alex. Is Scott content with half a home, Joan?" Then he switched. "You're not content."

"How could I know?" She paused. "I see dramas, too. In a movie called *House of Games* David Mamet has a murderess in an asylum say, 'I knows there are normal people outside but I don't know what those people do.' It's like that with me. My parents and I, then my ex-husband and I, looked for normality. Is there such a place?"

Petrie smiled. "Lord! I just wanted to say good morning, Joan."

"No, you didn't. You want to know about me. It's my turn. Do you have parents? Do you have a wife?"

"My parents are dead. Even when they were alive the three of us never knew what to make of each other. I'm not married and never have been." He paused. Then he stared at her only slightly. "I've known a lot of women."

"I won't care about them. What about your parents?"

"My mother was sick and exhausted. In the end she was, what? Without contention. She couldn't decide what she wanted. My father couldn't help. He was distant, silent. He'd been a prisoner of war under the Nazis." He paused again. "Maybe that explains his silence. Some thoughts must come out as screams."

She felt guilty all of a sudden. Domestic difficulties in Walnut Creek and Berkeley sounded like a soap opera compared with the horrors of the Nazi war. She tried to make amends.

"Listen, please. In my family, we were never silent, however trivial the issue. Accusations and recriminations needed sound. More than that, it was orchestrated. Every wrong was remembered. Every little victory recalled. We were quite adept—never missed a heartbeat."

"My God, Joan! What a burden you are carrying! Can't you one morning just start over?"

"You are an innocent."

"Tell me."

"People talk of parents not letting their children go. It is usually the other way around."

"You sound like a sixties flower child. You're too young! When were you born?"

"Nineteen fifty-three. I saw enough of the sixties and early seventies. And, after all, I went to Cal, to Berkeley."

"That's why you make your intimate complaints into public events?"

She began to cry, the tears filling her blue eyes, spilling over onto her sweater. She was alarmed by remembrance. Just as he rose to come to her, the snap of a rifle shot was heard and a pinking of the window as a bullet burst open the cable stitching over her shoulder, carrying away woolen threads with bits of bloody tissue. Petrie bent over and brought her to the floor by pulling her knees away from the bench.

He lay on top of her, whispering, "The rifleman is no farther than thirty yards." Keeping low, he seized her feet and drew her along the floor until they were directly beneath the shattered window, closer to the sniper but less accessible to him. Another shot splintered the floor at the entrance to the bedroom.

"His angle is not acute enough. He'll come closer."

"Is he alone?" Her voice broke from the pain. She had managed not to touch the wound.

"There's got to be a backup. There always is. But that one, he can't shoot from the bedroom side because of the shutters. They'll set fire to the lodge."

Another shot rang, this one thudding into the outside wall below the window. He motioning to her what to do, they rolled over and over across the floor, the pain renewed repeatedly in her shoulder, until they reached the bedroom door and could descend into the cellar. She was breathing hard now, her wound pulsing, her mind fearfully forming the worry that he'd try to survive a fire in the cellar—a probably fatal move because in fires most people die from lack of oxygen.

Now he took time to slip a handkerchief between the sweater and her skin. It abraded the wound and made her cry out. He kissed her wet eyes. Then he led her along a low passageway whose stone walls sweated. When he struck a match, she saw steel steps leading upward and above them a cover made of what looked like a barrel top. Petrie motioned her to stand aside and tugged an automatic from where it nestled under his sweater at the hollow of his back, then climbed the ladder quickly, pushing off the lid and diving into the open in what seemed to her a continuous motion.

She pressed upward and stuck her head out, surprised to see only a dense thicket of branches and leaves. The barrel top, painted green, was in the center of a thickly planted circle of cream bushes—plants she recognized from the days at Sea Ranch. She felt isolated in the bushes, left behind with uncertain choices—like halting in a room when the lights go out—and so she started to step off the last rung and climb out, anticipating the pain that radiated when she braced her elbows on the ground.

He lay on his stomach about four yards ahead, the gun held in both hands. His grip kicked once, then twice, the shots sounding very loud. Then he was up and running, crouched. She waited—either he freed her or he widowed her. It seemed five minutes before he returned and took her hand to pull her up out of the thicket. As she steadied herself standing, she heard a car sideslipping on the wet ground in the distance. Looking back, she realized that the tunnel ran under the lodge, so that they had emerged toward the sniper. About ten yards ahead a man lay on the ground, the back of his jacket pierced by a hole that was edged with threads stiff from drying blood, threads like splinters. Petrie bent to pick up a rifle.

"Is he dead?"

"Yes. The other sure isn't. And for sure he has ruined my regulator or cut the steering cables."

He picked her up, cradling her, and took short steps downward onto the porch of the lodge. Inside, he sat her on the bench and probed the crease on her shoulder where the capillaries were torn, the nerve ends confused. It sickened her and she vomited. He held her forehead as, finishing, she dry-heaved. He dried her mouth with a clean handkerchief he'd been holding to serve as a new bandage. Then he drew her to his chest to allow the pain to creep away like a villain.

"I've got to get away fast, Joan. I don't think I've compromised your son. Those gunmen weren't here yesterday. Otherwise, they would have held you and Scott as hostages to bring me out. They won't know your license plate. Let's work on getting you back home."

"But I'm an accomplice. The man is dead!"

He smiled tightly. "Are you still citing the Constitution? I shot him in self-defense. You'll have a scar to prove it."

"But he was shot in the back."

"The people who sent him are not much concerned with legalities. That's why I've got to get you home under cover. My valuables don't take any room—a lot of cash, in hundreds, a couple of small things belonging to my mother and father. I'll take only my jacket and raincoat. We need a car. Then we'll drive you home."

"There's another choice."

"There can't be."

She reached up to kiss him but held back at the last moment, aware her breath was sour. "There is. I'm coming. I'm coming with you."

He sat there in a brown plaid lightweight suit with a button-down shirt, a gray-green tie, and a white handkerchief in the breast pocket that showed three points at exactly one inch. He was a fed all the way. You could tell a fuckin' fed easier than a wise guy. Where, Renato said to himself, do they get these guys who all look English or Scandinavian? Some of them had to be Italian or Polish or Greek. Were they signed up because they looked like that? No, they must all go to a boot camp to learn to dress like squares and practice talking nice while acting shit mean.

"Mr. Mortella, we know all about your friends in Houston and Phoenix who launder your money and deposit cashier's checks in the Caymans. The Treasury needs only a word from us and you go to jail downtown on an arraignment without bail for maybe three or four weeks. The trial will last, say, eighteen months and by then Houston and Phoenix will be closed down."

It was unbelievable, this speech. Renato thought it sounded like a news announcement on TV. It sounded certain, inevitable. How could anyone walk into a man's office and deliver a speech like that without pausing, or blinking? It was like a death sentence—not because violence was threatened but because there was nothing else to be said.

"Who did you say you worked for?" He hated these blond goddamn guys who just stared and seemed never to sweat.

The commission inspector's name was Carl Hansen. He'd flown to Las Vegas from Santa Rosa in a Commission Lear 35-A, having been in Petaluma to see the real-estate woman whose name was on the card Alcarita had found. The woman remembered selling the lodge to Alfred Porter, but by the time Hansen reached it, now joined by another CI, he found "Porter" had fled. Fingerprints from the dead man had been faxed to Washington and he had been identified as one Andrew Chiaffo, many indictments, few arrests, originally from Detroit, recently of Las Vegas, and known to be a soldier of the Mortella family. Near the dead man was a disabled car and tire marks of another. Hansen had learned about two visitors to the lodge by asking the nearby residents, the "silver boys," who knew Joan Dunworth and her son, Scott. Of Porter they knew only what he himself had told them. From Washington it was verified discreetly, secondhand, that Scott Dunworth was at home with his father, an attorney in Berkeley, and that his mother, Joan, had not appeared at her parents' house in Walnut Creek or at her own apartment in San Francisco. It was assumed she was now with Petrie.

Hansen had called the Chief of Operations while Research was working up details of the threat he was to deliver to Renato Mortella. There was a fine point to be discussed. Chiaffo's partner might be chasing Petrie right now, seeking revenge. Should Hansen call him off or let him run?

"Mr. Mortella," Hansen continued. "Let's ride around town. There may be a way I can help you with the IRS about Houston and Phoenix."

"I'm not leaving here until I see some ID!"

That's when Renato was handed the Great Seal, the same one everybody saw on TV when the President spoke, and underneath was this guy's lodge number and name, with the words "Under Commission to the President of the United States" and a date. The piece was real gold and real silver, and it was engraved; it weighed almost a pound and must have cost at least two grand—like a Tiffany brooch. The leather folder that carried a card showing the fed's photograph and name and a Washington, D.C., telephone number even had a Mark Cross label!

They rode around Las Vegas in a green Grenada that looked like a Budget Rent-A-Car gazing at the tourists in their purple and yellow slacks and passing those vans with peace symbols painted on their sides, the ones in which teenagers like goddamn gypsies ate and screwed on the same flatbed.

"Your man Chiaffo was aced north of San Francisco, shot in the back. His rifle was on the ground next to three empty shell cases."

"I don't know any Chiaffo."

"Once more. Only once more. Where is his partner?"

"I can complain to my senator."

"You can. And one telephone call from the President and your senator won't remember having heard of you. Where's the partner?"

"He's out looking for the bastard who killed his friend."

"What state? What road? When did you last hear from him?"

"I don't know."

"One more answer like that and you are in a holding tank downtown with drunks and queers and bikers."

"Goddamn, goddamn, you guys do whatever you want. I know how innocent people must feel!"

Then Renato suddenly comprehended the questioning. He looked at the fed triumphantly. Obviously, the Mortella organization was more efficient than the government's. *They* had found the guy at his lodge ahead of the feds, and now Lou Torcello, Andy Chiaffo's old sidekick, might have a notion where he was.

Renato said, "Why can't you find Chiaffo's friend? You're a hotshot with a fancy badge."

Hansen stepped on the brake suddenly, throwing Renato into the dashboard, and at the same moment cuffed him on the neck with the side of his hand. Renato reared back, his nose gushing blood. For Renato the sight of bright red blood covering his two-hundred-dollar tailored shirt and two-thousand-dollar silk suit was horrifying.

"We know where the man is running to and we can pick him up there. We just don't want your man to slow him down.

We've checked up on Torcello and know from his old days in Detroit that he's a hothead and might shoot. He's your problem. The minute the runner stops, you telephone this number, to say you called off Torcello."

Renato was trying to stanch his nosebleed with a handkerchief and had reared his head back—the wrong way to stop it. Hansen took another shot. He cuffed Mortella's throat with a light karate edge, not hard enough to wound.

"Jesus, Mother of God, okay, okay."

CHAPTER EIGHT

———•———

PYOTOROV SAW TURCHEFF FREQUENTLY—AND FOR LONGER visits—during his second stay in the Soviet Union, in part because Pooley's business had fallen off. A sure sign was that spare parts were now mentioned more frequently than whole units of energy-processing equipment—turbines and transformers, heat exchangers and booster pumps. The two men walked constantly, as before, and on this trip they occasionally entered familiar public places, the Tretyakov Gallery with its collection of Orthodox art and one of the four lobbies, north, west, south, and east by name, of the world's largest hotel, the Rossiya. One night at the Rossiya Pyotorov felt they were intimate enough to relate that on his first trip in 1978 he had repeatedly been accompanied by an agreeable and energetic man named Efimovsk who, despite his title as a commercial attaché, was plainly KGB. They had become friendly and took lunch together now and then. Efimovsk had spoken of his parents and showed photographs of his wife and two daughters. On one of the last nights of that first trip, Pyotorov had returned about eleven o'clock to the West Rossiya and found Efimovsk seated on a bench in the lobby.

"What are you doing here so late? Are you in need of anything?" Pyotorov had asked.

"I came to take you to dinner."

"But at the desk they must have told you I had gone to dinner and was not in my room."

"They said you weren't even registered here," he said, motioning toward the six bulky, henna-haired women who sat stolidly behind the counter.

Then Pyotorov had made a gaffe. "My God, Efimovsk, why didn't you show them your KGB red folder?"

"Do you think *that* affects such people? They are absolutists! Immovable peasants!"

Turcheff laughed. "What did you do then? No, let me guess. You took him to dinner."

"Yes, my second of the night."

The two of them talked incessantly. A comment by one was made into a counterpoint by the other, and there emerged after several hours chords of logic and rhetoric. Turcheff was offended—the right word—by the sadness of lives in his native land and was especially reminded of it painfully on seeing public displays of drunkenness or boorishness. He spoke like the patriotic poet Mayakovsky—in a tone of despair spiked by affection.

During one of their conversations Turcheff said, "You must understand our agony. Three generations of Russians have been lost to Lenin's ideology and Stalin's dogmatism. *Three* generations!" And then, "It saddens a parent when a child's life is wasted. But what of wasting three entire generations? In the Soviet Union we have proved Hegel's definition: tragedy is waste, the sheer waste of human possibilities."

Turcheff's mother and father had been peasants from near Volvograd and both had died of starvation during the Second Soviet Five-Year Plan. His sister had frozen to death in Leningrad in 1943, during the German siege, just after Viktor Ivanovich had been wounded at Stalingrad. His wife had died of a brain clot in 1975 and left him without children. Had there been children, they would, like others, now be occupying nine square meters per person and spending a fifth of their daylight hours standing in queues for chicken or toilet paper or cleansing powder—whatever, under a lunatic system of distribution, was available that day.

"Alexandr Vladimirovich, I sometimes think that God since 1905 has on three occasions stacked on end a huge domino set in Vladivostok and then, at an exquisitely awful moment, has pushed the first domino so that, successively, people have been crushed under the weights marching across Siberia and over the Urals to collapse at last on the dreading, waiting populations of Moscow and Kiev, Leningrad and Minsk. Your writer Mark Twain could comprehend that. Can you?"

On this second visit Turcheff took his friend to see the University, that enormous, ornate, ugly building, and as they stood on the eighteenth floor looking out at the horseshoe bend of the Moskva River and the Komsomolsky Prospekt that leads straight to Red Square, Pyotorov told the Professor the story of a wealthy Princeton man who had visited his mother in a new apartment building in Monaco and had complained to her that its wretched architecture spoiled the skyline. His mother had replied, "But only here can you avoid seeing this building!"

As they stood, the Professor asked him if at Princeton he

had known of experiments with hydrogen as a fuel. Pyotorov said yes, both at Princeton and at Pooley. Turcheff then explained that while he had been peripherally involved in the Soviet experiments to devise aircraft powered by hydrogen, what interested him more was the use of hydrogen-generated fuel. The principle was simple: charge plain water with an electrolyzer powered by solar energy, which separates the water into oxygen and hydrogen. Then burn the hydrogen by recombining it with oxygen in a reaction that creates energy.

"It works," the Professor said. "Although my colleagues contend it will never be cost efficient, which is to say, one will never be able to get more energy out than one puts in. But it interests me because of certain primal qualities: first, it is local; second, its sources are abundant because water is everywhere; third, it does not pollute a room, let alone the world's atmosphere."

"Viktor Ivanovich, it's no secret that at Princeton we had your Russian Tokomak to use in our experimenting with nuclear fusion. Can I tell you, out of my ignorance, what I thought was its problem? I am an engineer, not a physicist or chemist, and so I can ignore lofty questions. It seems to me that the Russians and Americans need to figure out how to set up a magnetic field in order to hold the gases steadily small and in a regular shape."

Turcheff was amused by this simplification of an enormous scientific problem. The Tokomak was a machine that looked like a giant doughnut, which heated deuterium and tritium into a hot gas called a plasma. Lithium was present, too, in a kind of blanket surrounding the inner doughnut called the Torus. At tremendous levels of heat, the plasma fused and released *more* tritium, therefore more energy.

"Well," the Professor said, "you forget that one of the Tokomak's two magnetic fields already in place, so to speak, does more than hold the plasma steady. It *squeezes* it into a small shape. In any event, Alexandr Vladimirovich, there's a much more promising line of inquiry. It is not the use of heat to produce heat. Fusion at room temperature is the real mystery."

"I've never heard of that. Is it a secret?"

"Not that I know of. There are people at your Los Alamos as well as in India and Canada, and of course here in Russia, who are working on it. Since it doesn't exist, it's hardly a secret!"

Pyotorov said, "I've heard it said that if heat could be triggered over and over, you might be able to achieve a fusion of the deuterium atoms if you take out the deuterium and oxygen gases that are released in the breaking up of the heavy water."

"Yes, they talk of that here, too. But into what kind of container would you draw the gases? How you hold heat is the question," Turcheff replied.

"It's temperature that you meet at every turning, isn't it?" Pyotorov added after a pause.

"Of course. There is a good theory that the earth's core is molten because hot fusion keeps being triggered and the metals can't cool."

"Is low-temperature fusion even remotely possible?"

"Yes. And what will concentrate the attention of scientists is the urgent need to produce energy easily, plentifully, locally."

Pyotorov realized then how deeply committed the Professor was to his belief that human misery could be relieved by a science that was, in effect, homemade. Pyotorov had never before heard of science and sociology being treated together *as a mechanism* to solve ordinary needs: food, housing, celebration, art.

"Let me explain something that happened right here in an amphitheater on the eighteenth floor of this building only six months ago. The Provost had urged his natural and physical science faculties to be joined on this particular occasion by others—sociologists and psychologists and economists and administrators. We were to commune over many days on the subject of a worldview of the future. We were adjured to wed the several scholarly disciplines."

Turcheff then explained that the biochemists, physicists, and mathematicians had balked at accepting the participation of sociologists and psychologists because (although it was not said explicitly), with their Marxist training, such teachers tended to be dogmatic. But in the end they had given in to the Provost's request.

At the seminar, Turcheff had spoken at length. He began by saying that while scientists could comfortably assume the usefulness of their work, regardless of how immediate its applications were, it was not so easy for politicians and officials, who had the problems of dealing with today, with "right now." Leaders of people and nations, Turcheff said, feel an urgency about what they do, especially since they know that in fact most of their promises will bear concrete results *not* for people of their own age but mostly for the still unborn. In a meager economy, ordinary survival—just the gaining of food and shelter and health care—consumes most of the resources, energies, and hours of the present. Indeed, Turcheff confessed, the claims that better living has come about through grand scientific discoveries are often suspect. At the seminar, and now in recounting it to Pyotorov, Turcheff said that simple devices probably have had more influence on people than grand ones: the horse collar in the fourteenth century, movable type in the sixteenth, and in the nineteenth the steel plow and barbed wire.

"It takes a long time for the poor of the earth, the vast populace of the deprived, simply to reap the rewards of thinkers. Time is the unwelcome guest at every table and it wears the grin of irony. In the Occident, time is always on the mind as well as on the wrist. History is largely uninstructive because it's late."

"In the past," he continued, "some historians were willing to risk *speculation*. They were willing to admit that they saw patterns in human activity that just might make typicality into predictability—projecting the ordinary into the long term. Among them were the American Admiral Mahan, the geopolitician Mackinder, and those historical theorists Spengler and Toynbee."

Now they were largely forgotten. Geopolitics had fallen into disgrace, mainly because Joseph Chamberlain and others laid claim to it and put forth hateful predictions that were quickly seized upon by bigots, Hitler particularly. This abandonment was a great pity, the Professor said, because in fact geopolitical tendencies are known. People *still* do migrate along rivers, despite the air age; mountains *still* are barriers, whether economic, religious, or political; highlanders *do* think differently from lowlanders; north and south are similarly different in most countries; television and wireless *have not* lessened regional accents.

"In short," Turcheff said, "there are *notional* lines on earth that often correspond with geographical ones."

Now, charged up by his own thoughts, feeling himself in a dramatic mode because of the hush in his seminar audience, Turcheff proceeded to say that great changes in science, even if less fruitful to ordinary people than is supposed, were said at least to help bring harmony or accord among nations. "Even here," he declared, "the matter is doubtful. Only the nuclear bomb has brought agreement among the powers of the earth in our century. The bomb, only that! The tendency toward the local and parochial is evident even in advanced technology: the English still drive on the left; the Europeans use a different scanning speed for sound and pictures in television than the Americans do; and meters and grams are rarely to be found in the United States, the country on earth that has more material things to count than any other!

"Comrades, we avoid simple answers because we fear to ask the questions. What does it really take to feed ourselves? With enough energy and with only a minor amount of equipment, *and with incentives to produce more than the farmer himself needs,* any nation can, given some decent soil, straighten out its agriculture within three seasons. *Three seasons!*"

Geopolitically, Turcheff went on, one ought to judge nations by what they *consume.* The West was wrong to accuse the Soviet Union of glorifying "the Economic Man." That accusation had to do with religion and esthetic objections more than with economic issues.

"It becomes clear, does it not," he told his startled audience, "even if we will not admit it, that it is a mistake to think universally, globally. We must renounce imperialistic science, which, like all empire dreaming, ignores the common, the lowly, the meek. Nuclear power is global thinking. Vast agricultural units are global thinking. Power grids covering millions of square hectares, thousand-mile pipelines, whether elevated or buried—all these are based on the old notion, voiced by capitalist and communist apologists both, that science beneficially leads to central production and to nationwide distribution and therefore to universal benefit. No. What proves to be most important to people is not the imperial but the local and the singular."

Turcheff praised the French historian Fernand Braudel, who refused to accept as a general proposition that as science and technology advanced, people prospered and life necessarily got better; and who said that from 1350 to 1550 economic conditions were far better throughout most of Europe than was assumed and, further, that common people had less food and clothing *after* the Middle Ages—indeed into the nineteenth century. In some regions of Eastern Europe, certainly in the Balkans, the worsening had continued to the middle of the twentieth century.

"Why do we always look for grand solutions or, else, explain with grand excuses?" he asked his audience. "The Mongols didn't stop their westward march because of meeting armed opposition. No. They ran into a plain and simple *economic recession.*" He paused. Then, "Comrades, when you examine history, count granaries as well as armies! Comrades, look not just to the routes of war and religion to tell you how people live. Look to the routes of contagion, to the migration of the starving. Let me emphasize that global travel and global communication do not make nations equally free and equally prosperous. We must find ways to make a person, *a single person,* healthy, busy, and safe where he lives, in his house, in his garden, on his street."

Turcheff's two-hour presentation at the seminar on the eighteenth floor of the University building had caused confusion, indeed alarm. He had disturbed his scientific colleagues and confounded the sociologists and economists and engineers. His bold remarks had caused gossip everywhere in the University and of course had reached many ears in Moscow that were not attached to scholarly heads. Geopolitics! His audience thought the famous Professor Turcheff had come perilously close to dealing tarot cards or reading palms. He had been protected, ironically, without his knowing it, by his former pupil, the Deputy to the President. The Deputy knew that Turcheff was through and through a Russian patriot—and trusted him.

Pyotorov was himself puzzled when he heard the recounting. And he showed it that evening, his very last in Moscow, when he arrived at the Professor's apartment with a bottle of French brandy, caviar, paté, and a box of Cuban cigars—all bought in the store where only foreigners with their hard currency could trade.

"Viktor Ivanovich, I'm dismayed every time I reflect on that seminar speech of yours. I myself sell electrical long lines and large generators to service vast areas. Am I obsolete? You know something new, do you? Something imminent?"

The Professor laughed. "You mean a government secret, Alexandr Vladimirovich? No. I have thoughts, no secrets."

Pyotorov ignored that bit of sophistry and asked, seriously, "But there was a scientific thrust to what you said?"

"There are scientific studies, some you know about yourself. Indeed, some at Princeton."

"Hydrogen fuel? The Tokomak?"

"And other things."

"Let me stay away from science, then. Did you ever see the film *Lost Horizon*? No, you can't have. Let me explain. It's a banal story of an Englishman who stumbles into a hidden valley in Tibet called Shangri-La where abundance is everywhere, cheap energy and plenty of goods and no strife. While I watched, I couldn't help noticing how idiotically the natives were portrayed, grinning away in the midst of plenty. I wondered, does abundance make husbands any kinder or wives less quarrelsome? Can it abolish irrationality and boredom? What do ordinary people do for melodrama?"

Pyotorov stopped when he saw tears in the Professor's eyes.

"My dear Alexandr Ivanovich, I know well that art is said to thrive on conflict; and that Western religions were born of it. But do think about a child with a swollen belly, arms and legs like strings, and eyes so old that you are made ashamed of your own years! Think, too, of the waste of tens of millions of lives! I will not argue that Mozart is worth a million peasants. It's a false question. We cannot forgive the monstrous, the inhumane, in the name of art or, worse, entertainment."

"I'm very sorry. You're right. Forgive my glibness. It's just that I don't see a solution. I think you do."

"I'm getting close."

"Tell me when you can."

"Will you return?"

"Of course."

But of course he did not. Soon he became a member of the Commission and as part of his oath was forbidden foreign travel.

More than eleven years later, curtains twitched on the upper floors of a building on one of the two "Georgian Streets." Not every day did a Ziv limousine arrive carrying, next to the driver, a uniformed man who stepped out and held the rear door open for a passenger, in this instance a tall, lean man wearing a tailored raincoat and a fedora. In these days of open discourse it was curiosity more than fear that twitched the curtains. The dread "official visits" to citizens in their homes had largely ended with *glasnost*. Two hours later, the elegant slim man emerged smiling. Someone watching might have asked: had he heard good news? Well, good news in Moscow was still a matter of degree—not waking with a cold in the head, not waiting all afternoon in a queue, not arguing with the bookkeeping department over your expense vouchers, not being harried by your wife to brave the *maly persuloki*, those side streets always clogged with snow, to visit her sick brother who in his weakened state had developed an extravagant taste for tobacco—yours. As for the official, these days the government didn't have a lot to smile about.

"You will have some mint tea, Deputy?" the Professor asked.

"The last time you were here, almost twenty years ago as a student, you liked it."

"Twenty years? Incredible. I see you still smoke cigars, Professor, and from the aroma they are Havanas, not those nasty little Anatolian ones."

"You know, Deputy, an American once gave me a box as a farewell gift. Americans overrate Havanas because they are forbidden fruit."

The Deputy put down his glass of tea, looked at his old instructor quizzically. "Professor, you know that I came to ask about the American, Pyotorov?"

"I've been asked to report on a stranger or a foreigner—or on anyone at all—only once before."

"He came to Moscow, altogether, three times?"

"No, twice. But I was asked to observe him only on the first occasion. We often walked the city streets."

"Alexandr Vladimirovich Pyotorov—a name that when said in the United States must sound like that of an exiled prince! He talked about fuel and energy, did he not? His company, Pooley, built fuel lines over great distances, as in Alaska, and water-generated power plants along the northern tier of American states."

"Yes, he told me of that. Did you know, Deputy, that Canada holds a ninth of all the fresh water on earth?"

"Amazing. He also worked on accelerators used to smash electrons and neutrons?"

"The colliders? Yes, Pooley built a four-mile accelerator in the state of Illinois. As you know, Deputy, these accelerators, or colliders, are very expensive. You recall the Americans stopped building one in Long Island, off New York City."

"They stopped because of our own accelerator. But American scientists have of late started to build what they call a supercollider in Texas that will be fifty miles long and cost thirteen billion dollars."

"Expensive, Deputy, but perhaps not paranoid. Physicists keep wanting to get inside matter and to do that—at least so far—they must smash matter with energy. A thousand volts to break into an atom and detect a nucleus. A million volts to find protons and neutrons. Then, billions of volts to find quarks inside protons."

Turcheff relit his cigar, offered his guest a refill of tea and was refused, then resumed his seat, stood again, moved his own tea glass twice more. The Deputy did not believe this was an exercise in stalling for time. Twenty years earlier, he'd watched the Professor as a lecturer pace, smoke, fiddle with papers on the lectern, scratch his ears—it was one way of holding the attention of his students, like the stage business used by actors in a play.

"Is there no choice but these huge tunnels, these supercolliders?" the Deputy finally asked.

"Yes, Deputy, there is. Some of *our* scientists have been experimenting with wake-field accelerators, by taking a tube made of clay into which is inserted a large number of electrons. As these pass through the tube they leave a wake—much as a boat does—and the smaller number of electrons that trail then draw energy from those that have already passed. A great amount of energy could result. That's using electrons. There's a sort of football match going on nowadays among physicists: some favor protons because these constitute a far greater mass than electrons."

"Pyotorov worked on this, did he?"

"Deputy, we didn't talk of colliders. And then, in 1979, wake-field wasn't known. He had small interest in grand theories. He was a salesman with an order book making very good money. He liked tangible things."

The Deputy rose, looked out the window silently, then came back to stand close to the Professor. "Tangible. You mean local things, local devices? Did you not yourself dwell on the concept of locality at that famous seminar at the University?"

"I did. But I was not then talking of electrons, protons, quarks, and all the rest. I more or less redefined science on that occasion and some of my colleagues called it bad sociology! May I ask, Deputy, why Pyotorov is of any interest? It's been more than a decade since he was here."

"He no longer sells for the construction company. Now he has scientific secrets to sell. And the Americans want our help."

"My dear Deputy, it must be a hoax! There are designs and variations in technology that are guarded, say, by the Japanese, but there are no major scientific works that can be secret." He paused, searching his mind. "As you know, Einstein worked in a patent office. That seems altogether fitting, does it not? Patents make new things public."

"Patents are not what Pyotorov is selling. He did, after all, attend the American university, Princeton, where both fission and fusion have been experimented with. Also, hydrogen fuel has been studied there. The Tokomak was experimented with at Princeton. Did he mention the Tokomak?"

"He did. He said that as an engineer he couldn't understand why all the Americans, Canadians, Frenchmen, British, and Indians couldn't solve the problem of balance. But he didn't have any notion."

"Balance?"

"Yes. One problem in the Tokomak, Deputy, is to create a balance, or equilibrium, so that the hot gases, the plasma, will fuse in perfect order. It's like a top spinning. It takes a lot of force to keep it true: if it loses balance, then it loses force.

Every researcher is bothered by that. It's one reason why practical fusion has not been achieved."

"Perhaps it's chemists like you who will succeed, not physicists?"

Turcheff managed to achieve a bantering tone in reply. "All this cold-fusion business one reads of these days is embarrassing to chemists like me. It's as if the chemistry department in a university wanted a toy of their own. As it is, the physicists have both hot fission and hot fusion, with all the glory—except for Chernobyl, of course. I'm retired, Deputy, and out of the mainstream, but I cannot believe that Soviet chemists would make fools of themselves as the Americans have done with their failed kitchen experiments. Ha!"

"Well, Professor, it's not we, but rather the Americans, who are concerned over Pyotorov. You are perhaps the only person who might think of some event, or discussion, that could be useful to the Americans. If you can recall anything, telephone this number. My driver will pick you up."

Handing over a slip with the telephone number written on it, the Deputy rose, took up his hat, and thanked his host for the tea. He moved to the door, pausing only long enough to ask, "By the way, where did you walk mostly?"

"We sometimes walked over the *Preyesenskaya*, on the grounds of the old Armenian cemetery, a quiet place, of course."

Turcheff sat a long time without stirring after the Deputy left. He didn't rise to prepare supper. He didn't even turn on the lights. These days, he only rarely saw colleagues from the University and the Chemical Institute. Being alone, he lived without schedules, unforced by time. He rose whenever he awoke; he did not watch the clock to make appointments; he even ate unregularly. But today he had found a purpose and a schedule. The Deputy, a clever man, one rather well informed in science though he pretended not to be, had asked what Pyotorov knew. But that was like a card already showing in a stud poker hand. The Deputy had in fact come to inquire what Turcheff himself knew—the hole card. After all, in earlier days, in aid of his research he had been given all kinds of assistants and equipment. And it was known that in the course of various projects he had stirred and mixed ingredients in aid of that great question in science: how to create power cheaply, safely, locally, without pollution of the atmosphere. Had Turcheff gone beyond mere nibbling? Had he in fact in his kitchen mixed ingredients and succeeded in baking a cake? And perhaps, just perhaps, let the American Pyotorov take a bite?

The Professor sat without rising, hour after hour, smoking cigars, taking his glasses off and putting them on, running a heavily veined hand through his thick gray hair. By the end of eight or nine hours, he had decided. Yes, he could surmise certain things, certain causes and effects, and yes, he could conceive how a certain technology, if it could work, would be incredibly bountiful. But he had never before conceived of his intellectual self-debate as "official" and certainly not as dangerous. Clearly, he was now at risk. Was Pyotorov also? Yes, he was. Even if Pyotorov had no notion of what he, Turcheff, could surmise as a possible and practical technology, he could be in danger because he was the American friend of Professor Turcheff. What was it the Americans called it? Ah yes, guilt by association.

He decided he must flee his homeland, but in so doing he might have to flee his own identity. It bothered him that to do so would in some part obliterate his wife's. Tanya Irinovna had never been considered beautiful, even pretty, yet her always willing ways had made her lovely in his eyes. She had never complained, not about fate, nor even about minor annoyances. She had made his days comfortable, though not eventful. He had loved her constantly.

But on the desperate matter of flight, he didn't doubt that the Americans these days cooperated with the Soviets. If the KGB searched for him, then so would the CIA. If he left, he knew where he would try to go. Long ago, as a boy of sixteen, he had clandestinely been an admirer of Leon Trotsky, a man of physical courage and great intellect, the soldier and the thinker. Now he found a certain symmetry in considering a place of exile. Trotsky had gone there. So would he. Mexico.

CHAPTER NINE

NSIDE THE OLD MASONIC TEMPLE, THE COMMISSIONER ASKED wearily, "Do we know who the woman is? And who owns the house?"

"The woman is thirty-seven, divorced, one child, lives in San Francisco. As for the house, Petrie bought it two years ago. It's a monk's cell with nothing personal in it, not even anything with a store label whose bar code could have told us something." Tannenbaum concluded, "The novel he was typing is from a *published* book."

"Why did Petrie keep all those confidences?" Haagstrom asked. "Speaking Spanish and owning that hideaway near Petaluma—and whatever else. Could it be that ten years ago, when he joined the Commission, he and Turcheff had already lit on something so grand that he decided, as it were, to get inside the government for his own purposes? Or maybe only for his own protection? Keeping confidences of a minor nature could suggest a conspiratorial tendency."

Tannenbaum saw that Matthews, sitting nearby, was about to treat such a question superficially and he spoke quickly.

"Commissioner, I always regarded Petrie as entirely normal. He was far brighter than most of our staff, and certainly more confident in his personality. We now know that he attracts women without half trying, but he's no satyr, not like President Kennedy, who told Prime Minister Macmillan he needed to take a woman just to get through the day."

Coming from Tannenbaum, a strict, ascetic man, this was not mere gossip—despite his dislike of the way the Kennedys had, in his view, turned the White House into a locker room. He had a point to make. "This confidentiality in Petrie means to me, sir, that we don't really know why he joined the Commission in the first place. He was suited to our organization because he's discreet. Yet we must have suited him also. If you want to hide yourself—or hide something you have—then join an intelligence agency. Matt, your 'Purloined Letter' analogy, it now occurs to me, is about right."

Matthews was pleased. "Maybe so, Chief, but Petrie is also capable of saying too much. He quoted to me once something Batista said. I almost made him a Spanish speaker."

The Commissioner had waited to reveal the bad news— the reason he had called this 6:00 A.M. meeting. He'd heard it from the President's Chief of Staff after midnight. "Professor Turcheff has stayed ahead of his pursuers all the way. They have traced him through Poland and East Germany and then to Toronto. They think he's in Mexico now."

The Chief was dumbfounded. "Who could have helped him cross so many borders? Even continents?"

The Commissioner replied, "He seems to have found where

all the liberals have gone. Environmentalists nowadays, it seems, have become so radical that they run an underground."

Matthews made a shrewd guess. "This happened more than a week ago. They waited to tell us because they hoped to find him."

As the three sat in the Commissioner's office, each felt different in his own way. Matthews thought it another patch of bad luck, ice on a roadway. Tannenbaum believed that poor consequences came of dubious motives: he turned to strictures when distressed. Haagstrom, his temples anticipating the arteritis metronome, wondered why it was that people assumed that those engaged clandestinely were more crafty and efficient than others. Darkness never illumined.

The day following, the Commissioner arrived at the White House in the late morning, wearing a bowler hat. When he first became a district court judge twenty years earlier, then forty-three years old, he had decided to wear a bowler in the winter and a straw boater in the summer—and a vest during all seasons. It was a habit whose beginning was an admonition from his father: "At sixty wear a hat; by seventy carry a stick." When it came to the hat, Haagstrom had been precocious. On entering the Oval Office he typically did not extend his hand until bidden by the President's own welcoming gesture. Then he asked permission to refer to notes—on the ground that a man ought not look bureaucratically threatening, like a process server with paper in hand. The President listened earnestly, his thumb under his chin, forefinger pressing his cheek next to the sympathetic eyes—grandfatherly eyes practiced in letting misdemeanors slip away without notice.

"If Petrie talks to Turcheff, two things can happen," Haagstrom said. "Petrie will tumble onto the truth, if he doesn't already know. Or each may act as a catalyst on the other, and together they might seek to inform the whole world."

"The Soviet President presumes Turcheff is headed for Mexico. I persuaded him *not* to send anyone in."

"Mr. President, the Commission is prevented by its Charter from going outside U.S. borders, as you know."

"Of course. That's a point of law. But then, the way you sent Petrie into that hospital so he could be captured was also a point of law."

It stung. "Sir, at the start, the operation was entirely genuine. We'd capture Petrie in the midst of an operation with our own people present. I hoped he would volunteer to stay under keep, or else we'd make him do so until the Protocol went into effect. That way, no outsiders would be involved. As you know, Mr. President, Congressman Miroset is Petrie's friend. We needed a plausible story."

"But it went wrong."

"Yes. Nobody knows it went wrong but the three of us, my Deputy, the Chief of Operations, and me. The CIs involved think Petrie is a hit man who got away."

The President looked intently at Haagstrom. Now it came clear to him. The Commissioner had gone ahead because there had risen before Haagstrom's eyes the specter of the Watergate hearings. It must be so. Haagstrom had sought an involving circumstance.

"Commissioner, I quite appreciate your telling me this. But my hearing it doesn't alter the circumstances."

The President leaned back, closing the case by placing his opposing fingertips together: here's the church, here's the people. It was obvious to the Commissioner that the President would not now speak of what was next. For all his decent demeanor, his splendid public personage as a husband, father, and grandfather who disliked no one on principle, there was also a certain secretness about him.

"I prefer, Mr. President," Haagstrom finally said, "not to ask for an order."

"Of course, Commissioner, you do what *you* think best."

There it was, an exchange of genuine sentiments and acceptable axioms that was the nub of the unsaid and therefore, in strictly evidentiary terms, proof that no conspiracy had begun or ensued. The Charter cautioned against contingency plans tested in the field and strategic games played to the point that they became real through inadvertence or miscalculation or malfeasance.

Of course, a conspiracy was always at risk of exposure. The world might not be big enough to hide in, Haagstrom thought. He recalled talking to a Soviet official at a reception, years ago. He was called the commercial aide at the Soviet Embassy but was a KGB man who didn't know a bill of lading from a serving spoon. This official had told him about the Soviet consul in New York trying to teach his wife to drive by taking her to practice on an empty ten-acre parking lot at Jones Beach in the dead of winter. As it happened, the only other car on the lot was the caretaker's. "Would you believe, Mr. Director of Information Theory, that the wife managed to hit that single car? It's a small world, is it not?"

After Haagstrom left, inclining his head slightly with his habitual courtesy, the President reflected that he treasured this man for his genteel forthrightness and, unlike others in the White House, did not find him a strange bird despite his bowler hats and boaters and other niceties. The Chief of Staff and most of the National Security Council were suffering doubts not only about the competency of the Commission to keep the invention secret, but also about the Commissioner himself in guarding the explosively controversial Protocol. It was a little late for skepticism, the President reflected. The invention and the Protocol would be known publicly in another sixteen days. The Commissioner knew the schedule of course. It *was* odd, the President noted, that during his visit today Haagstrom had shown no anxiety about timing.

They crossed the Golden Gate in a new Buick that showed but four thousand miles on the odometer and held nearly a full tank of gasoline. The car with its keys in the ignition Petrie had found in front of a bank in the town of Novato. He and Joan had reached there by walking on secondary roads southward; and on the way he had taught her simple tricks of how to escape surveillance, such as her walking five hundred yards ahead of him and on the opposite side of the road, ready, on hearing a car coming either way, to reverse herself and so appear to be passing Petrie. The tricks were fine, but he knew that the point of them was to avoid questions by local or state police, not by the Commission. He'd found out in Littleton, and in traveling without incident all the way from Philadelphia to the coast, that the CIs were not using the police or any other federal agencies to track him. As for the wise guys who had shot at them, he couldn't guess what their organization's capacities in surveillance were. He assumed that they were allied to Shurtz, who was by now probably free of prosecution, with Hentleman dead. He knew that a Las Vegas Mafia family was Shurtz's backers.

At Pacifica, on the oceanside just a few miles south of San Francisco, Petrie abandoned the Buick and hot-wired the ignition of a Chevrolet parked in an employee lot near a Sam Goody's store. As he did this, Joan was, on his instructions, buying a streaked denim suit, high-heeled pumps, a purse, cosmetics, Band-Aids, peroxide, black hair dye, and shears. At dusk, still following the coastal highway, they proceeded toward Palo Alto. The quarter-moon bays below the road had gone gray and the beach was streaked black, dense, forbidding. On a headland at least a hundred feet high above the road, Joan pointed to an abandoned lighthouse. In the twilight, the high cypresses looked like black sentinels and the strips of bark on the gum trees hung like serpents on a staff. Familiar scenery had turned foreign. Because she didn't know their destination, every place was tentative.

At Palo Alto, while he swiped plates off a parked car and put them on the Chevrolet, she entered a fancy shop not far from the Stanford campus, still attired in jeans and running shoes, and bought panty hose, an overnight bag, some skirts and blouses, and for eleven hundred dollars a raincoat with a fur lining. She watched the saleslady smirk ever so slightly.

They stopped for dinner just outside of town and then turned into a motel next to the restaurant. By driving the perimeter slowly, Petrie determined that there were no cars on the far row away from the office. Then, with the lights off and the engine barely turning over, he parked on the near side, where other cars were parked outside occupied rooms. He led Joan, with her shoes in her hands, back around the building to the empty row of rooms and used a credit card to spring the lock on one of them.

"We'll have to be out of here before dawn. I'll look to your wound when you wake up. Let's give the capillaries a little longer to close. I know you'd like a shower, Joanie, but we can't afford even to flush the toilet. In the office the pipes might rumble like thunder."

She didn't reply. There was no small talk, or even big talk, that fit such an occasion, she decided grimly, especially since she knew practically nothing about him and his enemies. As her eyes closed, she observed he was dozing with his right hand gripping the automatic. When he awoke in the gray, false dawn, he saw that she'd gone to sleep in the raincoat with nothing on underneath. The tender skin under her eyes was dark from fatigue and even in sleep she seemed to be frowning. Did she realize how badly their escape had been managed so far? How could she? It wasn't her trade to be clever, but, rather, his. He'd taken too many chances with the cars, stayed too long on the coast.

"Listen," she said with a hoarse voice, startling him as he gazed at her closed eyes. "When are you going to tell me why they want you dead?"

"Soon, I'll tell you all of it, but for the moment would you believe me if I said I don't know who was shooting at us?" He asked the question as he came over to touch her hair, a gesture one might make toward a restless child. She pulled on his arm and brought his head down to kiss him with her mouth open. He was startled and for a moment resisted reaching for her shoulders or thighs, which showed like cream, soft and undulant against the fur that lined the raincoat she'd slept in. Her body was gloriously full, free of that tendon stringiness that occurred in women who kept themselves fanatically trim.

"Maybe,'" she said, hoping it was brave, "I don't need anything special from you. We're trying to be together, that's all. People are searching for you but not me. I called my mother when we were in Pacifica. I told her I was going to stay with a friend in Seattle."

They made love finally, and afterward he lay admiring her body. It was as extravagant as he had first surmised. Rounded and hollowed in the right places, it changed hue where smooth or shadowed. They lay face down and, heads together, whispered. Her breasts pressed into ovoids against the coarsely starched sheets.

"I feel old. People ought to fall in love young. Have you been in love, Alex?"

"No. I've tried to pretend."

"Pretending isn't the worst thing, Alex. I hate people who *summon* feelings." Then, without a change of tone, she startled him. "Do we have time to fall in love?"

"We're headed for Mexico, Joan. Let's pray there's room and time enough."

Once she had changed into fresh clothes bought in Palo Alto—without the bath she wanted so badly—they were back on the road.

Inside the car again, she studied him with sideways glances. What kind of boy had he been? A studious boy, surely. Had he been, early on, vulnerable in friendship? That cabin of his, the "safe house" as spy novels call such places, told something of him—as does any place where someone puts down. He could not obliterate all signs of himself. She had deduced from the lodge and its contents that he was familiar with loneliness, a terrible skill, that. Just looking at him, before the bullet had interrupted their first acquaintance, she had known he was bright of mind and fearless in a quiet way, not needing to be noticed or regarded—or avoided.

Put down. Joan had put down in lots of places and now was all too aware of how intimacy can hurt. From the age of thirteen, when her personality was definable, her parents had been scared stiff of her. Storms of recrimination at home had begun when she was seventeen and had just enrolled at Cal, in Berkeley. Her mother had found out that within weeks she was living with this man, then another, off and on. Arguments swelled and crested. She hadn't returned home for long periods and, finally, had left for good after she married a man six years her senior when she was twenty, in 1973. In her family's home in Walnut Creek, especially on those occasions when families stoutly insist on being festive—birthdays and holidays—there was always the sense that Joan and her mother and father were watching each other for new signs of contention and that Scott, from the age of five or so, was their referee. Everyone believed that everyone else should behave better, it being Christmas or Easter, yet the celebrants were alert to signs of treachery, that awful subversion that arises when a shared blood colors everyone's remembrance. Joan was an only child and Scott was the only grandchild. There were too few distractions.

"Joan, we'll talk when I can put it forth as a consecutive story. I'll let you hear the worst. I need you to tell me if I'm paranoid."

As the light sent strokes across the dull hillsides, Joan felt oddly content—a change from earlier. Looking at the blooms of jimsonweed and daisies along the highway, she realized she was making observations that were not critical to herself. She saw flowers. Violet was an intercessionary color: it introduced day to a departing night.

CHAPTER TEN

———— • ————

ALEX, WHY ARE WE GOING TO MEXICO? WE COULD HAVE headed for Canada. From your cabin, it wouldn't have been any farther. Are you meeting someone there? Do you speak Spanish?"

"My trouble with the Commission—it's the watchdog organization I work for—has to do with Professor Turcheff, a scientist in chemistry I met on two different trips to Moscow, in 1978 and 1979, while I worked for a New York engineering company."

She was puzzled by the dates. That was more than ten years earlier. She asked if he'd been in touch with the Professor since then.

"No and yes. I joined the Commission in 1980. Not only was I an inspector, a CI, and therefore by regulation not allowed to travel abroad, but also I was warned by the Chief of

Operations, a man named Tannenbaum, not to keep up any correspondence with him."

"They thought he might entrap you?"

"No, not really. The Commission is anonymous even within the United States. I'd told the Chief that on my first visit it was clear that the KGB had asked Turcheff to report on me. Viktor Ivanovich admitted it at the time. We both thought it was absurd."

"Why would the KGB think you were a spy?"

Joan was that someone who could cause oddments to rise through the cracks, half-remembered circumstances. For the first time he comprehended that the KGB had been just as interested in what Turcheff said to him as it had been in his own comments. Maybe the Russians had been killing three birds with the same stone: finding out about Pyotorov, finding out what Turcheff knew, and warning Turcheff generally.

"Neither one of us was a spy. I'm not one now. And I'm sure Turcheff isn't. Something enormous has happened. I keep wondering if it is part of a U.S.-USSR collaboration. After all, we are going to hold joint maneuvers with the Russians!"

"Who will attack? Peru? Or Jamaica?" She laughed. "Alex, if you're hoping to meet Turcheff in Mexico, how do you know he's there?"

He told Joan about his last evening in Moscow in 1979, when he had come bearing brandy, caviar, cigars, and, unknown to Turcheff, two thousand dollars in cash. "I made him promise to write me a letter containing a code if ever he needed my help. He *did* mail the letter. After I left Denver I telephoned my friend in Fairbanks. He read me the letter. It had just arrived, which means Turcheff is already running. And I know where to find him in Mexico."

"You were already planning to join the Commission, the last time you saw him? You knew you weren't coming back?"

"No. I hadn't even heard of the Commission then."

"He was a dissident, back then?"

"No, he wasn't, Joan. He was a scholar who was quite open. He held views that had to do with all of humanity. He was against what he called imperialist science. He wanted scientific research to create goods using local energy."

She objected. "Certainly they wouldn't jail him for *that*!"

"No, but his zeal *may* have led him into areas he thought experimental that were already real—and secret. He talked a lot about using hydrogen as fuel, about cold fusion—cheap energy generated locally without long-line transmission and without causing air and soil pollution."

"Academics talk about those things like a party platform at election time. None of it seems real, does it?"

"Joan, it's *not* unreal. When I was at Princeton I helped out on the Tokomak, a huge doughnut-shaped machine that produced hot fusion. Not fission, splitting atoms, but fusion, bringing together particles by overcoming the forces that separate them. In the 1950s both countries tried to achieve hot fusion. Princeton was the American center of this. All the experiments I knew about to create energy involved hydrogen, either as a fuel component itself or in altering the hydrogen atoms in heavy water.

"Nobody, Joan, no Russian, no American, no one else, was or is trying to invent a bomb. The thermonuclear bomb—the H-bomb—is hot *fusion*. We've already got the bomb."

Joan was not familiar with the physics she heard. Even so, she thought it puzzling that such information could put both men at risk. But she was also inspirited: his confidences lessened the distance between them.

She took his chin in her hand and turned his head toward her, saying, "And now you and I have something else. We've achieved our own fusion. It's not earthshaking—but it will do." Her eyes were moist. "Please God, give us a little time together."

Like Petrie before he found Joan, Turcheff needed a listening companion, someone who would approve or contest the various schemes he was conceiving on how to escape to Mexico. He'd once been told that the chief engraver at the University was expert in using lasers that could almost simultaneously erase and reimpose words and numerals on documents—for example, on passports and visas.

Turcheff held a passport still in force because he'd been invited to a conference in Romania in late 1989, but just before his departure the government in Bucharest had collapsed. How many visas did a man need to get across two continents? Let's say that you drove your Lada into Poland and, farther, into Germany, after carefully rigging it to hold tins of petrol— as a chemist he knew how to ventilate the tins to keep the vapor from exploding. You'd need two visas in that case. Say you took a train. One document could get you into Finland and, if you could then fly to Canada, only one more would be needed. But, on inquiring, Turcheff found that the engraver was now hospitalized because he suffered from palsy. An engraver with palsy!

What if he drove his Lada to Baku and there boarded a freighter for Vera Cruz? He'd read that ships of Mexican registry regularly plied a trade in minerals, outbound hauling cargoes of nickel, chrome, and titanium, the last used both in tempering other metals and in calendering paper. Unfortunately, a captain of a ship was the worst type of official to try bribing. After he took your money, he still had you in custody, on his vessel.

Whatever the route he took, he held seven thousand dollars in U.S. currency, the two thousand that Pyotorov had left in his cigar humidor (without telling him) that last evening in Moscow and five thousand he had exchanged on the black market over a period of fourteen years. He was prepared to leave everything behind, his books, his metal icons, his paintings, the three sculptures in vermeil and the alabaster flasks his wife had collected over the years. Leaving without suspicion was also not a problem: he had only to tell the nosiest of his neighbors in the apartment house that he was off to visit some cousins in Volvograd.

Ronald Reagan and Margaret Thatcher had, in the end, shown him the way. He would get in touch with one of those groups of environmentalists who used to be political leftists. *They* could help spirit him from country to country!

Communism had crashed as a dogma and there was no other clear-cut workable system other than free-market capitalism. Even Sweden, once called "the middle way," was not much of a model: its cost of government was the highest in Europe, as was its suicide rate. Where could zealots now gather in the righteousness of a radical cause? The environment, yes. Capitalists oppressed the people because they polluted the soil, the water, the atmosphere.

The Greens had become a potent political force in Germany, the Netherlands, and elsewhere. In Great Britain, Labour had turned its coat from pink to green. What's more, some environmentalists were like the syndicalists of old, quite ready to commit violence in the name of truth and goodness. Recently, bombs had been found in California stores that sold fur coats, bombs that could maim and kill adults and children nearby who wore nothing more sinister than jeans and sneakers. Would such militants want to smuggle out of the Soviet Union a scientist who said he could furnish irrefutable proof on how precisely the United States was devastating the U.S. and Canadian countryside with acid rain? Some concessions *had* been advanced by the U.S. government, but the precise scientific proof was still lacking. It was still a big issue!

Petrie had pulled off the highway twice during the day to change the dressing on Joan's shoulder, wetting the old bandage with peroxide to keep it from sticking. The wound was not infected, although he'd told her it would leave a scar. The fact that such stops were uneventful, that their progress south toward the border was unimpeded—so far—was a continuing proof to Petrie that whatever was at stake was too big to be shared with outsiders: this he saw as both a blessing and an awesome curse.

"What happens now?" Joan said. "In the backseat are those shears and some black hair dye. I figure that one of us will soon give herself a haircut and dress up like a tart in a denim suit, high heels, and a fuzzy raincoat. Aren't I entitled to hear the name of the play I'm dressed for?"

"My agency is called the Commission, just that. It's charged with keeping all other government agencies—including the FBI and the CIA—from breaking U.S. laws. Five days ago in New York City, my bosses, in the course of an operation to secure the testimony of a witness against some corrupt Treasury officials, went to elaborate lengths to set me up. They tried to capture me, maybe wound me, possibly kill me."

"My God, Alex! That's simply awful!"

"And this is going to blow your mind, Joan. I was christened Alexandr Vladimirovich Pyotorov." He laughed as he lifted both his hands off the steering wheel—like a blackjack dealer in Las Vegas whose gesture at the end of his shift is a sign that he's hiding no cash or chips as he leaves the table. "I was born in a little coal-mining town in Colorado called Frederick. I speak Russian. My parents were Russian—and Russian Orthodox."

"You're still Alex, then. The silver boys called you Al."

"I gave them a pseudonym. What's more, the Commission gives one to each of its inspectors—there are forty of us. Most of us have seen or worked with only ten or so others of the total, if that many. My name in the Commission was, is, Mark Petrie."

"It's a lot of names. But no worse than your average old-time Russian novel. The Commission hired you because you speak Russian, is that it?"

"For that in part, even though the Commission can't send anyone outside the country. Also, I'd gone to the Soviet Union while working for that construction company."

"You're a patriot, is that it? You enlisted."

"I think I wanted to become a functionary. I left Princeton in 1976, when I was twenty-two. I was offered a job with the construction company at a big salary and could have stayed on, receiving good raises—much higher than the Commission pays. Sometimes I think I joined the government because it was the first wholly unconnected event in my life after my parents died. I had gone to school, gone to college, gone to work. I didn't go to war because there was none. The only other routine thing I didn't do was get married."

Was he, at bottom, cynical? Joan looked at him searchingly as he stared through the windshield. "Maybe not going to war and not getting married were part of what you missed. A secret government agency is always at war with someone, isn't it? And a secret job is as demanding as a wife. Your bedroom is the office." When he didn't reply she took the plunge. "I saw that place of yours on the coast. All those cans without labels! Were you looking for a way to become another person?" She then added, hurriedly, "I'm not baiting you, Alex, really I'm not."

Then he frowned. Too often in the past, and now, he wasn't

able to match motives to his actions. "I don't know what I was running toward. I didn't hate my times."

"I hated the times. I didn't run through the streets of Chicago during the Days of Rage. I saw a few stragglers, those flower children who disappeared into ashrams in Oregon and Idaho. About ten years ago, I went to one. It was awful. The people all looked like refugees from a terrible battle that took place only in their minds."

After they'd driven a while longer, he pronounced, "Joan, you will be at a terrible risk. There's Scott."

She began to cry and she was glad he didn't slow the car or make consoling sounds. The miles passed. She dozed. Then she came awake with a start.

"I got married in my junior year in Berkeley. I married a man six years older who was in his senior year of law school at Boalt Hall. He had passed the bar and started practicing in San Francisco when I graduated. My parents didn't like him because he was Catholic. I began not to like him because he was dogmatic about everything except religion. He cared about large issues but couldn't remember the baby-sitter's name or what we paid her or how much it cost to feed a child. Scott was born early, six months after we were married." She paused, started to speak, then stopped. "Why do people give better odds to make a marriage go than they do for other relationships? Parents and children, unofficial lovers, friend to friend?" She interrupted herself again. "I guess I thought that just being together, day in and day out, in the kitchen, bath, and bedroom, would convert proximity into a lifetime love."

"That's alchemy!" He laughed.

He'd dismissed her complaint, making her defensive, acerbic. "Speaking of odds, who said that not betting on a whole series of women makes you a winner with the last one?"

"Who is the last woman?" he asked, fascinated by the concept of love as a terminal condition. "I'm not sure, Joan," he said somberly, "that I'll know if I'm in love."

"Don't worry about it. I'll tell you."

Turcheff knew one longtime radical environmentalist, a sociologist named Nikolai Garbacz, who was frustrated by Soviet indifference to his causes. Garbacz kept in touch with like-minded people in West Germany, the Netherlands, and Sweden—by what means, Turcheff had no notion. When Turcheff approached him, he sent the Professor to see a Greenist woman who was a medical technician in a city hospital. They met on Dzerchinsky Street in a philatelist shop, the only one in Moscow where high-quality stamps were sold to foreigners. It was a cover that enabled persons to speak of other countries as if only their stamps were of interest—just in case they were overheard. Even after *glasnost*, it was hard to break old habits of secrecy. As it turned out, the technician found a nook where she indicated it was safe to talk. She was thin and wore square-rimmed glasses and never once smiled.

"Canadians suffer from acid rain from the United States," the Professor began. "But they can't measure the amounts carried. The main reason they have failed is that they are ignoring the alkaloidal compounds that are also present. I've found three such compounds outside Moscow and Kiev."

"Why has no one discovered this before?" she asked in German. He realized then that she was a descendant of German colonials in the Ukraine, whose presence dated from long before World War I. Nowadays one was hearing German for the first time in half a century.

"I must talk with my colleagues in Bonn," she said then. "Are you in danger here?"

Turcheff replied, "I've been unwise. I told the Provost at the University I had new information on Chernobyl."

Three days later, he was directed to proceed to a housing development twenty miles from Moscow. As instructed, he parked the Lada under one of the buildings cast in gray concrete rectangles, the windows the same size as the abutting walls, the whole of it like children's blocks someone had forgotten to paint and letter. The environmentalists were not only conspirators but also bargainers. The Lada would pay only for his passage to West Germany and a forged passport to Canada; and he'd have to pay fifteen hundred dollars more for his coach airfare to Toronto. Before dawn, he was led by a blond-haired youth of about twenty to a truck parked near his Lada. His suit and shoes and fur hat were placed in a cheap suitcase and he donned a set of work clothes. He had grown a two-day beard, had blackened his fingernails and neck with dirt, and carried an unlit cigar in one side of his mouth. He rode alongside the youth until both driver and truck were exchanged in Brest, where they went through customs without trouble. Then a Polish driver took over all the way to Warsaw, where he boarded a train to Frankfurt-an-der-Oder, then on to East Berlin. Turcheff crossed over to West Berlin—wonder of wonders—as a pedestrian. At Templehof airport he went into a men's room, shaved, and put on the suit, shirt, and tie in his suitcase, which in turn he filled with a fairly full set of clothes he had bought in West Berlin. The suitcase he checked through to Toronto. It had gone off without a hitch. Maybe the Greens *should* become administrators.

In Toronto, he was met by two young women, one who wore long hair that, spread, looked like the hood of a cape. The second woman wore Levi's and Adidas running shoes and looked as if she'd just quit smoking because she repeatedly put things in her mouth: pencils, toothpicks, her fingers. They installed him in a cheap motel on Spadina Boulevard halfway between the airport and downtown, and after an hour's talk they said they'd return at noon the next day, after he was rested.

"Your reputation has certainly preceded you, Professor Turcheff. How did you come to work on acid rain? It's not a Soviet problem, is it?"

"Oh, yes! It is not publicized because there are so many other environmental issues at home: no prohibitions against the killing of seals and bears for their fur, no electrostatic scrubbers installed in smokestacks, no ban on asbestos, and so on."

"How does your equipment work?" the precise, jittery thin woman asked.

"Distillates of pollution are placed in a container made of clay in which electromagnets keep all the distillate in balance. A series of these samples can show the pollution routes precisely. Like drawing a straight line from dot to dot, as in children's art."

As science it was sheer nonsense, of course, but it seemed to satisfy the two women. When they left, Turcheff didn't wait for the next day. He took a Canadian Pacific train to London, Ontario, and then a bus to Windsor, across from Detroit, where he caught a commuter bus that went under the Detroit River and into the United States. In Detroit, he bought more clothes and a better suitcase. He took a series of buses, to Chicago, St. Louis, and Santa Fe, and finally to Tucson. In Tucson he signed up for a three-day bus tour of Mexico beginning in Nogales and proceeding to the Sea of Cortéz.

CHAPTER ELEVEN

———— • ————

AFTER BEING DRIVEN AROUND LAS VEGAS BY THE MAN WITH the silver and gold Presidential Seal, Renato Mortella had telephoned Gunther Shurtz.

An hour after Shurtz heard the receiver slammed in his ear, he said to Calvino, "Nick, my boy. I'm afraid your relatives have ended our business relationship. You will do well to tell your lady that you are moving to Las Vegas."

"Gee, Gunner, I'm real sorry. What're you going to do? Go home?"

"A splendid idea, Nick. I'm giving you and Angie a going-away present. Twenty thousand dollars. Now, don't spend it all in the same casinos, my boy."

"Twenty big ones! Gunner, I appreciate. I know it's kinda like severance, like the plumbers' union ya know. But I can't take it."

Alone, Shurtz pulled the handkerchief from his sleeve and wiped a thin ridge of sweat from his boar's head. With the Mafia there were scores of ways to call it off, all of them bad. The Mortella brothers for some reason hadn't broken his arms and dumped him in Jamaica Bay inside a drum filled with concrete. They had just packed it in, nice and neat as Bob's your uncle. And they had almost forgotten to pick up their idiot nephew on the way out.

Shurtz was in fact buoyed by Renato's rage. Someone had scared Mortella off and shut him up instantly. It could only be the United States government.

Renato had said to him, "You got us into this crazy goddamn scam—following that bastard from the hospital. And what we got was a dead soldier, a good man. If I had time I'd make you dead too. You're dead on the docks and airports right now, this minute, you fuck, you."

The feds had scared the Mortellas so bad they weren't even going to avenge their dead soldier. Ha! So much for their bleeding brotherhood, so much for the ties that bind. No, he wasn't going home to South Africa. He had friends in Mexico, especially in Tijuana, and, who knows, he might set up his business there. Moreover, Mexican officials were said to be always glad to hear bad news about the United States.

When Shurtz reached Tijuana the next day, he found the street where eight pharmacies in a row were hawking wares mostly to American buyers, went into the one called Los Tres Americanos, and asked for Señor Gomez. This was where Shurtz had previously bought hormones, anabolic steroids, and other drugs banned in the United States by the Food and Drug Administration. The clerk asked him to wait. Soon, a middle-aged man who was not Gomez emerged, a man in a neat suit and foulard tie who invited Shurtz into his car.

"You know that the government has confiscated the Noriega factory?" the man said.

"It's not about that I've come. I need to see the Minister for External Affairs in Mexico City."

"You can tell the Northern Baja California Administrator. I can arrange it for you."

Shurtz, on the way to his appointment with the Administrator, felt no fear that he was in danger of arrest. He had not once taken possession of his medicine deliveries inside Mexico, but always across the border at San Ysidro. The Administrator's office was in a large building—one forgot that if Tijuana were in the United States it would be the ninth or tenth largest city. Shurtz told his story of the events: Harkness Pavilion, the Mortellas following the fed, the dead soldier. He told it to the Administrator and to the tape recorder the Administrator had running. He told it all and he offered to pay his own way to Mexico City.

"We'll put you on the flight and have you met. And, Mr. Shurtz, you are *not* to resume your old business in Tijuana."

"Of course. I plan to deal in large dollar amounts in Dominica."

"When you return, perhaps we can, after all, discuss it."

Shurtz was met at the airport in Mexico City by a limousine carrying a driver and a front-seat passenger, both wearing shoulder holsters. On arrival at a tall building on the Paseo de la Reforma, which had originally been laid out by the Emperor Maximilian, Shurtz shuddered at the daring of the Mexicans in building on a dry lake bed that was in an earthquake zone. He sat in a reception room for more than two hours. Shurtz was familiar with the techniques that induced a man to talk for the mere sake of company. These were pretty much the same the world over—except in some nations of the Far East, where the inquisitors, out of racial bewilderment, immediately harass a stranger. The man who finally appeared was short, squat, with heavy arms and full jowls, his eyes like marbles set in dark aureoles. Shurtz noticed that his shoes, thick soled with silver metal tips and heels, were good for mucking or kicking. He sat down on a table at the opposite end from Shurtz and lit a cigarette and placed his pack on the table with an old Zippo lighter squarely on its center. After he inhaled and exhaled three times, like an artillery man counting off between rounds, he began to speak in excellent English.

"Your business with General Noriega is over with. Why did you return? Was it your gun-smuggling business?"

"Governor, why don't we save a lot of time? I never smuggled guns, from Mexico or Mars. I don't own a gun. I've never fired one. *You* do know, governor, that Englishmen are not shooters. Mainly, we're burglars. What I have is information on maybe billions of dollars. I need a friendly government to tell my story to. If some of that money comes loose, that particular government could keep it."

"And what do *you* want?"

"If that government is satisfied, then I'd expect to resume my business, only this time I'd live and work in Tijuana and let someone else in San Ysidro do the selling."

"You're talking about cocaine."

"No, governor, we both know what I did—and do. I'm talking about prescription drugs. Drugs for AIDS, for cancer, for muscle building, for reducing weight, growing hair, and eliminating wrinkles. I don't try to make people deliriously happy."

The squat man left and shortly, in his place, there arrived a thin, tall man who wore a dark suit with a polka-dot tie and an expensive watch on his wrist. His shoes were thin soled.

Shurtz was at last ready to recite. "I figure that it's like after World War II, when the Russians captured German scientists and the Americans did too. It's how they both made missiles, isn't it? Only now, the scientists have been studying something *together*. And maybe they've found it. You no doubt heard the tape of what I said in Tijuana. There's more."

"What's the more?" He didn't look hostile, Shurtz was pleased to note, only skeptical.

"The more, governor, is this. Back at the start, an FBI man I pay to talk told me a fed agency put my hired gun somewhere after they captured him, before he could do the job, *and they put their own man in.* But no one knew *which* agency. Then a fed showing ID from the President of the United States calls on Renato Mortella and scares him out of his bleeding guinea mind. He doesn't right out prevent the partner of the dead man from trailing the guy who's on the run. Now, what do you make of that? There's some terrific secret the United States has, so big, so terrific that only a small group in the government knows about it. How do I know it's small? Well, the United States has got at least thirty thousand federal police of one sort or another, and enough computers to hold a billion Chinese names. Blimey! They ain't using all that force!"

"And you think it's military secrets?"

"Well, governor, no I don't. The Russians are broke and aren't paying for military secrets. The Japs can't attack anyone. The Germans are busy making Marks. And the Chinese never leave home to fight."

"And why," the Mexican said with some sarcasm, "would this exciting chase end here? Why not in Canada?"

Shurtz was pleased that they were talking how and where, not why. He was quick to answer. "A bloke on the run doesn't go to Canada unless he is a draft dodger. If you want sanctuary, you go to Brazil or to Mexico. I think the United States will watch your borders. I think the Las Vegas partner will find out where he crosses but won't follow.

"Governor, some agents visited my lawyer in New York City. They showed him the same ID as the ones who scared the Mortellas shitless. They are the President's own secret agents. They didn't ask about smuggling. They just told him never to repeat my theories. That's all!"

The Mexican, Carranza, was in fact not in doubt about pursuing this weird story. For a Mexican, the notion of intrigue in governmental affairs was too familiar to be dismissed out of hand. Shurtz was a crusty crook, really a throwback to simpler times. The man's persistence was not manic, he thought. No, it was fueled less by greed than by the hope of gaining a new home country—a more reliable motive in his own circumstances.

Renato Mortella was sitting with his brothers Mario and Roberto when the Mexican official was ushered into Renato's office at the casino in Las Vegas. Roberto's presence was not usual for him in family strategy sessions. He was there because he was the least profane, the least threatening, and the most professional looking of the brothers—a calm man who came to work at the casino as to a bank, promptly, quietly. Renato sat behind the ornate desk with its heavy brass pulls and pad feet, his chair pushed a good three feet back from the edge, with his arms circling his middle, fingers joined, a gesture that should make a man look pacific but not so in Renato's case— the color in his face was brewing and any semblance of patience in him was but the eye of a hurricane. The Mexican introduced himself as Luis Carranza. He was slender, graceful, with small hands, expensively outfitted. Mario thought him almost a WASP.

"Gentlemen," Carranza said. "There is in the State of Sonora Prison a cousin of yours, one Alberto Corcini. He's serving twenty years. And in a warehouse in La Paz, in Baja California, there are slot machines you've already paid for destined for Mexico City and Vera Cruz. It's possible the Mexican government could confiscate the machines. And of course no one survives many years in a Sonora prison."

Renato was outraged. Imagine! A spic was telling him that he could kill people and take over property just like that! And he wasn't even a wise guy! What was happening to the world?

Roberto spoke then, not his usual role. "Mr. Carranza, what is it that we can help you with?"

"One of your employees is following a man who shot his partner. The Mexican government would like to know where the man is now." He smiled, a thin smile that showed more menace than mirth. "The Mexican government *can* be lenient."

Mario spoke quickly, wanting to forestall Renato, whose temper was moving off center and gathering the force of a gale. "Did Gunther Shurtz tell you all this?" And when Carranza didn't reply he exploded. "Why would a high official like you believe an old fuck like Shurtz? He's gone off his rocker over that fake fed. He's lost his business, lost his friends, lost his bearings. He's like an old dog without teeth that keeps chewing on a bone."

Carranza was seeking verification of Shurtz's bizarre story, yet he could hardly ask Mexican intelligence to investigate— the matter might be too sensitive even for *them*. Far more important was his desire, in verifying Shurtz's story, to see faces and hear voices firsthand, to see the shadings of feeling and opinion, and to hear the half notes.

"But the American government *did* come to see you," Carranza said quietly. "And American agents, whoever they are, haven't hurt *your* business. Shurtz's lawyer lost his fees but not his license."

Roberto spoke now, much to Renato's displeasure. "Our man following the killer is named Torcello. The last we heard was when he called in from south of Los Angeles. It's Tijuana where the killer and his blond girlfriend are going to cross."

"Excellent. And when you tell the American government what it wants to know, you will tell me." It was said with the smile of the contented and the damned.

When Carranza had gone, Mario said to his brothers that if they couldn't themselves avenge Chiaffo, there was someone else who could do it for them. "Why don't we let that woman in Denver—the one the guy was shacked up with—know about the blonde? We can start her up and she might just shoot his balls off. It ain't much, Renato, but it's *ironia*, like the old man used to say. The Mexicans will never buy Shurtz's shit. That fed, he's like Dillinger. He's only famous because he hasn't been caught."

The day after the talk in Las Vegas, a soft-spoken man knocked on the door at the terrace of apartments on Twenty-first Street.

"Señora Obregon? You are a friend of an Alex Hoffman. No," he said, seeing her eyes narrow and her hand tighten on the knob of the half-open door. "I'm not police. Only a friend of his who knows he's in trouble."

"I don't know where he is."

"Señora, I do. He's in Baja California. He's there, somewhere, with a woman."

"A woman?" Carita asked, loosening her grip on the door but still not inviting him in. He looked prosperous but he had a weak face and knowing eyes.

"She came with him from a place he owns near Petaluma, in California."

Carita's face flushed and she considered, for a moment, closing the door on this man—just as she had closed that part of her life that had begun on Stout Street and ended in the kitchen in Pueblo. But now, that painful past had suddenly burst open, like a rotten fruit. Before her stood a man she didn't trust, yet whose intimate knowledge beckoned her.

"He lost most of his money in Petaluma, where he lived with the woman. When they came for him, he fought it out and he killed a man. And the house burned down."

"How do you know all this?"

"A woman telephoned to say Alex wanted to see me. I went to San Diego but he wasn't there. A blond woman met me. She said he couldn't come himself but had sent her with five thousand dollars in bearer bonds for me to cash."

"Why didn't he do it himself?"

"Señora, bearer bonds are pieces of paper that can be cashed by anyone who holds them. If Alex was in trouble in Mexico, he wouldn't want to go to a bank and make his face known."

"What did you do?"

"I cashed the bonds but gave her only five hundred dollars. I knew nothing about her. And I remembered that two years ago, Alex said that if you ever needed money I should take care of it."

"I don't need his money."

"Señora, I've got the forty-five hundred dollars." He paused. "Señora, I am sorry you don't trust me. It is hard to talk like this on the sidewalk."

She let him in.

Americans could enter Mexico for seventy-two hours without showing their passports or obtaining tourist visas. Other foreigners could obtain tourist cards by merely showing their passports. Using his USSR passport, which by Soviet custom was stamped with his vaccination certificate, Turcheff had an easy time of it with the tour bus company in Tucson, which routinely handled scores of tourist cards a day without taking any interest in where its passengers hailed from. At the border the number of cards was simply matched against the number of passengers. No inquiries were made of the passengers.

On the bus Turcheff studied maps and guidebooks. Baja California was a peninsula more than 750 miles long, longer than Italy, and was separated from the Mexican mainland by the Gulf of California, called the Sea of Cortéz in its midsection. Baja seemed to Turcheff to have not much connection to the ancient and turbulent history of Mexico: no Olmecs or Toltecs or Mayans or Aztecs had settled there; no revolutions were born or persisted here. Perhaps that was why, Turcheff speculated, Baja was an excellent escape route, in effect, a back door. At Guaymas was the terminal of the frequent ferries across the Sea of Cortéz to Santa Rosalía, astride Mexican Route 1, which ran all the way up to Tijuana, the city that was plainly named "Aunty Joan's place."

That last evening, long ago, in Moscow, Pyotorov had given him the advice he was now following. He'd said, "If you ever start running, have in mind the place to go."

"But why do you speak of my running? I am comfortable. My work at the University goes well. My colleagues are at least tolerant. I still write scientific papers. I have stopped collecting things, even books, especially since my wife is no longer here for us to discuss at length why we should buy something inessential. That's always a luxury, that kind of talk, isn't it?"

"Humor me, my friend. I'd feel happier if I knew where you would go if forced to leave Moscow—for any reason."

"I have no such plans!" Turcheff protested.

"Just name a country where you'd go if forced to flee—

for whatever reason." His repetition was a measure of his insistence.

"If you must know, then let me choose Mexico."

Pyotorov immediately was convinced it was a favorable omen: he knew some northern parts of Mexico and of course he spoke Spanish.

"Now, if you *must* leave, here's what I'd like you to do. Write to me care of Nikolai Miroset—use the English, 'Nicholas Miroset'—and write on the envelope 'Hold. Do not forward, please.' "

Turcheff, still uncomfortable, retorted, "You want me to post a letter to an official in Washington, D.C.!"

"No. Here is his home address in Fairbanks. Memorize it."

As close as Pyotorov was to Nicholas Miroset, very close to this day, they had rarely seen each other after Miroset went to Fairbanks and there married, raised four children, and on his first try, at age thirty, became a congressman. They had met twice in New York while Pyotorov worked for Pooley and three times in Washington after he joined the Commission—though Miroset had assumed he still worked for the engineering company.

"Alexandr Vladimirovich, what should I say in a letter? I can hardly say I'm leaving for Mexico and will meet you there next Thursday."

"Of course not. But in such a letter we can agree *now* that if you say certain things I'll know what's happening. Speak of platitudes, the weather, your health—everything sounding normal and generally unimportant—and amidst these mention several books and say, 'I've never managed to find the book you like so much, *Catch-22.*"

"What will that tell you?"

"It would tell me you are on your way to a place in Mexico I know well."

"Which place? My God, I've no head for such intrigue!"

"There's a city called Guaymas, in the state of Sonora. It is the largest mainland port on the Gulf of California opposite Baja California. It's a tourist haven—the whole coastline is— so the people there are used to seeing foreigners. If you speak English only, you'll be okay."

"How do I get into the United States with no visa?"

"You can cross the Canadian border, believe it or not, without showing a passport. And you can enter Mexico without a visa if you take a tour with a group that's assembled in the United States. You could leave the tour and stay behind. You might have to bribe the owner of a small hotel if you have to stay a week or more."

Turcheff had been dismayed by his persistence. What had happened to make Pyotorov so anxious? Had it been his account of the lecture at the University? There had been no repercussions from that. Most of his colleagues had dismissed it after a while as eccentricity, an academician's grazing far from home out of either boredom or senility.

This tense conversation had occurred eleven years earlier! The Professor had been alternately alarmed and disheartened over not hearing from his friend. He'd armed himself against fear and regret by resorting to several explanations. For one, Pyotorov might have joined a government organization that didn't allow him to stay in touch with a Soviet national, however innocently. Moreover, he could have decided to run for public office, like his friend Miroset—and, given the American public's paranoia about things Soviet, he hadn't dared to correspond with a Russian scientist. Or he could have been stricken dumb by a stroke or even have died of a heart attack; and if so, since he was unmarried and without any relatives, no one would have thought to notify Turcheff.

Now, it was late in 1990. The letter was sent by Turcheff

the day after the Deputy called on him. He didn't mail it from Moscow, however. He waited until he'd reached Berlin and posted it from the airport, Templehof. When the letter reached Fairbanks it was fortunate that Congressman Miroset was at home—Congress was briefly out of session. When he was telephoned by Alexandr and asked to read aloud the letter, the confidentiality of the proceedings was made safe—even from Miroset himself, as it turned out.

After he'd left Alcarita Obregon's apartment, he had planned to call Fairbanks, convinced that if the Commission was in search of him, then the Soviets would begin questioning Turcheff—even though they'd not seen each other in eleven years. He made the call from a public booth in Sausalito, north of San Francisco.

"Nick, it's Alex. I'm lucky to have caught you at home. But then, it's Christmas. How is your family?"

"Fine. You want to know about the letter, right?"

Nicholas Miroset didn't waste time if he thought something important was afoot. His concentration had made him a formidable football player, one who rarely fumbled.

"Open it and read it to me, Nick."

After he'd read it, Miroset asked, "Who is he, a spy?"

"No, he's one of us, a good Russian. He's a professor of chemistry who had permission to leave the USSR on a sabbatical to the U.S. I told him to write the letter so that I could help him if he wanted to stay here permanently. Nick, he isn't even a dissident!"

"So, what's the code in the letter?" Miroset was hanging tough.

"Have you forgotten our summer in Sonora? *Catch-22* and all that?"

"Alex, are you sure you're not doing this for the CIA?"

"I'm not CIA, Nick, for Christ's sake! I'm doing it for an

elderly Russian who treated me kindly on my several selling trips to the USSR. He's retired. His wife is dead. He has no children. When he gets here, he might want to stay—if not here, then in Mexico."

He laughed then and added, "Jesus, Congressman, I sure wouldn't want to appear before one of your hearings! You'd cite me for contempt just for exhibiting charitable impulses toward the old and friendless."

Miroset relented then and soon was relating the successes of his four children in school, his wife's obtaining an M.A. from the University of Alaska. And he chided Alexandr on not having married and formed a family.

It ended amicably, each promising the other a visit as soon as things allowed. But in fact Miroset doubted they'd come together until his friend was domesticated. Alexandr was plainly ill at ease the two times he spent in Miroset's house in Washington. He was not, as it were, housebroken.

Turcheff's tour bus passed from the American town of Nogales to its Mexican counterpart. Lunch was taken in the village of Santa Ana, notable for its Seri Indian crafts and a mission built in 1596, also a grove of cacti. It was a small town, where no doubt the tour company took a percentage of what the passengers spent. Turcheff and the other thirty-two passengers spent the night in Hermosillo, the capital of Sonora, which sat astride Route 15, running from the border to Guaymas on the Sea of Cortéz. The next morning they proceeded westward to the shore town of Bahía Kino, whose hotels showed spectacular views and offered fine fishing and swimming on gentle beaches. Opposite the town was the largest gulf island, Isla del Tiburón, once inhabited by the Seri Indians, now a nature preserve to which no admittance was allowed.

At Guaymas, Turcheff separated himself from the tour group

to walk along the shore where clumps of fishermen, mostly tourists wearing rubberized waders, stood at the water's edge. He was fortunate to find an American who said he lived in Phoenix and several times a year took a bus down here to fish, sleeping in a "bag" on the shore to "save money." The man was nearly seventy, Turcheff estimated, but hearty. Turcheff explained that he had come to Guaymas to see a young friend who was having a bad time with alcoholism and hadn't been able to find him, yet he had only a three-day pass. Would the fisherman be willing to take his place on the bus, so the tourist cards would add up to the same total recrossing the border? The favor was worth four hundred dollars. The fisherman admitted he could "use" four hundred and, when Turcheff asked what should be done about the tour guide, his newfound friend said, "Give me one hundred dollars more. He won't be any trouble."

His bribe's success lessened the tension he felt and now made it possible for him to revel in the cool and almost crowded shoreline. Behind was the Sonora desert, a smooth, flat plain that ran eastward up to the western range of the Sierra Madres, tilted like a great platter that was brick red in daytime and at twilight a deep hue of orange shot with blue. It was, Turcheff thought, like a giant satellite that caught no earthly signals.

CHAPTER TWELVE

I N THE COMMISSION'S BOOT CAMP IN HIS APPRENTICE DAYS Alex had learned how to disable a man with his hands without making a fist; and how to join his hands to club a man's neck when he bowed it from having been kicked in the groin. He had taken target practice with revolvers and automatics and rifles with scopes. He had been taught to tail a car and spot a tail. Usually, a single car couldn't tail another for more than a half hour without being spotted. Petrie had ignored his training up to this point because he didn't believe CIs had been alerted to his escape. But now, making a run for the border, he had to presume the worst. He took a chance crossing the Dumbarton Bridge, open to view as its roadways are, and in taking secondary roads southward to reach U.S. 405, the San Diego Freeway.

He spotted them: a 1990 green Olds, a good car for a tail, a car that a dentist might drive; and a poor choice, a cherry-

red Infiniti. It was clear that the Infiniti driver had been recruited in a hurry. Did they have walkie-talkies? Probably. About
every fifteen minutes they went about switching positions, with
one four or five cars ahead, the other six or seven cars behind.

Alex hadn't told Joan of the tail, not even after they stopped
early, about three o'clock, at a motel in Del Mar, about thirty
miles short of the border. Alex picked a room at the end of a
row. Once they were registered and parked and inside the room,
he looked out and saw the green Olds enter a space opposite,
the driver obviously using his interior and side rearview mirrors to keep watch. Cherry Red was not in view. After unpacking their few belongings, Joan went into the bathroom to
freshen up, while Alex peered through a half-inch space between the drawn curtains. Returning, she sat on the only chair
in the room and began methodically to remove all her clothes,
drawing or spilling her body out of the constraints of blouse,
brassiere, skirt, panty hose. Then she put back on her pumps
only, looking at Alex the whole time, and when done, said,
"Well, shucks."

When afterward he sat up and lit a cigarette from a pack
on the bed table next to his automatic pistol, he told her that
they'd been followed and that one of the two drivers was parked
in the motel lot directly across the way. He told her to pack
quickly and to stay by—he wasn't sure whether they'd run or
fight.

"Damn it, Alex. You mean we made love on borrowed
time? Are you certain they are out there?"

"I'd stake my life on it."

"'And mine."

The driver of the Olds was, he had guessed as he looked
through the curtains earlier, a man of about fifty-five—the age
of the man he'd shot at the lodge. He was gray-haired. Alex
was perplexed. The Olds was now unoccupied. Alex stepped

out quickly, staying close to the door, an automatic at his side. Down the row, four car spaces away, was the Infiniti and a driver, parked tail in, ready for a quick start. Crouched, Alex drew himself past the rear bumper and saw that the driver's window was open. He guessed that the driver had been instructed not to make a cocoon of the closed air-conditioned car. Otherwise, he might not hear any movements emanating from the motel room. His forearm rested on the windowsill, his fingers holding a cigarette. Alex reversed the automatic and brought the handle down on the man's braced forearm, numbing it instantly but not breaking bones. He reached inside to remove from the driver's belt and golf jacket an automatic and two clips. Opening the door and disentangling the driver from the gear shift, brake pedal, and steering wheel, Alex pulled him out, straightened him, poked the gun in his back, and marched him into the room past Joan, who had watched from the doorway, fascinated and horrified. It turned out that Cherry Red was no older than twenty, a kid with a mass of black hair who wore an expensive sport shirt open to the navel. Flopping against his suntanned chest was a gold chain holding a medallion that looked like an Olympic medal. Alex made him lie back on the bed, tied his shoelaces together, and brought him up to a sitting position—ready for interrogation.

Gino Torcello was confused by the pain and even more by the suddenness. Here was the famous fed who had shot his uncle's partner, Andy Chiaffo. He was a big man and quick, but he seemed not excited or even angry. Gino had been called by his uncle to help him tail this guy and the blonde, which made it fortunate that he lived not far from U.S. 405 and could join the parade at a freeway entrance his uncle named for him. But where was Lou now? He'd said he was going for a bite and to call Las Vegas. But that was forty minutes ago.

"You killed Andy Chiaffo!" Gino said.

"That was his name? We weren't really acquainted. Where's your partner?"

"Fuck you."

Alex quickly chopped the kid's bad forearm with the edge of his hand, and then, as if to complete an established routine, he made a lateral chop against the Adam's apple, causing Gino to moan in agony and gasp for air.

"When did you start tailing us?"

"On 405. My uncle picked you up earlier."

"What about the lodge?"

"Lodge? I don't know nothing about any lodge. What is it? Like the Elks?"

The kid was serious. Joan could hardly believe that the ludicrous could intrude on so awful a scene. Alex saw no point in going further. The kid had been enlisted in a hurry, which explained their using a car that looked like a tropical bird. He switched the gun to his right hand and brought the barrel down on the crown of the kid's head, a simple motion producing a concussion that made a hollow sound and caused Joan to wince once more. She found it unpleasant to admit to herself that Alex was capable of such clinical cruelty. He went about his torture like an orthopedic surgeon!

Unconscious, Gino was dragged into the bathroom, where Alex tied his hands with a skimpy towel. Then Alex looked through the gap in the curtains again and stepped out, going up briskly behind Lou Torcello, who had returned and was bending to look through the window of the Infiniti on the driver's side, as if hoping to find his nephew not gone, only asleep. Alex broke Torcello's right collarbone with the handle of the automatic, then with his left hand swung Torcello around and removed a Beretta from his shoulder holster and three clips from his coat pocket. Alex was impressed: Torcello didn't scream or curse or fake falling to the pavement. He took it like a soldier, a Mafia one but a soldier nonetheless. Inside, Joan feared that the older man might die, looking at his graying face.

"Now, your nephew is out cold," Alex said. "And so beat up he'll probably never surf again. We can do this quickly or we can play cops and robbers. Your collarbone will need setting soon. Make up your mind."

Torcello wanted to dream himself into the past, long ago, when things were simple, when he and Chiaffo used to go to Briggs Stadium of an afternoon, when Andy used to kid, "Let's go down and watch the Tigers and have a few beers between hits."

"Where did they start trailing me?"

"Omaha."

"Who are they?"

"The Mortella family. Las Vegas."

"And where did *you* pick us up?"

"At Pacifica. I watched you cop a car in Novato. Then another one."

"Why did the Mortellas tell you not to shoot me?"

Torcello shut his mouth, squeezed his eyes shut for a moment, and looked at the blonde. She might help him. He could see she didn't like the torture her boyfriend practiced. Then he felt a chop against his throat and, from it, a pain in his chest. Jesus, he was having a heart attack! He had to make it stop. So he talked.

"Mario Mortella told me a fancy fed of some kind came to call on them. The fed told them to get out of the game."

Alex didn't wait for more. He gagged Torcello lightly with a cord taken from the curtains, allowing him air through the mouth but making it hard for him to yell. He bound Torcello's ankles, put a pillow under his head, and covered him with a blanket—the broken collarbone would make him start to shake soon. He picked up their luggage, led Joan to the red car, the keys in the ignition, and drove off. Joan didn't ask if the men risked dying: she hoped he'd tell someone about them. She thought about Gino in the bathroom. Whoever found him would also see an empty bottle of black hair dye, shears, and a conditioner that was used with hair coloring. In the motel she'd become a black-haired woman with a chopped, punk hair style. When they reached National City, three miles north of the border, Alex came off the main highway, Route 5, and parked on the skirt of the access road. At a nearby public telephone box he called the Del Mar police, dropping in seventy cents in coins, and told them two men were kidnapped at the motel. After a 360-degree glance about, he opened the car trunk and folded his large body inside, bunking down the lid and tapping it—a signal for Joan to head for the border.

The guard at the Mexican station readily accepted Joan's explanation that she was going over to shop for the evening. With the denim skirt hitched above her knees and the carmine color of the expensive Japanese car she was driving, she looked cheap and, in the right circumstances, available. The officer didn't ask Joan to open the trunk—she looked like a consumer who'd fill it with Mexican goods before she returned home. Let the American guards check her goods when she recrossed the border. It was just as well: Alex was sweating from cramp and heat, gun in hand, ready to shoot.

She knew not to stop in town until she got free of the main traffic heading southward. She finally found a street that was almost empty, lined by small houses with no porches and warehouses with no front windows. When Alex climbed out, he felt crippled, so stiff were his legs.

He complained of it when he got out. She found it inequitable that he should do so.

"You're not even disguised and disfigured like me. Jesus! I forgot to get rid of my braids. They're in my bag. I suppose they're relics of a sort. Secular ones. It isn't much of a disguise anyway. My pubic hair gives me away."

He smiled, kissed her, got in the car, and took the wheel. He decided to put her in the mood for the kind of dialogue that once had been second nature to him and Viktor Ivanovich.

"Joan, when you are listening to Viktor you feel that information is a weight. The great Russian poet Mayakovsky said to Maxim Gorky, 'I want the future today.' That was in 1915. Then the future fell on the Russians, crushing them, like a load of encyclopedias."

"Did Turcheff tell you that?"

"Yes. He's candid but also cautious. He said that whenever someone asked him if he could keep a secret, he replied, 'Why should I? Obviously, you're about to break one.' "

She laughed. "Did you two always talk in metaphors? In riddles? It sounds like great fun on a warm night."

He caught the sarcasm. "Okay, Joan, so we're Russians. Viktor told me once that revolutions begin with small circles and end with long queues. It's happening now in Eastern Europe. He was a prophet. He said it eleven years ago." A pause. "You know, Joan, Viktor Ivanovich Turcheff can be an engaging man, but he's under pressure just as we are. Each of us is at the other end of a desperate dialogue."

At the White House, at about 9:30 in the evening, the meeting continued after Haagstrom left. The stream of discussion on policy was narrow at first, dealing with the Mexican development, then broadened into a delta that encompassed no less than the world itself. The Protocol would shock all and please none. It would be *misread* unfavorably or, otherwise, be *read* unfavorably. It would immediately start endless argument and afterward would cause endless evaluation. It would be blamed for all the world's ills, even bad weather. The Protocol listed those countries that would receive supplies and equipment, on what schedule, whether to be delivered by truck or ship or barge or airplane, and how distribution would be monitored by platoons or companies of the regular armies of the two powers. Among the nations excluded from receiving supplies were Great Britain, France, Germany, the Netherlands, Ireland, Norway, Denmark, Sweden, Luxembourg, Spain, Portugal, Italy, Austria, China, India, Israel, South Africa, Japan, Korea (North and South), Iraq, Cuba, Libya, Australia, Turkey, New Zealand, and others. The list had kept changing from the moment the first one was compiled. It satisfied no one.

"All lists are eccentric," the Secretary of State had told the President when the fourteenth version of the Protocol was approved by the Soviet Supreme Council. "Clubs are designed more to keep people out than bring them together. Groucho Marx said he wouldn't join a club that was willing to take him as a member."

On being summoned to the White House at 8:30 that evening, Haagstrom had assembled in his dispatch case the pertinent data, including the KGB's report that it had taken them three days to trace Turcheff's route to Berlin and then to Canada. Haagstrom knew that the Presidents of the two countries had decided to let Turcheff become a Judas goat to lure Petrie to his side.

The Commissioner could now furnish more information on Joan Dunworth. She was a bright woman who was only periodically ambitious, a caring mother to her sixteen-year-old son, and at times a political radical who had, curiously, never joined political organizations. She had been divorced seven years earlier from an attorney. Ms. Dunworth had in the past year been paid $1,200 a month to prepare a catalogue raisonné for a collection of eighteenth-century handbills donated to the

University of California by a wealthy alumnus. She also received $800 a month for child support from her ex-husband, who lived in Berkeley with a second wife. Her parents deposited $2,000 each month into her checking account in San Francisco. Since her divorce she had not lived regularly with another man, but she was known to have embraced, or consented to, a series of lovers.

Seated in the Executive Wing, in the small conference room, the group meeting with the Commissioner consisted of the President, the Secretary of State, the Director of the National Security Council, and the President's Chief of Staff.

"There's a new development," the Secretary of State said, almost as a matter of fact. "The government of Mexico says it knows where Pyotorov is and that it knows he holds 'industrial secrets.' "

The Commissioner said that he knew from Hansen and other CIs that Luis Carranza had called at Las Vegas. "We know what set the Mexicans off," Haagstrom now reported. "It was Gunther Shurtz, the importer of medical drugs we have been watching for a year or more."

"Let's assume that Petrie and Turcheff meet, and let's assume that they are prevented from talking—talking to anyone at all." It was the Director of National Security who said it.

Every face in the room was focused on Haagstrom and no one spoke. The silence continued because no one wanted to break it. The unsaid was safer.

"Something must be done to neutralize the Mexican government—discreetly."

After several matters relating to Canada's being one of the four privileged nations, Haagstrom suddenly said to the President, "May I be excused?"

He didn't put on his bowler hat until he was outside the building, walking along the short path that led to the western gate of the White House on Pennsylvania Avenue. At the curb he raised his hand, a cautionary gesture, as his chauffeur quickly rose from the driver's seat and got out to open the limousine's rear door.

"Go on, Mr. Jordan," he told the black man. Jordan was his own age, also gray-haired, a man who spoke only when something needed to be addressed. "I'll walk."

Later, he couldn't recall the streets he traversed or what turnings he made, yet he found he'd made his way to the Mall and then to the Vietnam Memorial. Near it a few couples walked and next to the black marble lay a tattered man insulated with newspapers stuffed inside his coat and with a piece of tarpaulin covering his legs. Then Haagstrom found himself on Constitution Avenue across from the navy buildings of World War I, the ones built as temporary offices more than seventy years ago that had continued to hum inside over the course of four major American wars. Suddenly he saw Jordan, who was once more holding open the rear door of the car.

"Mr. Jordan, I forgot. Did I ask you to come here? I mean, to this place?"

"No, Mr. Commissioner. I just thought you might want to talk."

"That's kind." Inside the car, driving across the Memorial Bridge on the way to Alexandria, where he lived, Haagstrom said, "Mr. Jordan, you fought in Korea, as I did. You suffered more than I because you endured and survived capture. Did the killing ever seem to you justified?"

"I killed two men in that war. But I never excused myself."

"Did you forgive yourself?"

"That I did, Mr. Commissioner."

CHAPTER THIRTEEN

THEY HAD ENTERED BAJA AND CONTINUED ON ROUTE I TO Ensenada, then headed southeast on Route 3 toward San Felipe on the Gulf of California. Outside of town in a village called Punta Estrella they found a small hotel where they dined and spent the night. It was very late when they arrived. He wanted to reach Punta Estrella so that they could stay off the main highways, and accordingly the next morning they proceeded along the gulf on two-lane roads, some unpaved, until they reached Puerticitos, where Alex entered the post office and asked to place calls to several hotels in Guaymas. It was midmorning, with only a few tourists around. He told the postmistress he was trying to find his father, who had business in Mexico City but might have taken time to stop in Guaymas, in which case the dutiful son, himself, would cross over at Santa Rosalía to meet up with him. Alex gave her the names of four major hotels and one small one outside Guaymas, having studied the tourist guides carefully. He gave his own name as Alda Turcheff and handed over two hundred pesos as she placed the calls, each to the reception desk of a hotel. On the fourth try she came up a winner. Señor Turcheff was indeed a guest, only at present, the receptionist said, he was walking on the docks, his favorite pastime. Of course the receptionist would be glad to book a double room for his son and wife for tomorrow.

"He's at a hotel. We'll work our way down the coast to Santa Rosalía, spend the night there, and cross on the ferry in the morning," Alex told Joan.

In this place of huge volcanic peaks and a bay so deep that only the edges seemed penetrable by shades of light, Joan felt that it would be right to stop and stay, not to plan and move on. The gray-red rock and cobalt-blue waters overwhelmed her senses and made her want to stop. She wanted to get straight with Alex, to be intimate without interpretation. But he was compelled to move and urgent.

They drove on, some six hundred miles from the American border, to reach Santa Rosalía. Like Puerticitos, it held an old mission, although most missions on the Baja were on the Pacific side of the mountains that ran the length of the peninsula. Looking out to the Sea of Cortéz, Alex realized that Santa Rosalía was connected to Guaymas by more than a ferry. Both were large ports lined with docks from which copper ore and other minerals were shipped. Both held large fishing piers. Both bore the stamp of French colonialism. Eiffel was said to have designed the galvanized iron for the Santa Rosalía church; and Guaymas had three times been invaded by Francophiles, once by the Emperor Maximilian's French guard. Both beaches were black, not from volcanic deposits but from the residue of ore trolleys.

Alex recalled one difference: Santa Rosalía, when he had come here for two days in 1970, had showed wooden houses and buildings, unlike other Baja towns on the Sea of Cortéz. He recalled sleeping one night on the beach in front of a splendid hotel called El Morro on the southern arm of the bay. This was not the hotel to enter now: its expensiveness alone might draw among its clientele some Mexican or American officials. They chose a place not far from the Eiffel church. The next morning they crossed to Guaymas.

At La Colineuse, a small hotel about four miles from the center of town, below the ferry terminal, they found Turcheff, seated on a patio and reading an American newspaper. Seeing this stolid man of over seventy, with the plain European cut to his suit, sitting on a terrace of concave brown tiles under balcony railings painted a childlike pink, Alex thought Turcheff seemed much changed in face and figure. He was recognizably *old*. The two of them greeted each other somewhat circumspectly, shaking hands formally, talking without animation. Alex introduced Joan in English. Then Alex left to register them at the desk, where the clerk asked for tourist cards. Alex said he and the lady, both American citizens, were returning to the States with his father, the old gentleman, the following day. Leaving the old man below, he took Joan upstairs to unpack. She was relieved to find the room had a shower. The trip down Baja had been brutal for her skin. Now, she felt querulous. Suspense had been their constant passenger, hastening them to their rendezvous; and unfamiliarity was her destination, stranger meeting stranger.

"Why can't we just keep going all the way to Brazil? No one can extradite you from there," she said to Alex before he returned downstairs.

"I've committed no crime."

"You are talking about the letter of the law. The way I did when you caught us in your lodge. They are trying to *kill* you."

"I've got to see Viktor now. He'll be nervous."

"Odd. So am I!"

On returning to the terrace—no one else seated there but Turcheff—he ordered drinks for them both.

"Don't be concerned over money, Viktor. I've brought with me all I own, over two hundred thousand dollars in big bills." He switched to English. "Money is no object, people always say, but of course it is always the subject."

Turcheff smiled, uncertain of the joke. Then he turned serious. "Is this woman someone you can trust under present circumstances?"

Alex was aware that Turcheff had no way of knowing that he also was on the run, and said, "You left Moscow when? No more than ten days ago? I've been fleeing my own government for the past seven days. *Your* flight induced mine, although you could not know it."

"Alexandr Vladimirovich, I've heard nothing. When the Deputy came to my flat to question me about you—more than eleven years after I'd last seen you—I suspected you were in trouble, and of course immediately I knew I was also. I presume it is the *same* trouble."

"It must be the same. Ten years ago I left Pooley and joined a government agency called the Commission, which is empowered to investigate *other* agencies of the United States government when officials are suspected of acting illegally. Then, seven days ago, my own organization set up an elaborate scheme. It had a legitimate purpose but it turned into a maneuver to capture or kill me. My own agency! I've been running since."

"But about the woman, Alexandr Vladimirovich?"

"I met her four days ago, just as two gunmen were firing at me. I killed one of them. She was slightly wounded. She decided to come with me."

"She's married?"

"Divorced. She has a sixteen-year-old son. She comes from a family with money and social status, but by nature she's been rebellious."

"What is her cause?"

"Everything and nothing." He saw alarm in Turcheff's face. "No, she's not disloyal to people just because of their beliefs. She is a victim of her own seriousness. She's not sure how she proceeds from day to day without always summating her life-time. And she hasn't come this far for the thrill of it. She's searching for her own answers—and, now, my answers too."

There followed general talk later at dinner in the hotel. It was conducted in English for Joan's sake. Turcheff spoke of archaeology and the history of Mexico, almost as if he were the lecturer on a tour. Alex was puzzled. Joan was soon offended.

"The Mexicans are deadly serious about their *Indian* past. Once I attended an international convention of chemical scientists in Warsaw and at the start of the plenary session the official languages were chosen. The Mexican delegation agreed to Spanish only as their second language. They declared themselves Indians.

"Since I've been here I've read, quite superficially of course, about Mesoamerican archaeology, about the later ancient culture, Mogollon, which had an interesting turn of events. About 1000 A.D., the Mogollon stopped living in pits and in caves and began to live in aboveground structures. It was the women who made this come about."

"Are there records of that? I mean, about the women?" Joan asked.

"Only signs of a sort. The men dug holes, kivas and the like, for their secret male ceremonies. But the women seem to have sought the light. Perhaps the men sought to prolong youth and the women, tending infants, were willing to be weathered—is that the right English word?"

Did Turcheff resent her presence? He had looked disapprovingly at her casual clothes. Alex immediately changed the tone by inquiring into the matter of Turcheff's documents.

"You had to use your own name?"

"As you know, a foreigner has to have what is called a tourist card. The bus companies handle the cards. I bribed an American fisherman to get on the bus in my place—thirty-three passengers, thirty-three tourist cards. I told the concierge here that I would leave tomorrow morning or the next morning."

As they lay in bed that night talking to the ceiling, Joan was intensely aware that something was not right. The two men had spoken only briefly alone, in Russian, after first greeting each other, but they had spoken much longer while she was showering and getting dressed for dinner. Then, when she joined them, the Professor had turned formal and distant, talking of how women aged and of plenary sessions.

"Did he tell you what *you* are supposed to know?" Joan asked Alex now.

"Not enough. He was too nervous tonight."

"It's kivas and caves, after all. Buddies. I look like a tart! You told him you've only known me a few days. Did you tell him in Moscow of your other women?"

"Joan, give us a break. I mean, give one to all three of us. The old man is puritanical and he's wary. Mainly, he wants to find out if I'm safer staying somewhat ignorant, or safer becoming somewhat informed."

"How will he decide?"

"He knows we are all fugitives. And he'll talk now. He left Moscow because he was worried not only over himself but also over me. He had a visit from the Deputy to the Soviet President, who told him that I'd gone bad and was selling scientific secrets."

"Joan, please don't judge him just on tonight."

"But he does know the secret? The one everyone thinks you have?"

"Yes."

"It must be something tremendous."

"It is. Earthshaking."

They didn't make love that night.

Alex recognized the toll of indecision, the debt that inaction exacts. A man waits and soon begins to doubt his judgment. A man waits and people who depend on him soon begin to wonder if he is confused, or timid, or afraid. Many times he had heard the axiom "Act, even if wrong, act," and had thought it naive or footless. Yet it had a ring to it, especially if one was watching a leader and depending on him. He decided suddenly not to tell Turcheff or Joan what he proposed to do. He rose before dawn and drove away from the docks of Guaymas northward, crossing the small peninsula separating Guaymas from Bacochibampo Bay. On the beach was the Hotel de Cortez, a resort that was almost a village in itself, self-sustained, with a fishing pier, golf course, riding trails— the whole enchilada. He followed the shoreline until he came to Bahía San Carlos, where an immense volcanic peak guards a landlocked bay. Americans filled the marina with their costly yachts and were the clients of a huge Club Med resort. He chose San Carlos because practically all the cars he saw on the town streets and on the roads leading out bore American plates. He would be much less noticeable here than in Guaymas.

As he had discovered at Puerticitos, telephone calls were

still made by radio transmission in Baja California and on the mainland opposite. Now, he placed a collect call to the Commission number and it was accepted when he told the operator to say that it was Mr. Tannenbaum's brother who was calling.

Mrs. Alberts said, "Is that you?"

"Yes, it's me. It's been a while. You checked my voice print."

Soon Tannenbaum was on the line.

"Chief, tell the Commissioner I want to call him within a half hour. I don't want anyone listening in. I don't want it taped." He hung up. He went to a café next to a market and drank coffee as he counted the minutes.

The three of them sat in Haagstrom's office at eleven o'clock eastern time, ten minutes after Petrie's call. Matthews was dour and suspicious.

"Matt, we've been looking for Petrie. I can't lose anything by talking to him. I might persuade him against some extreme measure."

The other two left reluctantly, Tannenbaum at once curious and worried, Matthews outraged. Each day that passed had made Matthews blame Petrie more and more, even to the point of suggesting that he was a double agent. In 1980, Matthews reasoned, when Petrie first joined the Commission and there were no secrets shared by the two powers, Petrie could well have found, in the atmosphere of the cold war, a warm spot on both sides. Moreover, as a double agent, he could over the years have been Turcheff's collaborator.

When the telephone rang exactly a half hour later, Petrie was on the line. He didn't ask whether anyone else was listening. Haagstrom liked that.

"I've found out what is so terribly secret. I know what it is, how it works, whom it benefits. The knowledge makes me breathless, as if buried alive, as if the earth had fallen on me.

It is awful—in the real sense—and magnificent in its simplicity and bounty."

For his part, Haagstrom was struck by the eloquence of the man. This was the first time Petrie could describe objectively what he now knew from talking to Turcheff. What Petrie had learned must be almost like a hallucinogenic to him. He would want urgently to describe it—as if he'd seen eternity the other night.

"Commissioner, I know you used to be a judge. You must know of the English Petition of Right."

"Tell me about the Petition. Of course I know it. You have a point to make."

He then said somberly, "Commissioner, it has not to do with justice or mercy, but plainly with what's right. We all know in our hearts and minds what is right. Commissioner, let right be done—to me and all others. Come and talk. I know it's difficult. There are many catches when you stick too closely to the letter of the law, when you avoid common sense. Conundrums. Catch-22. Even a Catch-22 doesn't make governing impossible."

He paused. "For God's sake, let's talk before someone is shot. Everyone is innocent, so where is the crime?"

The Commissioner had told Matthews not to tape or trace the call. He said he wanted no record for the CIA to use. (And he had a personal reason.) Matthews had contravened Haagstrom's orders. Communications called the Deputy within minutes.

"Sir, the call was placed from a public telephone box in San Carlos, in Sonora."

But the Deputy had miscalculated also. To whom could he boast that he'd found out exactly where Petrie was? He could hardly tell the Commissioner. It was like the joke he'd heard on the golf course at Burning Tree. A rabbi sneaks off to play a round by himself on an early Saturday morning, breaking the Sabbath. His drive somehow ricochets off trees and takes other heavenly bounces so that he makes a hole-in-one on a 420-yard hole. Gabriel says to God as they watch, "It's the Sabbath. Will you punish him?" "He's already in agony," God replies. "About that golf shot, to whom can he boast?"

CHAPTER FOURTEEN

ALEX RETURNED TO GUAYMAS JUST AS JOAN WAS AWAKENING at La Colineuse. From the door he saw the sculpture of her shoulders and upper arms and the mound of her breasts. She sat up, propped by her elbows, the sheet slipped down. It was for him spectacular.

"Alex, I am so very sorry about last night. I'm scared. I behave badly when I'm scared. I know your friend is concerned about you—and you about him. I'm jealous. Men *are* buddies, even without the caves and kivas. Make love to me. I want us to have something of our own."

He went over and brought her to him, her cheek against his chest, holding her as if she'd just been found. She seemed not to breathe for a few seconds. Then he felt her tears.

"Joan, you can't catch up with your own life. There's an adding up of years, or a wearing away, either one; and that can't be helped. There's so little time. Forgive yourself."

"I love you." She looked at him and said what was hardest of all. "Don't tell me you love me. I can keep on."

Turcheff had risen early and in the hotel had had a breakfast of thick coffee, eggs, and *pan Bimbo*, plain bread. He had been told to stick to simple foods. Especially in the north, in Sonora and Chihuahua and Coahuila, the choices were not notable. "For a man of your years, it is best to stick to *tortillas de haring*, grilled meat, and beer." This had been said by the hotel manager, who was himself an old man and had watched too many foreigners founder on Mexican fare.

Alex and Joan found Turcheff on the quay, his head raised, drinking in the blue and gold morning light. He was watching as the ships entering the harbor steered past a headland, Caso Haro, then moved along a narrow island shaped like an iguana, its curved tail pinching the entrance to the port. Northward in the bay were resorts and yachts, southward the docks, a quarter mile of which held berths for fishing boats. Turcheff had become an instant expert and remarked now on the shrimp and the huge grouper called *cabrilla de astillero* and the Pacific amberjack and other varieties—in such abundance, he said he'd concluded, that the Sea of Cortéz made the Black Sea seem unpopulated. The volcanic black cliffs that overlooked the shore made the water appear bottomless. Joan, looking at the oatmeal-colored stone used to build the ramparts, remembered her honeymoon at Acapulco seventeen years earlier, a trip her parents had paid for, wanting the three-months-pregnant bride to feel "normal" or seem "typical."

In Russian, Alex said, "Viktor Ivanovich, please let us talk of matters in English now. I have no fears about Joan's discretion. She is important to me, apart from having been wounded in my company. Let's talk freely. If we are pursued, all three of us will run."

Turcheff said, in English, without wasting time on prefaces, "Your country and mine began to compete openly on their experiments with hot fusion, with almost immediately apparent results. The combination, or the fusion, of atomic elements—rather than their fission, their splitting apart—seemed a superior way to create energy because the source materials were commonly available, the fallout far less deadly. Your having attended Princeton made my government think that you would be able to comprehend things about the secret development that, they believed and feared, I may have revealed casually."

Looking at Joan, her large blue eyes now more noticeable because of her renewed and natural blond hair, Turcheff found her strikingly beautiful. Whatever else, Alexandr's attachment to her was not *nostalgie de boue.* Joan, looking at Turcheff, listened intently and was already worrying, as in climbing a slippery rope, that once you started to lose your grip, the fear of falling seizes not the rope but your mind.

"Is this, Professor," she asked, "the fusion in a jar that everyone was talking about last year? Those men in Utah— was it?—who said they'd created energy in their kitchen?"

"That's *cold* fusion," Turcheff told her. "Did you know, my dear, that, whether hot or cold, fusion has become part of grand arguments? Some women scientists say that there is no such thing as pure science because it has originated mostly from a male culture—inventors, university researchers, and bureaucrats."

"And what do men say to that?" Joan was fascinated that science was arguable in feminist terms, which was to say, politically.

"One of them, a scientist doing research on something we call the Standard Model, refutes this because he thinks things are real for everyone, whether man or woman or child, because all matter is made up of particles. He once said, 'There

is no such thing as a piece of string with only one end.' " Turcheff laughed. "Quarks can't be just theory without fact. We
know that particles are observable, and quarks exist only where
particles are."

"I refuse to ask what quarks are. I have a right to remain
silent."

Turcheff was puzzled by this until Alex explained, in Russian, that at their first meeting Joan had been literal about her
civil rights when he searched her body. Turcheff found *that* to
be typical of a wondrously odd nationality, the Americans.

"Viktor Ivanovich, you recall that time we stood looking
out at the Prospekt all the way to Red Square, when we spoke
of the loftiest result of the colliders—once one is built that is
large enough—which would be the ability to integrate matter
and energy into a single physical theory."

"Yes, it speaks to what you Americans call the Big Bang,
how the galaxy was born. Long before quarks, Montaigne said
that all things tend to be alike and all move toward decay.
Right now, I'm quite satisfied to accept that we know about
three kinds of matter and four forces of energy.

"But it's normal, is it not, to seek oneness? Religions arise
from that desire, Christianity, Judaism, Buddhism. And you
Americans keep talking about 'the whole earth.' Liberals
everywhere want equality, if not commonality, in living. It's
quite understandable, is it not? All reflection urges us toward
the center."

Alex spoke in Russian. "Let's walk a way down the dock."
Then he said to Joan, "Excuse us, Joan, for only a few minutes." When they were fifty yards down the dock, he paused
to make a point.

"It's room-temperature fusion, isn't it?" he said.

Turcheff replied, "Yes. American and Soviet scientists together have found a way to fuse particles in such perfect harmony that little energy is necessary to force them together. No disharmony is caused, and little energy lost, mainly because of the correct and multiphase structure of the container and a triggering effect that keeps repeating itself."

"I want Joan to listen. Do you agree?"

"It's all right, Alexandr Vladimirovich."

They returned to where Joan stood holding her shoulders with her hands, hugging herself against the strangeness. She saw the volcanic rock heights as impenetrable amber and the sea as cobalt, neither warming. The talk resumed after she was told yes, it was "kitchen" fusion.

"What is the container?" Alex asked, picking up the thread. "There was speculation that the researchers in Utah in 1989 were using clay lined with aluminum. That sounds too simple. Surely that can't be it."

"No. An electromagnetic field within a grid of crystals, ceramic chips in fact, surrounds the plasma. This is in connection with something that may be new to you, a wake-field function. Together, they manage to keep all the elements in a perfect balance without spending too much energy."

Joan knew she'd lose her grip on the rope but made one more gesture to hang on. "Is it like the human heart? If all the blood that it pumps were needed to keep the heart itself working, then the rest of the body couldn't survive."

"Yes, it's like that," Turcheff said. "What we now know is how to expend energy *not* in favor of its own device."

Suddenly, Alex said, "We're not in danger—right now, here in Mexico—because there's been a discovery! No, it's the deal over who shall own the means of production. That's the dangerous part of the secret!"

Joan heard it as she was staring out at the slow heaving of

the water beyond the island's iguana tail. The Professor's revelations had seemed to make her own presence of small import, but now Alex's statement made her feel seriously involved.

"You are quite right, Alexandr Vladimirovich, that there must be an arrangement between our countries. As I fled Moscow, my mind returned again and again to this suspicion. A scientific discovery is usually publicized once it is confirmed. The British journal *Science* or some American or Russian journal announces it once there has been sufficient peer review by fellow scientists who can challenge or confirm its findings. But no such article exists. No public disclosure has been made. I have known of the cold-fusion experiments, of course, but I assumed none of them had been finally proven."

"Viktor Ivanovich, we are part of the deal—accidentally. We'll have to hide first, bargain later."

"Bargain for what, Alex?" Joan asked. It seemed unreal to speak of barter when it involved one's own safety—unreal and frightening.

"Bargain for our lives."

"Is there a place to hide?" Turcheff asked.

"Yes," he replied, putting an arm around Joan's shoulders. "It's not far from here."

Now it came clear to Alex what the deal might be. "Viktor, there must be an agreement between the two powers to make the cold-fusion technology itself available to no other countries."

"Yes. I have come to believe it."

Alex left Turcheff and Joan and walked down the dock. He looked at his hands. Could these alone protect them from their pursuers? What could he hold? A gun. What could he write? An ultimatum. He recalled that on a visit to Leningrad many years before he'd met a woman in the electricity bureau who had told him of surviving the horrible winters while the city lay under the German siege. She'd told him that she had repeatedly thanked God she had no more than two children. You can give a hand to each of two children as you run, as you climb or fall, she'd said. But not to three, not to four.

Coming up behind him with Joan, Turcheff touched him on the shoulder. "My friend, forgetting diplomacy and speaking of science, it's unbelievable, is it not? We have found the way to make cold fusion work within small confines. Its ratio in energy output to input must be at least a hundred thousand to one. We can produce endless energy cheaply, safely, and, best of all, locally. This is the most practical discovery in the history of all the world's tribes and peoples. And our two countries own it. I'm certain that for a time they won't share it. Nothing so grand could be left to everyone all at once. The poor, if they inherit the earth, will not do so immediately and equally."

The morning after Petrie's call, at about nine o'clock, Haagstrom took up his bowler, looked around his office, closed the door quietly as one might leaving a hospital room, and walked down the main staircase of the building in Anacostia. Out on the circular roadway, Jordan stood holding open the rear door of his limousine.

"Where to, sir?"

"I'd like to go to Baltimore. And, Mr. Jordan, don't report our route to Security once we are under way."

At the airport in Baltimore, within a space of sixty-five minutes after leaving Anacostia, the Commissioner arrived at the departures area for USAir. He carried nothing but his dispatch case. Jordan was with him as he stepped toward the gate. He was not wearing his bowler. It sat in the middle of the backseat of the limousine, on top of the overcoat that was neatly folded so that the black satin lining showed. They shook hands. Jordan had no notion what was happening, only that it was an occasion that called for no necessary gestures, only genteel ones. The Commissioner appeared to be melancholy. It occurred to Jordan that he was so preoccupied that he might stumble over a suitcase or luggage cart. He assisted the Commissioner with a slight hold on his elbow.

"Shall I call in your itinerary now, sir?"

"No, Mr. Jordan. Thank you. Just put the car in the garage and go home. I'll see you later."

At ten o'clock in the evening of the same day, Tannenbaum said, "He's gone."

"What do you mean, he's gone?"

The Chief reported to Matthews that the Commissioner had been driven to Baltimore. At the moment, CIs were running down leads at three airports, Baltimore, Phoenix, and San Diego.

Matthews picked up the blue telephone on the Commissioner's desk and waited to talk to the Chief of Staff at the White House. He sat stiffly in Haagstrom's chair, uncomfortable only because the desk was without the accoutrements familiar to him—no humidor for cigars, none of the letter openers, magnifying glasses, and other items of "brass and glass," as the British Raj used to call them.

After telling the Chief of Staff of Haagstrom's departure and Tannenbaum's current reports on air schedules, he waited.

"He's probably on a mission of some sort," the Chief of Staff said.

"The Commissioner on a mission?" Matthews shot his eyebrows, even though no one was there to observe them. "That is implausible. He was a judge. He's not an operator. I don't understand your use of the word mission here."

The Chief of Staff leaned back in his chair and decided that the President would not, especially now, wish to hear any

contentiousness. As for himself, he was at the moment con-
firming his earlier impressions of Matthews, that he was stiff-
necked and would make a splendid colonel in another country's army.

"I'd like to talk to the President," Matthews said.

"He will call you."

Matthews rang for Tannenbaum to come back. He couldn't
bear alone the uncertainty of such extraordinary events, but
more, he suspected that Tannenbaum might know more than
he'd said initially. Matthews addressed Tannenbaum before the
door was shut.

"The Commissioner's absence doesn't seem to upset the
Chief of Staff. The Commissioner *did* go to a meeting at the
White House two nights ago at about eight thirty."

Tannenbaum waited. There was more to come.

"How is it possible that we learned this late of his being
taken to the airport in Baltimore? The time is crucial. He's
been gone from here over twelve hours. That USAir flight your
CI found he took, that flight stopped at Phoenix at four thirty
our time and got to San Diego at five forty-five our time. He
could have driven from Phoenix through Tucson and crossed
the border at Nogales by eight thirty, or, more quickly still,
gone on to San Diego and driven the fifteen miles to *that* border by six thirty."

Tannenbaum agreed that the border patrols couldn't help,
because they hadn't been notified until 9:15 eastern time. "The
Commissioner told Jordan not to log his movements. And Jordan did as he was told. He works for the Commissioner."

Matthews was weary of the impasse. He sighed, started to
light a cigar, then put it down. "What made you call Jordan
at his house, then?"

Tannenbaum said, "I really don't know. I felt nervous. Just
that, nervous."

"Do you really believe he would go on a mission? The White House used that word!"

Tannenbaum looked at the Deputy evenly and said, "I believe he was convinced that he was best qualified to do whatever he must do."

At the White House, the Chief of Staff went into the Oval Office to describe Matthews's reaction to the disappearance of the Commissioner. "Matthews won't let it be. He's harrying me on Haagstrom's defection—if it *is* that."

"He'll make a nuisance. The first thing he'll do is ask for a clear definition of his duties."

"Mr. President, we seem, throughout this thing, to be running through stoplights."

"It's the secrecy. It makes us suspicious of all those who don't know and embarrassed by those who do."

The Chief was surprised to hear a maxim like this from a man who was not known to be pithy in his expression. Then he recalled that the President had once been Director of the CIA.

It was midafternoon in Las Vegas when Renato Mortella picked up the telephone that was "swept" daily—to guard against bugs—and called the number that Hansen, the CI, had given him. After Tannenbaum's secretary recorded Renato's voice, she passed him to the Chief.

"I'm Renato Mortella. Are you the top man?"

"Start talking. If you lie, I'll know it."

"You guys! Jesus! I have to talk to you without a lawyer?"

"Listen, Mortella." Tannenbaum's voice took on a juridical tone that made his words fall like drumbeats on Renato's ears, like an oar master in a Roman galley. "In the interests of national security, you and your brothers can be held without habeas corpus."

"Wait! Wait! Jesus, Mother of God. What about the law?"

Renato already knew the answer to that question. When he had called one of the Nevada senators and mentioned the Commission, he had been told by the senator's aide that deportation hearings had been mentioned by the White House. Renato had been so enraged that for a moment he forgot that he and his brothers had been born in New Jersey. The seconds went by in silence and weighed like some threatening words: heavy.

Finally Renato spoke. "Okay. Our man followed the killer and the woman from near Petaluma to a motel outside San Diego. Yesterday, about four o'clock, the fuck attacked our man. He broke his arm and locked him in the motel room."

"Mr. Mortella, I advise you not to give this information to Mr. Carranza. Yes, we know about him. If you call him, it could be treason."

"I quit! I quit! One minute you are going to deport me even though I was born here. The next minute I'm betraying my country, which is New Jersey!"

He had in fact already given the same information to Carranza by calling a number in San Diego from a pay telephone near the pool at the casino. Fuck the feds. He didn't care much for spics, either, but let them fight it out.

Alcarita was debating with herself and that was a new experience for her. Being quick-tempered, and intolerant of time passing, her emotions usually settled things quickly. But here she hesitated. Alex had been kind. He had been loving. And generous. Yet he had within a week either found a new woman or rejoined one, having known her all along. Now she began to accept that he was so different from her as to make everything distorted and suspect. His Spanish was educated and he even had a Cuban accent, her brother had told her after taking his children to Tampa for a holiday. Alex read books and intently watched the national news on television but never the local news. He was not a plain man of plain tastes. Why, then, had he sought her? Why had he enslaved her?

Her father would say, were she to ask him, that there was no reward for envy, as there was none for revenge. Envying a beautiful woman didn't improve one's own looks. A knife-scarred face was a reminder of the original hate, not of its retribution. And so it went: loss, fright, disfigurement, even death were not made right by revenge. But her father would have left out of his argument the enormous force of pride. A proud person had to live with a decent respect for herself.

She would return to the homeland of her parents and grandparents, Sonora. She would take a bus to Albuquerque, then to Las Cruces in New Mexico, then over to Route 2 and down it to the Obregon village of Imuris. From there it was only two more hours by bus to Hermosillo, the capital of Sonora, where she would ask about him at the post office and telegraph office.

CHAPTER FIFTEEN

W E'LL LEAVE AT SIESTA TIME BECAUSE FEWER PEOPLE WILL BE around—especially natives." Alex had settled it thus. As he and Joan packed the trunk of the Infiniti, Turcheff told the hotel manager that they would be boarding the three o'clock ferry for Santa Rosalía. Establishing the alibi so precisely caused the manager to insist that they eat in the hotel first, especially as he worried over the delicate digestion of foreigners, and Turcheff particularly as a man of his own age, which is how they came to eat *caldo sudador*, made of shrimps and abalone, followed by a mild tamale and beer. It wasn't until they were driving away that Alex translated into English the name of the delicacy: "sweating soup." Joan said she didn't want to know the particulars of how it came by that name.

Under way, they drove along the quay road past the ferry terminal and kept to the shoreline until reaching a branch in the paved road: right went south to the airport; left went north to San Carlos, which it took them almost an hour to reach because siesta time didn't apply to San Carlos, which was full of Americans. Between the two volcanic peaks that dominated the great bay was a steep road they would take as soon as Joan had bought some supplies. Under instructions from Alex, annoying in part because he refused to say where they were headed, she went to four different stores in San Carlos, changing her appearance slightly each time by wearing a scarf or else a sun hat bought in Guaymas, either keeping on a denim jacket or going without it and showing an expensive white blouse.

The last stop was extensive and required three trips back to the Infiniti, which Alex kept moving so that it was always parked close to other cars and thereby stood out less obviously. By the time they were ready to drive out of town past the large hotels and also past the landlocked marina, Joan had bought and carried to the car two plastic containers, mosquito netting, a sleeping bag, cans of soda and beer and milk, cheese, biscuits, canned fruit, preserves, and two liters of bottled water. As Turcheff gazed back from the top of the steep road, San Carlos Bay far below looked to him like a highly colored poster. Then they headed for Los Algodónes.

"What is Los Algodónes?" Turcheff asked.

"Our side of the shallow bay is invisible to the other, which holds Rancho Los Algodónes, only a few tourist *pensiones*. The fishing is not good here and from time to time what's called the red tide—algae—makes both eating fish and swimming unpleasant. On the eastern side, where we'll hide, the access is not easy except in a four-wheel-drive vehicle."

"Which this car is not," Joan complained.

"No, it's not. Joan, you drive. Viktor and I will walk."

For Turcheff it was no hardship, walking, because he was enchanted when they entered a narrow canyon, lined densely with palms. The grove opened onto the eastern shore of the bay. As Alex stood looking down, he was enormously relieved. No one was in sight.

"What is this place, Alex?" Joan asked as the car came to a stop near some half-built or half-destroyed buildings made mostly of volcanic rock and concrete. "Was that a landing strip for planes at the left of the canyon entrance? If it was, it can't have been used in years and years."

"It hasn't been. It's an airstrip all right. World War II Liberator bombers could land there."

It was now patchy, broken in a score of sectors, some showing asphalt, others only the steel netting originally installed to support the now missing asphalt.

Turcheff stared. It was incredible, this place, made by a madman perhaps. "What is it, Alexandr?"

"It is the movie set for *Catch-22*. I came here with Nikolai Miroset in 1970, when I was sixteen, and we got jobs as hands."

"You're kidding," Joan exclaimed as her memory went into high gear. "You mean the movie with Alan Arkin and Orson Welles and, who else? Oh yes, Martin Balsam, Buck Henry. You were here?"

"I was. Mike Nichols, who was the director, spent a ton of money to make a set for an airfield and barracks out of World War II. The Battle of Salerno. The airstrip was used by the bombers in the movie, but also to fly equipment and actors in and out."

Turcheff was baffled. There was little wood left—no doubt taken by the natives—except for some planking, which Alex explained was mainly used as tracks for the camera trolleys. There were two latrines, with concrete walls but no ceramic back tanks for flushing, no seats, and no roof or doors. Only two buildings looked usable: one that Alex said had been a cutting room where a moviola once stood—this machine he described later—and one that had been the mess hall and now had a roof over only the middle section. Alex drove the car into the latter, covering the entrance with stones and concrete slabs, holding against them, as an interior lining, some tar paper he tore from the walls.

He arranged for the supplies to be stowed under the car and for the cutting room to hold the sleeping bag and most of the mosquito netting, the rest of it used to cover the three-quarter-closed windows next to the front seat of the car. They would stand watches, four hours each, in the cutting room, which had a view of the canyon, while the other two slept on the front and back seats of the Infiniti. Alex said they could cook nothing, else the smoke would give them away. The plastic containers would be used to bring up sea water so they could wash themselves and use the latrines as hygienically as possible—he had determined that soft paper would go down the bowls if they were flooded with water.

Joan, still wondrous, asked, "You found out about this place just from reading a magazine, or what?"

"No, my friend Miroset and I heard about the filming from a high-school history teacher who had flown Liberator bombers in the war and was being paid as a consultant. We hitchhiked through Raton, New Mexico, and down into Arizona, and crossed at Nogales, just like you, Viktor Ivanovich."

"Alexandr Vladimirovich," Turcheff asked, staring, "what is this catch-22?"

"It's the title of a novel and of the movie version of it," Alex explained in Russian. "It has now entered the English language, somewhat like Kafka's 'K' and Orwell's *1984*. In World War II a bombardier finds himself trapped by lunatic bureaucratic logic. No really sane man would risk his life day after day on orders given by someone thousands of miles away, day after day being shot at by enemy fighter planes and anti-aircraft guns. When he tells the command that he's insane to do this and wants to be discharged or put in a hospital, his superiors say that the fact that he can deduce the particulars of this insanity proves him to be competent and rational. So he must continue flying."

"What is a catch?"

"A conundrum or paradox."

"Ah, yes. This place suits us."

As they walked about, Joan thought it didn't look like a ghost town—a place people had left because the gold or silver had run out—but more like a place where there had occurred a series of beginnings without the means or will to reach the end, like a building with a staircase going to a nonexistent second floor, a road that stopped short of any buildings, a tower that could not have held fuel or water or even guards. It was a place of false starts.

"Alex, how will we get away?"

"Joan, the question in the minds of our enemies may not be what happens if we live but what if we die. Death here, and now, may not put paid to anything."

Turcheff, listening, his face revealing nothing, asked, "Alexandr Vladimirovich, are you armed?"

"Yes. One automatic of my own, two I took off the crooks who followed us, and about a hundred rounds."

"And have we enough petrol to reach the ferry to Santa Rosalía without stopping?"

"I filled the car in San Carlos. We've got at least fifteen gallons. Enough to reach the California border, assuming we have to."

"Who will come?" Joan asked.

It was later. Her question was asked in the confines of the car, as in a bunker. Outside it was black, making footing dangerous. Turcheff stirred in the backseat, pushed himself forward, and put his face close to hers as she sat in the front. He cleared his voice and sounded decisive. His mood was hard for Joan to interpret.

"Who will come?" Turcheff repeated. "Americans. Soviets. Mexicans. Maybe even those hooligans who shot you, Joan. Alexandr Vladimirovich's guns and hundred rounds will last ten or fifteen minutes, no more, if they mean to kill us. I don't mind dying. I'm old, there's that. But I do mind martyrdom. I'm not at all sure what it could mean for others if we died here, on this moonscape, on this movie set."

Moments passed. A wind came up off the shore and blew through the spaces between the stones, flapping the tar paper. After taking the first watch, Alex was lying on the front seat now as Joan slept in the rear. Viktor was in the cutting room on the sleeping bag, covered by mosquito netting, watching the canyon. Alex couldn't sleep. He recalled having seen Orson Welles here playing the role of a general who arrived to inspect the airfield command.

Welles hadn't returned to Los Angeles when he was done with his takes. He had lingered on, drinking, talking, reliving in a raucous remembrance his extraordinary public career, which began when he was nineteen and was more or less over by the time he was twenty-six. Only later did Alex read F. Scott Fitzgerald's maxim that "there are no second acts to American lives." Welles had been looking for new audiences so he could relate again the anecdotes that made his fallen star still glitter. He had left finally. In the end they had all left, taking with them their photographic and recording and editing equipment and the airplanes. The show was over.

Viktor came from the cutting room as small streaks of light pierced the crevices of the shed and were refracted from the car windows. Earlier in Guaymas he had said to Alex, "It's a different sky on this continent, you know. It's open, straight up, uncomplicated except for color. I saw it coming across the Great Plains. In Europe, the sky closes in. One could argue that the European sky is life-sized. But then, a life-sized sky can fall on you."

After Joan had fixed a cold breakfast and each had taken a turn at the latrine, then washed in an eddy that was not even visible from the buildings, Turcheff resumed his scientific discourse—on Alex's urging. The Professor didn't feel the exigency that oppressed Alex. Americans were by nature restless. Alex had once told him that they had invented the rocking chair.

"Why are you not elated?" Alex asked Turcheff. "Cold fusion is quite the opposite of what you once called imperialist science. It's local, even homespun. With it, at last, the Soviet Union can be populated by citizens who are *consumers*. In America we *teach* people to create a demand. That can happen now in Russia."

"First," Turcheff replied, somewhat irritably, "we must teach Soviet citizens to produce. A whole country after only *three* seasons of growing can feed its people—you give farmers an incentive and consumers a true pricing. After all, nature has laid it out quite neatly. Animals you tend daily, crops you tend weekly, fruit trees and bushes need care only monthly. There was no famine in Russia in 1880, but there were several in the 1920s. Communism stopped the seasons."

Joan was more than curious about the issue of deception in science: it bothered her a great deal. Having for a dozen years found herself scornful of what TV called public perceptions created by officials, churchmen, psychologists, and sociologists, she had clung to only one absolute: scientists didn't lie.

"Alex, I know you haven't heard it all"—meaning Turcheff's explanation—"but it really is beyond me. Can I walk around the back of this set, between those big boulders, and take a swim?"

"I'll go with you," he said, motioning to Turcheff that he'd be back shortly.

"We'll be out of here soon," he said as they walked.

"How? What's happened?"

"Nothing new. We'll have to leave here within a day, two at the most. And that requires logistics."

Something *had* happened. He was giving up! His voice was too matter-of-fact in tone, too reasonable. She gripped his hands in hers and said, fatefulness now become real and awful, "You're not coming with us! You're going to let Viktor and me go while you draw off whoever is out there."

"Joan, we've got to talk. The Commission may think I'm capable of revealing how the cold-fusion device works. But I'm not. I can see the edges but not the center. What it means is that Viktor has to be saved. He's got to get free."

"They'll kill you." She said it without feeling, the way one might say, "That's ten dollars for the spade."

"Not if I can help it. I'll surrender."

"You couldn't surrender before? Why have we been running? Alex, you've got to tell me the truth. I can't bear your being cautious with me. Tell me what you're going to do! Tell me what the rest of my life will be!"

He kissed her. Her mouth was open, her breasts free inside the man's shirt she was wearing. Then they were on the sand.

Afterward, she lay naked on the sand, motes of afternoon light touching her blond flesh like a yellowing brush. He stood looking at her. Nothing seemed to him as capable as a woman's body: it gave pleasure while engendering life. A beautiful woman went far beyond the demands of evolution: she was, in that sense, a glorious example of natural excess, a rainbow, or roses doubled on a vine.

CHAPTER SIXTEEN

———— • ————

WHEN ALEX GOT BACK, HE FOUND VIKTOR IN THE AUTOMO-
bile smoking, disobeying the injuction. Alex joined him in a
cigarette and in continuing the dialogue. Dispelling the smoke
by waving their hands, they took up the explication, Turcheff refusing the offer of tequila and limes, which Joan had
bought quite on her own initiative in San Carlos. Alex drank
to slow himself down. It was only a half hour since he'd left
Joan in her odalisque pose on the shore, golden and nude to
the world. She hadn't even looked his way when he left. She
knew he was a man who loved women and she wanted him
now to be sated and later to suffer the excitable unease that
she was absent.

"What happened in the Soviet Union on the early tests?"
Alex asked.

"Keep in mind, Alexandr Vladimirovich, that hot fusion is

physics, while cold fusion is basically chemistry. You know it, but let me lecture. It's my trade! When you bring together two positively charged deuterons—this, deuterium nuclei made up of a proton and a neutron—there's immense electrical repulsion, the Coulomb barrier. Pons and Fleischmann knew from the start they'd have to deal with it, so they started with lithium and heavy water. Then they took two electrodes, one of positively charged platinum, the other of negatively charged palladium. They decided on palladium because it's a crystal with a regular atomic pattern, constructed so that electromagnetic forces will crowd or compact the atoms, forcing them together in all the interstices, making it more likely to take them past the Coulomb barrier.

"Here's something interesting! In some of our experiments, if we put palladium electrodes into heavy water, with its oxygen and deuterium, then pass the current through, nothing may happen. Then, days or weeks afterward, bursts of heat are emitted. Odd, no? These bursts aren't regular. And they are not predictable. So where do they come from? To scientists at first it was like Saint Elmo's fire.

"We decided that the solution of heavy water was like a battery, releasing energy when triggered. You worked with the Tokomak at Princeton, so you may know that we proceeded to create another version of the Tokomak, a smaller igniter. Our idea was that you could achieve continuous firing, or triggering, so that as the charged particles fused they would leave a wake."

Alex felt an electric light bulb turn on over his head. "That's what the necessary element is? The wake field?"

Turcheff paused, opened the car door, and stood up outside, bending his knees. "Alexandr Ivanovich, it is really not a good idea for us to remain seated like this. You can throw a clot from cramped arteries. Then you can only hope that it lodges in your lungs, not your heart. What's more, if someone comes, we'd be cramped and couldn't run."

"We are not going to run. Our only way out is to drive out. It's rough country except on the shoreline, where, going away from the Rancho, you still have to climb volcanic rocks. When Joan and I were on the beach, we saw that there are boulders blocking off the sea's edge, so that the only clear passage is on patches of sand in between. It would take an hour. We'd be exposed both from the heights *and* from the sea. A rifle could pick us off at four hundred yards."

Joan had returned and stood straight next to Turcheff. Tears were brimming and her hands closed into fists at her thighs. "Are you saying we're waiting to be shot? That's crazy. That can't be. What's ahead of us?"

Alex bent over to her and held her, but she resisted, keeping her arms crossed over her body, as if hugging herself against harm.

"Joan, if we act rationally and turn ourselves over to the Mexican authorities, they'll sweat Viktor for his information, and me too. If our governments capitulate but want us silenced, they'll stand by while some *federales* kill us—by accident. This crazy thing is not to be cured by a rational act."

"So what do we do? Wait?"

"We're waiting for circumstance to work. A break, a chance, maybe an accident that befalls someone else."

"Do you believe in circumstance?"

"Yes. There can't be just one end to a piece of string."

Gunther Shurtz had plenty of money, yet he was vexed to be staying in a rather cheap hotel near the Plaza de la República where he'd been installed by Luis Carranza, who didn't want Shurtz to be seen by chance by any U.S. officials staying in one of the more luxurious hotels of Mexico City. Shurtz was, from any viewpoint, quite a problem. He had been involved with the Mafia, which was despised by Mexican officials and successfully kept out of Mexican affairs. He knew too much, even if most of what he knew was speculation. To deport him to South Africa was to let him convince *another* government that a great bounty was available—maybe. No, Carranza decided. It was necessary to hold onto Shurtz until there was no risk from him.

Oddly, the Mexicans did not want to kill him, risk though he may be—they thought him useful in case they could not enter into something lucrative. He was, still, an igniter of events.

Within weeks, the Mexican government would put the old boy under guard in a comfortable house in the interior—away from outsiders. He'd be promised a chance to renew his old trade, only this time from the Mexican side of the border. In any event, Shurtz was soon to be retired—not the worst fate for an oldtime "wide boy."

The fact that the man and woman had crossed into Tijuana had been all the information Carranza needed to alert the military. He had been instructed by the President of Mexico not to use local *policía*, only *federales*, in the search and capture. It had taken him only eighteen hours to trace the meeting of the two with the one, making three fugitives, at La Colineuse. But when the *federales* finally came to call on the manager of La Colineuse, Petrie and the woman and Turcheff had already disappeared. No one had seen them leave town. Inquiries at towns southward and northward, and across to Baja once more, had brought no results.

Would they stay in the Baja Peninsula, if they had returned there, crossed over as the old manager in Guaymas said? No, that made no sense for a trained officer like the American. He'd know that Baja was a pipe that could be closed at both ends. If they had stayed in Sonora, which seemed probable, given the time period, there were plenty of places to hide: the shoreline held a hundred isolated coves, north and south of Guaymas; and to the south was the Yaqui country, which, given that the Yaquis were the sole Indians in Mexico to maintain their sovereignty, was poorly mapped. Even the border was not much of a barrier except in Tijuana. It was fifteen hundred miles long, without fences (even if there were patrols) over long reaches; and the Rio Grande was hardly *grande*, but so shallow over large stretches that wetbacks waded across every night. To the interior were two mountain ranges, the western Sierra Madres and the eastern, the first a severe series of craggy heights with stone canyons.

Because the search was difficult and the stakes so high, Carranza was keenly attentive to the views of the Commandant General in Hermosillo. Moreover, Carranza was himself a native of Monterrey and was all too aware that the northern Mexicans were almost like another race. Historically they were rebels and seemingly always had been a dour and suspicious people. It was not by accident that so many renegades and popular heroes were northerners, Pancho Villa, Huerta, Obregón, others. The Commandant was a bulky man, his copper face so smooth, so taut that he looked as if he'd been skinned. His narrow green eyes moved guardedly but his body was motionless, his hands composed.

"They will stay to the shore, Minister."

"Why not try for the interior?"

"They would need proper equipment, a vehicle with four-wheel drive, guns, camping equipment, sleeping bags. If they had all that they could find a hundred places in the Sierra Madres, especially if they headed eastward toward Cochise, in the Sierra el Tegre. But I think it's too long a trip." He paused.

"And our questioning turns up no evidence of their buying the vehicle or the other gear."

"Then where? The gulf?"

"That's the best guess. From the north, beginning at El Golfo de Santa Clara, through Puerto Peñasco and Puerto de Lobos, to Isla del Tiberón, and below Guaymas to Potam, there are rock canyons, scores upon scores of caves, many trails leading up dry streambeds to the volcanic headlands."

"Who would be likely to see them there?"

"Not counting us?" The Commandant laughed for the first time, his square yellow teeth showing like tombstones. "Seri Indians. Yaquis. American tourists. Some of the few miners left in the mountains. *Policía.*"

Carranza wasn't getting quite the information he had hoped for, so he rephrased his question. "Would they be better off to appear to be tourists, riding buses in the interior? Or would they go to ground, like a prairie rabbit, and only look up once in a while?"

"There are no prairie rabbits in those rock canyons. The younger man is resourceful and trained in arms, in surveillance. Those gringo crooks couldn't catch him and he killed or wounded at least two of them. A man like that will not hide where there's only *one* way out. He'll stay on the gulf. His backdoor escape is by water."

"Then, how many men will you have searching?"

"A thousand. Our President said this was important. Important is not counted in hundreds."

"Mr. President," the Soviet President said through his translator. "May I tell you what I think?"

"Why, of course, as usual."

"No, no, please. I want this not to be official. What I say

now may not even be real, which is to say, true in every aspect. It may, in fact, happen only as I describe it."

Bush said then, "You mean you are guessing?"

"It strikes me, Mr. President," the Russian said, "that given what's happened to Petrie and Turcheff—and in my saying so please believe that I am not a determinist—it strikes me that things that happen are not unlike the very people they happen to."

"I don't understand."

"It's theoretical, of course. A man who doesn't want to win rarely does. Worse, a man with only halfhearted desires somehow seems always to fall victim to accidents that confirm his indecision."

"I'm not sure I understand. Could be the translation."

"Mr. President, you are uneasy. Let me say I'm just pondering the accidents that have befallen our Protocol so far. Your Commission is thoroughly reliable and competent, yet it has too few field agents. You have not called on your excellent FBI or Secret Service, which have thousands of operatives. And now, Mr. President, you tell me that the Commissioner himself— not a field operator, indeed a judge and a man over sixty years old—has gone off on a mission to deal with the fugitive."

"Are you saying that here in the United States we make our own bad luck? Why would we do that, Mr. President? We have the saying: shoot yourself in the foot. Is that what you think we've done?"

There was congenial, if also forced, laughter on the other end of the line. "Well, unlike one of my predecessors who is remembered for banging his shoe on the table at the United Nations, I don't have some homely peasant expression to use on an occasion like this. Let me say only that if some circumstance is blind—that's fate, is it not?—another circumstance is merely blindfolded."

The conversation on the delay decoder—which made it useless to monitor the airways since the voice signals were sent digitally on a code index that was charged to be reset every forty-five seconds—ended with terse pleasantries and a resolution to talk again within twelve hours. The President was well aware that his Soviet counterpart believed that consciously or unconsciously he was allowing the scientific secret and attendant Protocol to be broken—so that the bounty of the great technology would be dispersed to all people, without exception and immediately.

Could he be right? No, fair was fair. The visit of the Deputy to Turcheff had certainly been on the order of a blindfolded man allowing himself to fall down the stairs. Turcheff had been started up and set running by the Russians themselves.

The President immediately set in place the CIA and the FBI and the Secret Service. Matthews's worst fears were realized before he was himself told.

CHAPTER SEVENTEEN

HAT EVENING, THEIR SECOND AT THE MOVIE SET, ALEX AND
Joan took the chance to climb up into the grove that grew
so densely inside the canyon, shutting off eastern Los Algodónes from the outside world. When Alex had been here in
1970, during the filming, another road had been cut to Rancho
Los Algodónes to the west, which ran through and below the
red and black cliffs and was filled with more than a thousand
palms. The road was now blocked by metal gates, which made
the only access to the *Catch-22* shoreline the track where they
now stood.

"How do you remember it? I mean your coming here with
your friend."

"It was the most dramatic thing I ever did, coming down
here with Nikolai. I read all I could, started teaching myself
Spanish, and walked at least fifty miles. We even went over to

Tiberón. It's maybe forty miles long and twenty miles wide. Nikolai and I found it was only a mile across from the mainland opposite a small town called Punta Chuaca. We rowed over. And we got caught."

"Police?"

"Coast guard. The island is awesome, with one peak almost four thousand feet high and palm canyons like this one. The Seri Indians used to live there, but the *naval militar* evicted them. It's supposed to be a wildlife preserve."

Joan knew that Alex was not acting as tour guide, nor was he making small talk. He introduced even desperate subjects by means of detailed description. Was it his training? No, his disposition.

"Is that your ace in the hole? You think we can row over there and hide?"

"From the Punta Chauca point, you could swim it. In a boat, it would take less than ten minutes of rowing."

"You haven't told him about it?"

"No. I don't know why I haven't."

Below, the light failed and the waters were streaked blue and white and orange. There were no clouds.

"You can see all the way home," Joan said, after they'd fallen silent for several minutes.

"Do you want to go home?"

"I'd like to see Scott."

"You're a good mother."

"What was your mother like?"

"I don't really know." He waited and in the silence between them they heard the waves rush up gullies between the rocks to slap at the stones, then the sound of retreat, a slurring as the water left the sand between the rocks.

He thought of his mother in Denver during the days when

she was ill and stayed in her bed, sometimes entirely silent for a whole day. Ill, she had seemed resigned, yet she had reminisced because, he felt, she wanted the cancer not to waste her past as it was her present. She had told him about her childhood in Montreal as the daughter of Russian immigrants, and how her English was of course far better than his father's yet, oddly, his having been a German prisoner of war in occupied France had left him with more fluency in French than Alexandr's mother could command. His mother was not comely, nor particularly personable, but it was not for those reasons, he reflected now—more than twenty years later, as he and Joan stood looking at the darkening Sea of Cortéz—that she had seemed misplaced. Had she married someone of her own background in Montreal, she might have been cheerful, or at least hopeful. But she'd married a man fifteen years older than herself, a man gaunt and meager minded from five wartime years of suffering that had included three years of imprisonment at near starvation, a man too eager to make up in America for his lost life. That he had become an alcoholic Alex could now understand. He had regarded his father as reclusive, rarely speaking and never complaining, either. She hadn't loved him, her husband, Alex was sure.

Here on the volcanic desert by the sea, he reflected that nothing for him had so far been conclusive or even crucially important. He was a man waiting—what for, it was not clear. When tested in scholarship in a formal way, as he had been at Princeton, he had thought it perhaps useful to win honors, yet he'd felt no particular ambition; and later, it had made little difference whether he earned ten thousand dollars a year more, or less, at his work. As a son of immigrants, he respected work and had done his job diligently at Pooley, then at the Commission. Had he sought admiration? Not particularly, for that was ambition of its own sort. Women made him feel *present* in a conventional way. His being with a woman was almost like counting off, "present and accounted for."

"Mr. President," the American President said, "you have my report on our Commissioner. He's trying to meet up with Petrie and Turcheff. I believe he's going to get their silence— by whatever means."

"Could you be thinking, Mr. President," the Russian replied, "that he's joining their cadre and wants the world to know of our great and joint ownership of the energy maker?"

"The Commissioner was dedicated to the Protocol. I know he was."

The Russian asked, "The Commissioner is a jurist, is he not? He will presume that things can be made fair for everyone. Idealism is a privilege of the well-born."

"Mr. President, I should never have entrusted the security of this thing to our smallest and newest intelligence agency. I've let you down."

After a pause, calmed now, the Russian asked, "What will the Commissioner do? And here I'd like your own opinion, please—not those of others, of apparatchiks."

"Yes, I do have my own guess. I think he'll try to get Turcheff and Petrie to agree to our plan and then he'll help them escape. By calling on your consulate, or ours, wherever they are. Petrie respects the Commissioner. Turcheff will too."

"I must tell you that I have kept my promise to you when Turcheff fled. No Soviet agents are looking for him. I wouldn't allow it because the risk here is from the Mexicans. You agree?"

"Yeah. If I thought the Indians or the French knew anything about this, I'd really be worried. Both those countries are proudful when it comes to world public opinion. But you're right. The Mexicans wouldn't talk about the discovery. They'd just ask to be let in, like Canada and Poland, which would enlarge our syndicate from four to five. Luis Carranza, their State Security Minister, just flew into Hermosillo and is working with some general in the state of Sonora. He's mobilized a thousand Mexican army regulars."

"My God!" The translator put emotion into the English, hearing it in Russian. "The Mexicans can be dangerous. I've had some experience with them in our Soviet trade. They could quite easily kill Turcheff and Petrie in the act of saving them."

What was there left to say? The American, sitting in the Oval Office, was ashamed by the fact of inefficiency but not really by the result of it.

"We'll wait, of course. And hope for the best. But I want you to know that if the discovery *is* released around the world, the United States will pay for your fusion stations."

"How do you mean?"

"We'll give you a credit of three hundred billion dollars to buy the equipment and build the stations. You said earlier you would set up about thirty thousand of them. Our estimate is that a single cold-fusion station costs about ten million."

"A loan?"

"No, a gift."

The Soviet President was taken aback by the quickness of this reparation, if that's what it was in fact. He turned pragmatic because it was safer ground.

"Let's hope it doesn't come to that. That doesn't serve. No, it doesn't. We need the authority of controlling the discovery—not money. We have both the Germans and the Japanese to worry about, whereas you have only the Japanese."

"Not quite so. We both have Europe '92 to compete against."

"Please do not think me a cynic if I tell you that the dissolution in Central and Eastern Europe may largely defeat the original purposes of Europe '92. It is no longer a racing car. It has become an omnibus, perhaps overloaded. The original club of nations must now take in poor relatives, do you know?"

He paused, not in order to formulate his next statement, for he was by now versed in his own axiom, but because he wanted the American President's full attention—waiting made a man keen to hear what the other would say next.

"What we have here now are the issues of 1918, not 1945. Moldavia, Bessarabia, Transylvania, Kosovo, Macedonia. All are the jagged edges of the First War, not the Second. Europe, Mr. President, can never escape its past, just as America cannot escape its future."

Uncomfortable with this historical, almost mythical, speculation, the American replied, "Maybe Turcheff and Petrie aren't idealists. Maybe they're just fearful and don't know the way home."

"Like children?" the Russian translator said in English.

"Professor," Joan said on the second morning, "I believed that Utah news about the two professors who said they had created cold fusion in their kitchen. Everyone *wanted* to believe."

"You Americans have proved many times that if you give researchers working capital, they can create marketable products. Edison was incorporated by the Edison Electric Company. You have companies in medical technology: laser microsurgery, catheters that reach into the heart, epidural threads around the spinal column to reduce pain. All of them have prospered. Yet nothing happened after Utah!"

Alex not only had read the attacks on Pons and Fleischmann, but also had studied the scanty details they had revealed

about their equipment. As best he could reconstruct it, in a
container of layers of clay and aluminum they had put heavy
water, deuterium oxide, and when lithium was dissolved in it
the lithium became an electrolyte. Into the jar they had put a
platinum-wire anode coiled around a palladium cathode. Then
they had run electrical current through the electrodes. The by-
products of fusion simply hadn't shown up. There should have
been helium 3 and a neutron, or else helium 4 and a gamma
ray. But there hadn't been.

Even so, even given this initial failure, Alex knew enough
from working with the Tokomak that electrochemical science
was where most of the research was headed—away from extreme heat, toward chemical reactors. The Tokomak had used
hydrogen isotopes inside the doughnut, and when they were
ionized they created deuterium and tritium. In the Tokomak
one problem had been to keep the plasma shapely: if it got too
close to the walls of the doughnut, the magnetic field was distorted and the plasma became unstable. He said all this to Turcheff now.

"Yes, it occurred to some Soviet scientists—this I knew a
decade ago—that the container could not be made of material
such as clay and aluminum but, rather, should be formed by a
magnetic field within a grid. An answer was achieved only last
year. Ceramic chips were invented that hold digital signals
without using any energy, chips that can emit signals for ten
years without recharging. So, you create a latticework of ceramic chips along with palladium and, having created an electromagnetic field that is in perfect balance, you're now ready."

"Ready to trigger?"

"Right. The answer to triggering came from American scientists. They showed how over a short distance you can take
clusters of electrons and drive them along, leaving behind some
electrons that are propelled by waves in the electromagnetic

field—like the waves left by a boat. Each trailing electron draws energy from the larger cluster and pushes them along."

"What starts the movement?"

"Beams of light."

"What accelerates it?"

"A vacuum."

"I don't understand. Does it require something like a ten-mile-long accelerator?"

"No, no. This is all done in a short distance, no more than two meters."

"How dangerous is the process?"

"It's *not* dangerous. You use a radio frequency for the beams."

"Are you serious?"

"I'm deadly serious. It was all there, all the time. Except that the physicists and chemists weren't talking to each other. Hydrogen is the key. A perfectly balanced electromagnetic field is the key. Ceramic chips that don't need to be charged repeatedly are the key. The creation of a wake so that each wave triggers the one behind is the key."

"It's a lot of keys, Viktor Ivanovich. Do they really open the locked cage of cold fusion?"

"There's another key needed."

"Let me guess. Palladium is in short supply. The Soviet Union controls almost all of it."

Joan came into the cutting room, running, breathless. "Up in the canyon, through the palms, there's a man coming."

Alex pulled back the slide on his automatic and told Joan to stay next to Viktor. He stepped outside. He saw an elderly man walking toward him, hands in full view, a man wearing a suit with a vest, the chain of a pocket watch stitched across it. He was gray-haired, without eyeglasses, and without a hat or sunglasses despite the heat and glare of the afternoon sun.

Alex pointed the gun at him. The man didn't stop or even slow his advancement. When he was within eight feet he spoke in a calm voice.

"I am Arthur Haagstrom, the Commissioner. I'm un-armed, Mr. Pyotorov. And I'm alone."

CHAPTER EIGHTEEN

URCHEFF IN NERVOUS EXCITEMENT ASKED, "IS THIS YOUR superior, Alexandr? Why is he here alone? How could he know we are here?"

"I told him," Alex said, his gun still pointed at Haagstrom. "I telephoned him using the code I taught you in Moscow. I told him about *Catch-22*. Come into our conference room, Commissioner."

Once inside, Alex returned the gun back under his belt and gave the intruder an old car fender to sit on. The Commissioner in his meticulously tailored suit managed not to look absurd in this dusty half-built, half-destroyed structure, maintaining a composure more suited to a boardroom or concert hall. Joan thought his eyes showed a sympathy toward them with no tincture of condescension.

"I am glad to see you are well, my dear," he said to Joan. "If it is of any help, let me say that your parents and your son are in excellent health and not worried over your absence. We found that out, may I say, unobtrusively."

He then turned to Pyotorov with considerable interest. He had seen his photographs and of course had heard tapes of his voice, but only that. What motivated this man?

"Who is out there, Commissioner?" Alex asked.

"Out where? I saw no one. I got your clue on the phone— very clever, the movie-set idea—and came from Baltimore to Phoenix and then to Tucson by air. I drove a rented car through Nogales. It is now at the top of the canyon, hidden in the palms. I haven't been asleep since the night before last. No one in the Commission—nor anyone else—knows where I am. My chauffeur didn't report after he left me at Baltimore, which means that no border station and no car-rental agency can have been warned in time to trail me."

"Who is out there? CIA or KGB?"

"No. But I'm sorry to tell you, Pyotorov, that Communications has reported that one thousand Mexican soldiers are searching for you and the Professor. They are under a general who is the commandant of the state of Sonora. He is under instructions from a Mexican minister named Luis Carranza, who reports hourly to the President of Mexico."

"And the Mexicans found out about us from you?" It was Turcheff asking. If he was a target, he was entitled to know.

"Indirectly, yes. I'm at fault even for that. A man named Gunther Shurtz had been bringing drugs from Mexico into the United States illicitly. After Pyotorov ran, Shurtz got interested in him and persuaded his Mafia friends in Las Vegas to send men to tail him. Shurtz then convinced Carranza—he must have been very persuasive because he had no tangible evidence—to look for Pyotorov, claiming he holds vital secrets worth millions or even billions of dollars to Mexico."

Joan was terrified. One thousand *federales*! There was no

chance to escape! The Mexicans wouldn't kill the Commissioner or Turcheff because they held valuable information. And neither of these old men would try to shoot his way out. The Mexicans might kill Alex, and then they would have no reason to keep her alive—she'd be a witness.

"My God, Commissioner, why did you try to kill your own man, Petrie?" Joan's voice was low, but her eyes were wet from rage. "You started all this. Nobody would be at risk if you had let Alex alone."

Alex had to keep watch on the wooden track that ran thirty yards uphill from the building. Now he decided he needed a clearer line of vision and urged them all outside, quick-stepping them to the shore, around a series of boulders, to the small cove where yesterday he and Joan had made love on the sand. He climbed up to use the space between two boulders as a scope and turned his head at regular intervals to look toward the grove.

"Are the FBI and KGB in this now?" Alex asked again.

"By now, surely. The Commission was given the trust, by itself, to protect the secret. When the Deputy in Moscow called on Professor Turcheff, we knew we had to contain you." He saw the look of shock on the woman's face, the bewilderment on the Professor's, and Alex's scorn. He hastened to add, "The vice of the intelligence profession is to use words that are deceptively meant to put a proper gloss on improper events. Of course I did more than order you to be contained! I am deeply ashamed of that. I came here in part because of my shame."

"And more, Commissioner?" It was Turcheff.

"Yes. At various times I have lacked confidence in the Protocol between our countries. And before I left to come here, I began to think that the President, beneath it all, despite his declarations in meetings, was himself uneasy over the agreement with the Soviet Union."

"He knew you were going out alone?" Turcheff asked, astonished. "Leaving Washington?"

"No. But once they found out I had left, I've no doubt that some of his aides may believe I came to persuade you and Pyotorov."

"Before you do persuade us," Turcheff said, speaking slowly and distinctly, "please tell us the terms of the Protocol."

In Hermosillo, the Commandant and Carranza were speaking without urgency. The Commandant knew how vast the territory was—Sonora is the second largest state in a large nation—and he knew that the vastness favored him, not the fugitives. Carranza had over the past two days gained a sense of the Commandant's tendencies. He was single-minded and relentless.

"So, where do you think they are?" Carranza asked.

"They are on the coast, huddled in some cove, looking for another place. The American must be trained in reading maps. He's discovered by now that Tiberón has no tourists because it is a wildlife preserve. He may try to swim there and find a boat to bring the others."

"How quickly will we know?"

"There is a new element you should know about. A woman."

"A woman? He has a blond-haired woman with him."

"No, a *Mexicana*. A woman named Alcarita Obregon. She has arrived in Hermosillo to ask about the American. She is of a Sonora family from a small town not far from Nogales."

The Commandant stopped, as if to say no more. His impassive face was like a mask and his brilliant green eyes, while they seemed to notice everything, remained steady. Carranza was tired of his northern Mexican style of indirectly, or obscurely, imparting information. Why did Americans think

Mexicans were vivacious? They were dour, laconic, resentful, talented, artistic, proud. They were a mixed race with mixed emotions.

Finally the Commandant resumed. "She was the mistress of the American in Denver, although she knew nothing of his trade. When he fled, his superiors came to Colorado to question her."

"Does she know where he is?"

"No, but it becomes plausible. If I may proceed, Minister?"

Carranza had offended him. The Commandant would relate the story in his own way, in his own time.

"An attorney came to see her and said that her lover had entered Baja California with a blond woman and had sent the blonde to cash bonds. This attorney claimed he gave the woman only five hundred dollars. He left forty-five hundred dollars with Alcarita Obregon."

Carranza was now fascinated by this slow unraveling of an aspect of the story he hadn't known about. "Who would have spent so much money to make her worried? Jealous? What?"

"I believe, Minister," the Commandant replied, looking at the ash of his cigar, "it was the Las Vegas Mafia you told me about. They, of course, know you."

"The man Shurtz," Carranza said, reasserting his position as a minister acting for the President of Mexico, "told me about the federal agent and I was ordered by our President to verify Shurtz's story with his former partners. Is the woman here? Let's see her."

Alcarita, dressed in a simple black dress, her hair caught up behind with a red silk handkerchief, entered the huge office, where she saw a desk and chair with leather coverings and high windows with purple brocade curtains. She was determined not to show her fright. Her will was undermined almost immediately. The man behind the desk wore a rich uniform with shiny brass buttons and two stars on each shoulder epaulet. He wore medals in three rows on his strong, full chest. Had there been a war in Mexico? His head was bare but his black hair was so full and so neatly barbered that it looked like a crown. Less impressive but as frightening was the man who now stood, a tall, thin gentleman in a tailored blue suit with a vest who wore no jewelry, only a silk pocket handkerchief in his coat pocket. His hands were manicured.

"Please sit down, Señora. I am Minister Carranza. This is General Hernandez, Commandant of the State of Sonora. We wish to ask you why you are here."

She sat, took a handkerchief from her black purse, twisted it around the small finger of her left hand, and began to speak, clearing her throat repeatedly.

"The American I know needs help. I was given money to give to him."

"He's a spy."

"I'm glad."

"Why glad?"

"It means he didn't leave me over money or property. He must be political."

Carranza found that an intelligent rationalization.

"Do you know where he is?" The Commandant resumed the questioning.

"No, General."

"Why did you come to Hermosillo, then?"

"I was told he was in Tijuana, or somewhere in Baja California. I looked at a map. The other place he could go easily is Sonora, over the water. My family comes from Sonora. It seemed I should go where there are authorities, to the capital, and ask."

"Mexico is a very large country. He could be anywhere."

"Yes, General. But I came to the place I know."

Carranza spoke. "You did well, Señora. The Commandant and I appreciate your help. We would like you to stay in Hermosillo for a day or two. We will pay for a hotel room and meals for you."

"Thank you. I have money that Alex Hoffman gave me. I am here on his behalf. I would like to use his money."

"The forty-five hundred dollars?" the Commandant asked.

"No, General. I put that in a bank."

"What is wrong with the other man's money?"

"I didn't believe my man arranged it. I didn't trust the lawyer who came to me. If you will excuse me, General, I would like him to be safe."

"And the blond *Americana*?"

"If she is real, I would like to talk to her."

When Alcarita was gone, the Commandant said to the Minister, "I do not envy your living in Mexico City. Here, everyone was born centuries ago but speaks only of today."

At the White House, things were at sixes and sevens. The President was not at all content and hardly anything pleased him. The Secretary of State and the Director of National Security were allied, for a change, and reluctant to take strong positions openly—for the time being, at least. The Chief of Staff was busy and uncommunicative—for him a new persona. The President had been shaken by the telephone call with the Soviet President. He himself knew that the Commissioner was on a mission—but it was not to contain or maim the two men, Turcheff and the one called Petrie. No. He knew that the Commissioner possessed a juridical mind, a mind that admitted that, while everything is possible, only some things can be determined in favor of the common good. When they had first been introduced, he recalled, Haagstrom had said, clearly speaking of himself, "Power should be vested in those who understand its uses but do not seek its thrills."

"Yes, but how does that apply to the White House?" the President had asked, wary.

"I'd say, Mr. President, that Americans do not expect their President to be fair. That's for judges. They want him to act. It is quite impossible to be deliberative—to be thinking—and decisive—to be acting—at the very same moment. Only the press claims that privilege. They urge you to act and then blame you for not having considered those exact consequences that cannot be known until they occur."

It was, the President was told later, the longest remark anyone had heard Arthur Haagstrom make outside a courtroom—like holding a high C. That Haagstrom was didactic was obvious, but the President hadn't felt he was being lectured to. Rather, he had thought it was a rather eccentric way of complimenting him. But what if Haagstrom was now reverting to his old role as a judge and trying to bring an equable solution to what might already have gotten out of control? As for his Soviet counterpart, whatever had become of the Commissioner, he should wait no longer. The call was made.

"Mr. President, good evening. It's what, six o'clock in Moscow? I'll be brief. We know where the four people are. The Commissioner, Turcheff, Petrie, and a woman. The CIA warns us to proceed carefully. And," here the President cleared his throat, "as for the gift I mentioned, it is inappropriate. I regret mentioning it. It was like giving a man the deed to property he already owns."

He waited because the translator would have trouble with that metaphor in Russian. It had been a long time since it was common for anyone in the Soviet Union to hold a deed.

"What does the CIA say about the top general in Sonora?"

"He's competent, they say, and patient. They also say he's ruthless."

"How do you read the effects of *that*?"

"It's a toss-up. If the troops don't kill Turcheff or Petrie or the Commissioner right off, they can be made to tell what they know—under threat of some kind. On the other hand, if they are killed, the press will make an international incident of it just when we're ready to announce the Protocol."

"What is the worst case? I mean, if they stay alive?" the Russian asked.

"It becomes a five-nation pact. Mexico along with Canada and Poland. The Mexicans are generous giving people political asylum, but *they* want economic asylum. They nationalized their own wealth and then lost it."

CHAPTER NINETEEN

— • —

TURCHEFF SUGGESTED, QUITE IMPRACTICALLY, THAT JOAN NOW keep watch on the track up the palm grove while the three men talked. Alex immediately disagreed. As it was, they remained in the cove, where he could watch for invaders and still be attentive to the responses that were long overdue: why the Commissioner, the person in charge of protecting all the secrecy, had come here himself to talk with the fugitives.

Across the gulf, white clouds with purple edges hung high, motionless. The tide was out and the temperature about ninety degrees. No motors could be heard—no aircraft, boats, or army personnel carriers. Joan stood and sat, occasionally sifting handfuls of sand languidly. There was a world out there full of give and take, sorrow and joy, small victories and large defeats, yet in this tranquil cove there was a kind of stasis: an uneasy tranquillity.

Turcheff thought that the historians have it wrong: they keep thinking that people act in their own interests, when in fact they are far more often motivated by their attitudes. Would a sane man, *in his own interest*, take up a rifle and go off to a strange terrain to lose his life, as at Tannenberg in 1914, where two million Russians were killed or wounded or captured or lost in a single series of battles? No, a soldier went because he was patriotic, because he was taught there were higher causes than his own survival. He'd go, as Viktor had himself gone to Stalingrad, where a million Russians had died or been maimed or starved, because ideas were elevated into prerogatives and patriotic figures made into icons.

"Commissioner," Alex repeated. "It is time to hear what deals have been made over the invention."

"I suppose that some day what we call the Protocol could be looked on like a treaty of peace, say the Congress of Berlin in 1878. I mean, it will settle affairs among nations who weren't even combatants."

"Please, Commissioner."

"I know. The United States and the Soviet Union have agreed to keep their joint discovery secret for a period of three years. They will each build about thirty thousand power stations in their respective countries. The Soviet Union asked to share the secret with Poland."

"So that the USSR could build an economy against a united Germany in the west and against Japan in the east?" It was Turcheff who asked.

"Yes. But against China perhaps more than Japan. The Americans, as in a ball game when we were children"—he looked at Joan while saying it—"got to choose one partner, too. We considered Britain, that is, while Mrs. Thatcher was opposing some of the measures for Europe '92. But we ended with Canada, which is our leading partner and with which we share the longest border in the world, forty-five hundred miles in all."

"And," Turcheff said, "Canada guards against missiles from the East, over the North Pole.

Joan was enraged. "You mean poor nations would gain nothing?"

"No. It was agreed in the Protocol that the United States, giving two thirds, and the Soviet Union, one third, would make the goods gained from the energy produced so incredibly cheaply and easily available for three years to all poor nations."

Turcheff said, "Not to any of the Europe '92 countries. Not China or Japan or India or Pakistan or either South or North Korea, one because it's rich and the other because it's warlike. Not Australia or New Zealand. Almost every nation in Central and South America, yes. Every nation in Africa and Asia except Libya and Iraq. Maybe not Cuba or Israel."

The Commissioner was dumbfounded. With one or two exceptions, the Professor was right on. Had he any knowledge of the Protocol? How could he? Pyotorov didn't, for certain. Then he realized that, once the notion of exclusivity was sounded, any European intellectual could name combinations of nations. After all, Europe had been changing its borders since Roman times—and hadn't yet got them right.

Alex said, "Commissioner, Professor Turcheff knows what the discovery is and I know most of it—almost all of it."

Turcheff had walked into the small breakers with his shoes on, as if there were no change between land and water, as if all were fundament and familiar. He stood looking out at the Sea of Cortéz in wonderment. All was calm. All was seen. He turned and addressed them all.

"The President of the Soviet Union wants a head start. He wants his people to catch up after all the years of their deprivation. And he's afraid that it cannot happen with Germany next door, with Japan and the United States already having won every race since 1955. That's it, is it not?"

"That's it," said the Commissioner.

Matthews had returned from the White House, marched into the Commissioner's office, and called for Tannenbaum. He couldn't recall the drive from Pennsylvania Avenue back to Anacostia, to the fortress where only two weeks ago life had been orderly and never threatening even when unpredictable. He looked at the desk he had longed to sit behind during all those years he had been counting Haagstrom's birthdays and observing his appearance, looking for signs of fatigue or ill health. Now it was his desk, but he felt no glory. For one thing, he had won his seat by default, by Haagstrom's defection. For another, the Commission had just lost its greatest assignment.

"The President said he had to do it. I find it difficult to believe, this changing horses not in the middle of the stream but, in fact, near the opposite shore. The FBI and CIA! It's a great blow to the Commission. It's humiliating in its way. The Soviet President kept nattering at him about our forty agents. But I don't blame the Russians. The Commissioner let us down by running away!"

"Matt, let's not become Brutus and Cassius in the tent tasting our bile in defeat. The Commission will survive. Even the great discovery won't keep officials from getting greedy and committing crimes. We shall still guard the guardians. I worry over the Commissioner."

"Worry? Worry about us, not him."

"What about the CIs who are assigned to the fusion laboratories and to the important scientists?"

"They stay in place. The President threw us a crumb."

"Will the CIA go to Mexico?"

"Yes. It's there! Has it occurred to you, Chief, that our own people might kill Haagstrom so the Mexicans can't get to him?"

Matthews wasn't shooting his eyebrows for special effect, wasn't seeking the lurking ironical twist in an operation gone awry, wasn't seeking to put the Chief on the defensive. He was, to be plain about it, afraid. Tannenbaum, looking, saw it. For the first time in the fourteen years since he joined the Commission, he felt a certain communion with this normally haughty man. Matthews looked at him as if lost, confusion clouding his eyes.

They had walked back from the shore on the loose pebbles that were the vestiges of the movie company bulldozers' clearing away of the mesquite back in 1969. They ate biscuits and cheese and drank from cans of soda and beer, unappetizing because so warm. Alex explained the salt-water latrine system to the Commissioner as Joan went back to the small cove to swim in the nude—her only way of bathing. Turcheff, after he ate, went to read in the cutting room.

Haagstrom and Alex sat in the front seat of the car, each seeing flashes of the other's face from the light seeping between the blocks of concrete and sheared volcanic rock that formed the sides of the building. Light slanting from the uncovered ends of what once was the movie set's mess hall played off the cherry-red hood of the car.

"Pyotorov, do the others know what your fortified position—down there where we talked—really is? That the small eddy or cove is a cul-de-sac? That place is a trap, if anyone armed comes down from the palm grove, or comes straight down to the shore across all those boulders that lie below the old airstrip."

Without waiting for a reply, Haagstrom answered his own questions. "You were setting yourself up as the hostage. Your small arsenal of guns might buy the old man and the woman a little time. Not much."

"Something like that," Alex said.

"You have no means of escape."

"I made a mistake. I should have abandoned the car in San Carlos and stolen a power boat."

"You know this area *that* well?"

"I came down here from Denver to work on the movie, *Catch-22,* when I was sixteen, in 1970. On off days I scouted the gulf here on the Sonora mainland and across on Baja."

"Sixteen?" Haagstrom smiled. "Weren't you afraid?"

"Of what?"

"A foreign place? Or not being paid? Losing your money? Fights? Appendicitis?"

"You think a lot about what can and might happen, don't you? What can befall. How is it that at Harkness that kind of thinking wasn't evident? You could have captured me in New York by simply having Tannenbaum meet me in a hotel or at the Federal Building downtown."

"Yes, I cut the law too fine. When you do that with toast, it burns. I wanted to be able to say that you were captured during the course of a legitimate operation."

"You mean, you were unnerved about my Alaskan friend in Congress and anticipated what could be said at a congressional hearing."

Haagstrom nodded, looking through the windshield. Motes hung like question marks in the still, dead air.

"Would you have agreed not to reveal what you knew about cold fusion and, more, what you knew of Professor Turcheff, who was already on the run from Russian authorities? Would you, had it all been arranged properly?"

"I don't know. No, I do know. I wouldn't have agreed. I would have guessed the existence of a secret pact—just as I did on the run. I'd have considered it morally wrong. It would have been a rare moment in my life. A moment when I decided wholly in favor of something bigger than myself. Yes. I would have seized that moment."

"Your Chief, Tannenbaum, wasn't sure of your reaction. I was."

"You were a judge once. But you are not a judge now. When you enlist, you hand yourself over to others."

"And you enlisted, too. It's been ten years. Why did you join? And why did you stay?"

Turcheff had been right about Americans and Russians. Here Alex was, seated in a compartment before the train left the station, being asked to sum up his life. It wasn't military, a debriefing after a mission. No, it was a conversation that began with a melancholy question: why have you wasted your life?

"You asked about my coming down here when I was sixteen. I've never felt really alarmed, really afraid, for some reason. I somehow thought I could learn something, or pass a test, or get a job—always find a way in, find a way out. Yet I've never wanted to prove anything, or glorify anyone, including myself. I've always been without a cause."

"Do you *now* care what people think about you? History is supposed to judge us."

"Orson Welles was here on the set—these rocky half-built structures, the airstrip, the rutted roads—when I came down in 1970. *Catch-22* wasn't his picture. His last great picture—I mean as a director—was shot mostly in Tijuana.

"Welles plays a detective. In the end he lies dying under a dark bridge, shot dead by his oldtime fellow officer. Looking down, a DA says, 'He was a great detective,' and Marlene Dietrich adds, 'And a crooked cop.' 'Is that all you've got to say?' he asks her. She says, 'What difference does it make what you say about people?' She was right. What difference does it make?" Alex asked. Then he continued, "I don't think the world needs me. Whenever someone talks about free will, they assume you'll use it to perform an act of public consequence. Nobody assumes that you just take your free will home, like a fish wrapped in newspaper."

Haagstrom was astonished at the skepticism and felt that he had failed to understand someone like Pyotorov. He was not unique. There must be others like him.

"Ralph Waldo Emerson said skepticism is slow suicide." He paused. "I'm sorry, very sorry. I've lessened your chances. Lessened your life."

"Well, Commissioner," Alex said with an ironical smile. "I can't give you absolution. Anyway, the mystery is not in dying but in living. How do you explain what you've done? Was it right?"

Now they were down to it, to rock bottom.

"It's a mistake to equate age with wisdom. We know foolish old men. This cold fusion energy discovery rightly belongs to everyone. I was loyal. There's that. I was mindful of my pledge when I assumed my position. That too. But I knew it wasn't right."

"And that," Alex said, "is why the Commission went off the tracks so badly."

Joan sought him out and insisted on accompanying him halfway up the track, then into the grove of palms. It was dense underfoot and sticky, so that at times Alex carried her, taking mercy on her feet, ankles, and shins. They caught a glimpse of the Commissioner's car and Alex insisted that they stop and listen for sounds of cars or trucks. He didn't want to risk her coming upon sentinels that the Mexicans may have already put in place.

"Alex, I won't ask you exactly what you think is going to happen next. It's going to be bad, isn't it?"

"Yes."

He put his hands on her waist, his fingers almost meeting. And then he bent down and kissed her open mouth. She moved his hands down to her buttocks, so that he felt every yielding, fruitful part of her, lips, breasts, thighs. But he had to pull away, had to remain watchful.

The Commissioner and Turcheff were back in the cove seated on the sand, their backs against smooth boulders, catching the late-afternoon sun, when Alex returned. The Commissioner had been asking about certain techniques that the Russians had developed. Joan had gone to the cutting room to be alone.

"Professor," Haagstrom said now. "I must tell you we are precisely at the point where my leaving Washington needs to be defended. I was uneasy with the Protocol when I first was told of it by the President. I have continued to be uneasy. Harming Pyotorov, whom we called Petrie, made me still more uncertain."

"But," Turcheff said with a surprising vehemence, "this is what you call splitting hairs! It's only a three-year trust. And during those three years poor countries will be given supplies of equipment by both the United States and the USSR. Three years!"

"Professor, surely, as a distinguished scientist, you do not believe that sequestering research, denying to the world evidence of vast knowledge, is in the spirit of humanism."

"How many dead in the past make things equitable in the present? What is fair where there has been no justice? What is humanism when seen from the Gulag? How many Americans died in the second Great War?"

Haagstrom was taken aback by this last question. As a judge he would have asked counsel to state where this line of questioning was intended to lead. But as a witness in the box he replied, "Perhaps three hundred and seventy thousand in World War II, fifty-five thousand in Korea, about the same number in Vietnam."

"We lost twenty million in the second war, and twenty million more in the years between Lenin and Gorbachev. Alexandr Vladimirovich told me he was in Princeton when the Yugoslav dissident Milovan Djilas was let out of Tito's prison for a short time. He heard Djilas tell an American audience that Stalin had killed more people than Hitler. No one believed him."

"Yes, I would not have believed him then. Of course, now we all know it's true."

Alex told the two he was going to make a reconnaissance. They agreed to join Joan in the cutting room, but neither was convinced he should continue the dialogue without Alex being present. Alex took all three guns, the automatics and the extra clips, using his belt band and the pockets in his windbreaker; and after climbing high enough to see the far side of the airstrip, he headed into the palm grove. It was about four in the afternoon and the sun was rightly placed—at his back. As he climbed, zigzagging from trunk to trunk, like moving diagonally across a chess board, he asked himself the desperate question. If he ran into a military patrol, how long could he hold them off, so that the rest could at least drive far enough along the shore to reach the other end of the cove, Rancho Los Algodónes, where there would be someone to witness, and maybe to prevent, an attempt on their lives? Ten minutes. No more.

He had passed the Commissioner's car and come within twenty yards of the road when he saw Alcarita. She was alone, simply standing and waiting. She wore flats, a wraparound skirt, a Mexican peasant blouse, her thick long hair caught by a bandana. Had she eluded the *federales*? Or was she their point man?

CHAPTER TWENTY

HE STOOD AT THE TOP OF THE GROVE, ABOUT TEN YARDS off the verge of the road that in one direction led past the abandoned *Catch-22* airstrip, in the other up toward the volcanic ridges that overlook San Carlos Bay. The narrow road to Rancho Los Algodónes through the red and black cliffs made the approach to the beach that way quite formidable. His retreat was only the way he'd ascended.

Her loose clothing revealed little of her figure. They stood eye to eye since he was on lower ground, using a large palm tree as meager protection against being seen by an onlooker— or a sniper. They spoke in Spanish.

"Cara? Are you well? No one is bothering you?"

"Alex, there are one thousand soldiers looking for you. They knew you were here even last night. Around the bend of the road is a jeep with three *federales* carrying rifles. But I'm allowed to see you alone."

"I just walked up here to look around. How could you know I was coming?"

"I'm used to waiting. Things happen."

"There is a woman with me."

"I know. A lawyer in Denver gave me forty-five hundred dollars from you. He said he didn't trust the woman with the money."

"I know no lawyer in Denver. It's all a lie. The woman by chance came to a small place I own near Petaluma, in California. She came with her sixteen-year-old son the day I got there. She was shot in the shoulder by gunners trying to force me out of the house. Her boy is now safe, back with her divorced husband. She came with me. We've been running."

"The *federales* say you are a Russian spy."

"No. My parents were Russian. I worked for an American secret agency. All of a sudden, the agency wanted to kill me. That's why I left Denver."

"And the old man they talk about?"

"*He* is a Russian. But not a spy."

He moved away from the tree toward her, but they did not touch. She was motionless, her hands loosely clasped below her waist.

"Do you love this woman?"

"Cara, I have never told any woman I loved her."

"Can't you bargain with the *federales?*"

"No. And, Cara, when you go back, mention nothing. This is simply the end of a story."

"Who makes a story end a certain way?"

"God or the devil. I must go. Shall we kiss each other?"

"It's bad luck if it is good-bye. I'll wait for you in Hermosillo. I love you. Don't lose your life, Alex. Fight."

Joan stood on the camera-dolly planks waiting, looking up anxiously. Alex saw her and, outside the cutting room, he could see Turcheff and the Commissioner talking avidly, gesticulating. Either they were agreeing or they were disagreeing vigorously. At a distance it was hard to tell—just as a cry of grief or a burst of laughter can be mistaken one for the other in a photograph taken at a moment of climax.

"You stayed so long! Did you see someone?"

"Yes. A girl I lived with the past two years in Denver. She was alone. The *federales* brought her to the road just above the grove but they stayed out of sight around a bend."

"They have found us? Jesus, Alex! Will they rush us now?"

"Alcarita said they have known we were here since last night."

"Is she a Judas goat, Alex? Were you supposed to follow her scent into the slaughterhouse?" It was said bitterly. She was frightened.

"No, Joan. They let her see me hoping she would find out the relationship of each of us to the others *here*. She wasn't playing that game. She told me to fight for my life."

"She loves you. And did you love her?"

"No. And she knows that too. She's a Mexican. She's a realist."

"What's the reality, Alex?"

"The Mexicans will want to capture Viktor, I'm certain. And probably keep the Commissioner under wraps until the Americans can take him over."

"And what about us?"

"We are guilty bystanders."

"Then make Viktor protect us! My God, Alex!"

He drew her into his body, to sculpt themselves. He felt the tenseness in her back and the uncertainty of her fingers as she grasped his neck to bring his head down to hers. Then they walked down and Alex motioned the Commissioner and Turcheff inside the cutting room. He stood by an opening in the planks to glance at the track up the grove and then, as if on a policeman's beat, moved to another side to take a reading of the shoreline toward Los Algodónes. No one said a word. Joan couldn't read the expression on the face of either Turcheff or Haagstrom.

"There are hundreds of Sonora militiamen out on the roads above and below, on the shores both ways. They knew we were here last night," Alex said.

"Who told you?" the Commissioner asked.

"A Mexican woman I know. They let her through to talk to me."

"Miss Obregon from Denver? I'll talk to Carranza. He's the man who can turn the soldiers away."

"Commissioner, diplomacy won't serve here."

"Why will it not? Diplomacy works whenever one side wants something and the other side has the power to give it."

"And what have we to give or to sell?" The question came from Turcheff, who spoke for the first time, having taken off his heavy-framed eyeglasses, rubbed his eyes tiredly, and brushed his mustache with his fingers, repeating the odd gesture Alex had noticed in the old Moscow days.

"We have to offer a huge prize," Haagstrom said. "The certainty that the entire world will know of the new technology and share it from the start."

"I just told you—a dozen times!—I cannot agree, Mr. Commissioner."

"Professor Turcheff, and I repeat for the twelfth time, I've been uneasy since the time I was first told of the Protocol. It seemed to me morally wrong to ration the resources of the earth. It's just not possible!"

"Everything is possible," Turcheff replied. "I saw everything at Stalingrad. At Leningrad. And Tbilisi."

"But you are a scientist dedicated to open inquiry!"

"Why is it," Turcheff went on heatedly, "no one examines my country—even when it opens its doors and windows? Do you not realize that the Russian republic is the poorest among the more sophisticated peoples of the USSR—the Balts, Byelorussians, Ukrainians, Georgians, even some of the Turkic republics? My people must have their chance. Too many of us died in the darkness of imperialism, of absolutism—Lenin's, Stalin's, Hitler's. If the USSR cannot survive, then let there flourish a Slavic country stretching from Poland's western border to the Pacific."

"Professor, *that* is not the issue here," the Commissioner said firmly.

"Is it not?" Turcheff said angrily, his arms moving, his fists balled. "Should this great invention donate no more to its co-founder than it does to Portugal, which lives five times better than the Soviet Union and never lost a life in the two world wars? Should Venezuela, which has oil and not any hunger, be given immediate access to a discovery it spent no money to create? You, Commissioner, were once a judge, Alexandr tells me. But where is your justice?

"Alexandr Vladimirovich, please convince Mr. Haagstrom to stand by the Protocol. It's not the question of Mozart and the million peasants, Alexandr. Here it is real."

"There is another reality. Armed soldiers," Alex said.

He handed Turcheff one of the automatics and Haagstrom another, keeping the third and the two extra clips for himself. Turcheff held the gun at his side in his right hand, standing motionless. Motes of filtered light from the openings in the splintered walls played on his gray and weary face. Haagstrom stared at his gun as if it were something gross, human but disgusting like a shrunken head. He was appalled that Pyotorov could believe small-caliber weapons were at all useful. This was certainly not a moment for superficial displays.

"Professor, be rational," Haagstrom pleaded. "The world is not Babylon. Think of the world as a single place."

"Commissioner, in Mexico there is no single place, let alone in the world. Here there are white colonials, and blacks who were imported and enslaved and Indians who survived genocide—and half-breeds, because conquests leave a spore. And there are exiles, like us and, once, Trotsky."

It was on the last word that Turcheff raised his automatic and shot Arthur Haagstrom through the temple, killing him.

CHAPTER TWENTY-ONE

———— • ————

ORROR ARISES SO QUICKLY THAT IT MUST LIE JUST BELOW
the concourse of consciousness, Joan told herself after a
minute, as she stared at the body of Haagstrom. His eyes
were open but darkened, the pupils closing, and his skin
was already turning waxy from loss of current in both the nerves
and arteries. He lay on the cutting-room floor and because his
legs and arms were spread wide he looked oddly more energetic than when alive. There was little blood showing. The riv-
ulet that had started from the hole in his temple had pooled in
his ear and trickled to his shirt collar and stopped there.

Alex took the gun from Turcheff and said, "Viktor, this is
a terrible crime."

"I had to do it! I had to!" He said it in Russian and then
in English. "He would have revealed everything."

"Viktor! Consider the consequences! The Mexicans need
and want you. They won't want Joan and me to be witnesses

to your capitulation—and to the Commissioner's murder. You have condemned us to death."

"Please, Alexandr Vladimirovich! I will make the Mexicans keep both of you safe," Turcheff said in Russian, this time not translating afterward. "They will agree. Otherwise I'll tell them nothing."

Alex put his own gun in his pants pocket. He took Turcheff's and Haagstrom's and put them in his other pockets. He went to Joan and drew her close, kissing her eyes. She was suddenly frightened. It seemed symbolic of impending death, closing someone's eyes.

"They will promise you everything, anything. But there is no way you can keep them honest," Alex said. "How can you monitor their actions constantly? Once we are dead, Joan and I can't be brought back to life by a promise, Viktor."

Turcheff's shoulders were shaking, his hands trembling, as he drew near and said, "Alexandr Vladimirovich, my mandate was to help hundreds of millions of people."

"I know. I know. Neither you nor Haagstrom wanted Joan and me to become the victims of innocence. The two of you were like positive particles that repel each other."

No more was said because within a minute the sounds of the *federales* were heard, one platoon advancing along the shoreline from the east, two coming down through the grove, and a fourth clambering over the huge rocks that barricaded the eastern curve of the bay above the pool where Joan had bathed. Soon the Commandant and Carranza appeared. Then two coast guard cutters, each of about forty tons' displacement, took up stations at anchor a hundred yards beyond the breakers. It was high tide. Later, the cutters would have to withdraw another three hundred yards seaward.

In what seemed minutes but was of course hours, the logistics of the new situation were established. A large tent was raised on the sand, with a small generator resting on a wooden pallet next to it, furnishing power for lights and a refrigerator inside the tent. Two smaller tents covered portable latrines, ostensibly one for Alex, the other for Joan. Carranza and Turcheff had departed in a launch for one of the cutters. Alex watched with some astonishment as a lieutenant supervised four soldiers in removing the tires from the Infiniti. That it could become a getaway car was ludicrous! Alex assumed that two or three companies of soldiers were already billeted on the airfield, closing the roads, even the horse trails, in all directions. They would keep out journalists, tourists, and, God knows, spies.

Inside the tent, Alex described the situation to Joan. "They took the three guns and the clips, but they left me my money belt. They brought our clothes. No doubt Viktor and Señor Carranza are preparing a *maly protokol*—a small accord is what it means—that will be designed to protect us. We'll see it in the morning."

"What about the body? Will they hold an autopsy and an inquest?"

"After a fashion, yes. I heard a captain say that the death was one of misadventure. It seems that an automatic fell to the floor, and because its chamber mechanism was too loose a bullet was discharged accidentally. No doubt they have fixed the spring by now."

"Can they do that?" She was dumbfounded.

"Joan, this is not a game played by the rules of the U.S. Constitution."

"But we were witnesses!"

"That's our bad luck."

From the porthole of his small cabin on the cutter, Turcheff saw their tent lighted through the whole night. It looked like a pyramid on the sands bathed in orange light. He saw sentinels on the shoreline and also behind the tent. Farther up, beyond the grove, he saw more lights. Helicopters? Yes. He slept not at all: there was no way to lessen his turmoil. How could it be, what with his having killed a man, he was now a diplomat negotiating with one entire nation, Mexico, on behalf of another, the Soviet Union? All the while, in the folds of his conscience there appeared the cameo of himself, like a pressed leaf, as a fugitive seeking the help of a friend.

At eight o'clock, two hours past the dawn, the cutter's launch brought Carranza and Turcheff to shore, there to be greeted by the Commandant, who was attended by a captain, two sergeant majors, and a man of about forty-five in a business suit. The older sergeant major carried a military field desk into a second tent—this tent exactly like Alex's and Joan's. It had been erected at dawn. The desk was a splendid piece of marquetry with a leather writing surface and two drawers.

Carranza summoned all of them and presented a document of a single page, beautifully drawn by calligraphic hand, in three versions, one in elegant Spanish, one in mediocre English, and the last in execrable Russian. Both Turcheff and Alex grasped that the civilian in the business suit was a Russian-speaking Mexican official. Alex wore sports clothes, his money belt secure under his white shirt. Joan had dressed up for the occasion, in a cinnamon-colored dress with black flats and black panty hose. She also wore a single strand of gold beads that Alex had bought her in Santa Rosalía.

"Mr. Pyotorov," Carranza said in English. "You will be pleased to know that your superior, the Commissioner of the National Institute of Information Theory, has been given a proper ceremony on his return to his homeland. His casket of bronze was covered by a blanket of white gardenias and accorded a full military guard as it was put aboard Air Force II, sent by your President to Hermosillo."

The document, the *maly protokol,* was then read aloud, first in Spanish, then in English. Joan was handed a copy in English, Turcheff one in Russian, and Alex copies in all three languages. It provided for Alex and Joan to remain on Tiberón for three years.

Alex said, "I'd like to discuss this document with Professor Turcheff, if you please."

The Commandant's eyes turned cold, narrowing. Carranza quickly said that he was sure the Commandant would not deter them. The man in the business suit looked questioningly at Carranza. Should he accompany them, or trail them, or what? A gesture of Carranza's hand dismissed him. Soon the two men were alone on the sand, walking, talking, pausing to make a point, as on their Moscow evenings.

"You realize now, don't you, Viktor Ivanovich, that Joan and I will never leave that island alive? It's a prison. There is no one on Tiberón now because it was made into a wild life refuge in 1976. The proposed placement of the squads is a giveaway. There are only two ways off the island. One is to swim the channel where the old ferry was, a mile, or a mile and a half at high tide. The other is to try to flag down an American yacht off the south shore where there are a few accessible points, some spots of sand between the rocks. Tiberón—Shark Island in English—is just north of Bahía de Kino, a beautiful bay with lots of expensive houses owned by Americans who like to fish for grouper and rock bass."

"I know that their calling you and Joan 'wildlife wardens' is nonsense, but there *are* ways, are there not? For example, I could insist that the Red Cross monitor your safety once a month."

"Viktor, there'll be an accident one day. Joan will drown in some cove from the tide—it's as high as twenty feet in this part of the Sea of Cortéz. I'll develop a cut on the stomach, and by the time they get me aboard the cutter, peritonitis will have set in."

Turcheff was struck by the extraordinary detail of his friend's dreadful surmising. On the other hand, the *maly protokol* was also explicit, stating exactly where the squads would be stationed.

"They don't dare!" he protested. "I won't collaborate in that event."

"They won't tell you. And after six months they won't need you."

Joan, watching them from the tent through the mosquito netting that covered the entrance, heard the snapping of the canvas under the force of an offshore breeze: it was like those small firecrackers set off in series by children on the Fourth of July.

"Viktor, tell them no," Alex was saying. "Tell them that I'll sign—and Joan too—a notice that we understand from Professor Turcheff that the Mexican government has joined with the United States and Canada in a North American pact having to do with the production of energy. After signing, they can take us to the States with you; and then you can return to Mexico."

Turcheff walked away, looked at the midday haze on the deep blue waters beyond the cutters at anchor, took off his spectacles, brushed his hair at the back of the neck.

Joan was sure she knew what Alex was harrying the Professor about. He'd told her, whispering, as they left the tent, "Joan, the old man has lost sight of the schedule for the Protocol. I've got to get him to put time on our side."

"They won't trust you," Turcheff said now. "You could talk *later*, Alexandr."

"Viktor, it's only eight days away! Haagstrom told me that! The announcement will be made in Washington with the two presidents together, yours and mine. If we stay together, the three of us, for eight days, then Joan and I can cross the border under *your* protection."

In the Oval Office there was no air of crisis but still a palpable air of—what was it? Embarrassment? Doubtfulness? Mainly, a wish for it all to end. The President could not sit still. He paced, his slim body making turns around the chairs of his Chief of Staff and Director of National Security and Secretary of State. Everything was known. Yet there *was* doubt. Matthews was on Air Force II accompanying the casket of the Commissioner, along with documents relating to the autopsy and inquest that had followed on Haagstrom's "death by mis-adventure."

There were logistics left—and loose ends. As for the for-mer, the forty CIs and ten thousand FBI, CIA, and Secret Ser-vice agents were monitoring not only scientists themselves, and of course laboratories and assembly points, but also the begin-nings of military preparations. Eighty thousand U.S. troops were being mobilized to carry goods to poor nations in U.S. war-ships, AKAs and AKs, and even LSTs left over from World War II and Vietnam. Later, when everyone was a bit more relaxed, commercial freighters would be hired.

The Soviets had convinced two of their Nobel Prize win-ners to speak to Green parties in Europe and Canada to thank them for their aid of Professor Turcheff. Such aid had been valuable but in fact hadn't been necessary. Turcheff had mis-taken a request for information on Chernobyl as a threat to his earlier research. The Nobelists furnished a letter from the Professor admitting his confusion and saying that no better friends existed for scientists than the Greens.

Tannenbaum visited Joan's parents in Walnut Creek to say that their daughter was well and had become involved quite innocently in a matter that would aid suffering people every-where—a great technological event. She'd be home soon. Scott was present and was asked not to say anything to his father. Tannenbaum, citing Joan without her permission, wanted no part of a well-heeled radical lawyer in Berkeley. Her parents felt the same way—being asked not to inform their former son-in-law made them more trusting of what they'd heard.

Carranza was to arrange the affairs of Pyotorov and Ms. Dunworth now that Professor Turcheff had announced to all concerned that he would not cooperate with the Mexicans if they persisted with their Tiberón scheme. Turcheff had managed this because both the Americans and the Russians had told the President of Mexico that his country would receive no blueprints and be provided no materials, nor be granted an inspection of working stations in the United States, until Professor Turcheff was satisfied about the fate of his friends. Turcheff had used his leverage, just as Alex had asked him to.

CHAPTER TWENTY-TWO

I T WAS EXPEDIENT FOR THE MEXICANS TO FIX THE SPRING mechanism on the automatic and to publish an autopsy report and the results of an inquest, neither in fact undertaken. But this wasn't convenient for others. Despite orders that loose ends be tied up, one-two-three, in the Soviet Union, the United States, and Mexico, it was inevitable that a wake trailed the events at the *Catch-22* set: the death of the Commissioner, the intrusion of Turcheff into the Protocol, and the demands of the Mexicans, all the trailing traces of edged remarks and frayed tempers. Sooner or later everything shows and everything plays. Even the presidents of the two powers weren't content to let subordinates and supernumeraries expediently explain away these aspects in the fate of their nations—as if to assume that the principals themselves were too austere to be bothered with an unprecedented event.

In the White House, the resident asked his counterpart in

Moscow, "Are you saying this isn't over with? There's more to come?"

The Soviet President began to perceive that whereas earlier, while Pyotorov and Turcheff were on the run, the American President had been uneasy about violating the rights of individuals and was tortured by the notion of covenants not openly arrived at, now he was being testy about having his hand forced by a foreign power in Mexico. It had quite on its own hunted down those same individuals and used them to find for itself a chair at the feast.

They lay on their sides inside the pyramid on the sand whispering into each other's lips.

"Can we make love, Alex, with a hundred soldiers listening?"

"Why not? Just try not to make your usual noises."

"What do I sound like?"

"Contented. If sex were a season, you'd be autumn, ripe but ready, colorful."

"That makes me an old bag!" She drew back. "Here we go again. Tell me you love me. Can't you lie? Tell me you can't live without me. No, scratch that last bit—it's too close to the truth. Alex, I'm sick of generalities. I'm sick of causes. I want to marry you."

They made love then, not caring about the soldiers, and not fearing that Turcheff might come calling, arriving in the launch from the cutter where he slept and took his meals. They made love on the heavy woolen blankets placed over a woven pattern of ironwood reeds, surprisingly comfortable, resting on the sand; and the sounds heard outside were oddly like the creaking of bedsprings.

It was also comfortably intimate to walk on the shoreline, where the soldiers limited them to a range of a hundred yards, fifty yards in either direction from the center of the tent. The food was good, the wine only usual, Hidago. Alex told Joan that the yellowtail snappers they ate were a lazy man's fish: they could be caught with bait made of spoons or feathers or plugs, and they could be baked, broiled, fried, or made into chowder. When she asked how he knew this, he told her the stories of the Seri Indians that he'd heard on Tiberón when he'd gone there all those years ago with Nikolai Miroset. At first she thought he was playing fancies against their plight— they *were* prisoners for the time being—but he convinced her that had they gone to the island, as the *maly protokol* provided, he could imagine her becoming the second Lola or the returned Queen of the Seris, come to reign again on the heights and sands of Shark Island. The first queen had been Dolores Casanova, known as Lola, the daughter of a rich Guaymas family. She had joined the Seris, gone native, abandoning her rich Spanish family and marrying a shaman who, it happened, was later to kill her father. She had retreated to the island, where the Indians with their ironwood spears were shark hunters and deer stalkers. She had borne the shaman sons and then she had died before the Seris were finally humiliated.

Joan thought the legend crazy, but no more so than Alex's detailed descriptions of how he and Joan were likely to die on the island. He dwelled at length on the contours of the southern shore of the island, where American pleasure boats fished for 150-pound groupers, and on the dangerous effect of the tides on anyone who attempted to swim the narrows between the island and the mainland.

There were only three days left on the Protocol schedule when the Commandant, two captains, and three sergeants arrived at the tent to remove Alex and Joan and their belongings to the large cutter, *General Obregón*. Aboard they met Turcheff, who was to accompany them across the border into the

United States. From there they would drive away to northern California, while Turcheff, once he was satisfied about their safety, went to Mexico City to wait until the Protocol was announced. Then he could board a plane for Moscow.

"Let me put it this way," Tannenbaum said to Matthews. "Assume that the Mexicans won't trust Petrie and his girl once they are let loose in the United States. Let's say that Carranza can foresee the awful publicity if they talk, the whole rotten story."

"What would the story say? In detail, I mean?" Matthews was not unaware of the dread possibilities still lurking around the Commission and the United States.

"Petrie or Ms. Dunworth, separately or together, depending on how safe Petrie feels, could begin with the Commission's setup at Harkness Pavilion. Then talk about the Mafia, *always* good copy. Then move to that lodge near Petaluma for a dramatic scene—a hideout or a safe house, whatever, where there is shooting and a dead man left behind as the couple desperately escapes. Now the story could shift to Moscow, to the mistake of the Deputy and how Turcheff used the environmentalists as an underground. Then it moves to the old *Catch-22* movie set. The Commissioner defects, and in the interests of all nations is murdered by someone, preferably the distinguished scientist. Yet the murder is covered up by the Mexicans so they can blackmail the United States and the USSR."

Matthews lit a cigar with no ritualistic motives, not tapping it for dryness or cutting off exactly three eighths of an inch or replacing the cutter attached to the gold chain running from the slit in his jacket lapel to his lapel pocket.

"In this gothic tale of yours, Chief, you haven't even come to the secret technology and its cornucopia." He surprised Tannenbaum by his summing up. "You're right. The story is fabulous. A book publisher would pay at least fifteen million for U.S. rights. Foreign rights would be worth twice that much, counting newspaper serialization. Worldwide theater and TV and movie and videocassette rights ought to buy another fifty or so million. Altogether, yes, it's a hundred-million-dollar script. Having established *that,* what have you got?"

"What I've got," Tannenbaum said in a change of tone, "is that the Mexicans will get rid of Petrie and the girl without Turcheff's knowing it. Turcheff will be safe once he gets back to Moscow." His expression was dour. "God, I hope I'm wrong."

"And what do you propose? I cannot go to the White House over this." Matthews shot his eyebrows.

Tannenbaum almost laughed. Go to the White House! The Commission was at low ebb. Only the President had been able to stop the crisis of shame, the demands for dissolution. He'd already told Matthews that the Commission would in future not be allowed to deal with any persons or bodies designated by the National Security Council. Nonetheless, Matthews thought that the Commission's "splendid record" would enable it to survive the crisis, but the Chief found it more plausible to believe that the President felt a certain remorse over the death of Haagstrom and wouldn't let the Commission be buried alongside him.

Viktor Ivanovich Turcheff sat on the sunny side of *General Obregón* in a chair that was more suitable to an office than to a deck: tufted leather upholstery, large brass tacks holding it in place, and a mahogany frame. He wore a double-breasted lightweight suit that looked like linen—Joan wondered, had the Mexicans brought a tailor from Mexico City?—the color and texture of what in the old days was called an ice-cream suit. He was freshly barbered, his gray mustache trimmed, his hair in back shaped to the contour of his skull, not to fill the space between a fur hat and a heavy overcoat collar as was customary in Moscow. He was rereading Turgenev, a book he'd brought with him on his long underground journey from Moscow.

"Did they tell you the itinerary?" Joan asked, once greetings were exchanged, with Alex uncharacteristically not embracing Turcheff but shaking his hand.

The Professor rose to give her his chair, but she declined, keeping her back to the morning sun. *General Obregón* had sailed at about 0800 hours, departing the waters off Bahía de Kino and heading northward, keeping between Tiberón and the mainland. From Bahía de Kino to Mexicali on the border is about three hundred miles, but Turcheff said he had been told by the captain of the cutter that they'd head north-northwest to San Felipe on the east coast of Baja California, only about two hundred miles. There they'd board a plane and fly to the American town called Calexico across the border from Mexicali. Turcheff had already timed the journey. At twenty knots, they should enter the harbor at San Felipe by six or seven o'clock in the evening. Certainly they'd take off before dark. He told Alex he had insisted on landing inside the United States.

At midday, after their lunch on the aft deck, on what was in fact a helicopter pad where a table and chairs were set up for the three of them—the Mexican officials and the ship's officers ate in the wardroom—Alex led Joan to their cabin on the upper of the two decks that had portholes.

"Alex, you're killing him, being so formal and distant. Can't you let up a little?"

"He's not the man he was. I wouldn't have thought him capable of murder."

"He *is* the man he was. You're not the same. He is."

"What do you mean?"

"You are beginning to care about things and, better, about people."

"Are we talking about you and me?"

"God, I hope so! And you and Viktor. So talk to him now, while there's time."

Turcheff had always assumed that getting old was a phase in a man's life like others, growth and decay both being the normal order of things—Shakespeare's stages of man—but over the past three weeks he had realized that it was too glib a formulation.

An old man is an alien even in his own country. He is a person who will soon die and this identifies him specifically as nothing else does. "What will you do with your life?" is not a question addressed to someone who is seventy-two. Walking about Moscow, he often had stopped at cemeteries and occasionally had seen a headstone with all the letters incised and a photograph embossed and protected by a heavy plastic, but the grave was yet to be occupied. What did it mean? It meant that an old person did not trust even his friends and relatives to get his name and birth date right or to remember those of his children who had died before him. It wasn't a sign of vanity, these headstones. It was a sign of despair.

"Viktor, I have treated you badly and I apologize. Rudeness to an old friend is a form of treachery. I'm sorry." Alex said it in Russian, carefully not using Turcheff's patronymic, Ivanovich, and thus emphasizing his intimacy with the old man.

"You have done nothing. You have been shaken by the violent act of an old man who felt trapped and wanted to do something positive—yet did the opposite and took an innocent man's life. We could have been friends, Haagstrom and I, were time not so relentless."

"It wasn't history that determined your actions, Viktor, believe me."

"I know. I know. I don't believe in history any more. Neither did Mr. Gorbachev. No, I said *time*. Everything happens, only some happenings precede others. I am not now the man who shot the Commissioner, yet in that moment I was myself entirely. I was impelled to act by a force that overwhelmed my senses. Regret. That was the force. Regret. Isn't *that* a terrible irony!"

"I was angry," Alex replied, "because I thought you put Joan and me in danger. But that's nonsense. We were already at risk. And we are now."

Turcheff's head snapped upward, his eyes focusing on Alex with a fearful intensity.

"Now?"

"Yes, now. We will go ashore at San Felipe, as the Commandant told you, and we'll take a plane out to Calexico. We must now insist on Yuma, Arizona."

"Why?"

"Because once we part in the United States there'll be a surprise waiting. An automobile will be offered to Joan and me that is wired to explode a half hour after the ignition is turned on. Or a pair of assassins will be waiting to attack us as soon as you've left for Mexico City."

"I can insist that I talk to you from Mexico City, say, the day after I leave you."

"And if I'm not available for the call, then what?"

"Alexandr, it's Joan you are worried about, isn't it? This is the first time you have loved a woman."

"Yes. But it's more, Viktor Ivanovich. I'm ready to rejoin humankind. I've bragged that I have been generally fearless. That may be a matter of glands, not character. But one ought to be fearless in the cause of another person, apart from oneself alone. I know now why I joined the Commission. I was able to perform legal and moral acts without *initiating* them. Now, it's different. I've seen what an action that is deemed correct can do if the perpetrator fails to obtrude his own views and his own feelings. I've seen that looking after yourself can be dangerous to others. Yes. Viktor, I'm back."

CHAPTER TWENTY-THREE

———————— • ————————

S AN FELIPE IS A TRICKY HARBOR TO SAIL INTO BECAUSE THE
tidal changes can be as much as twenty-five feet, but it is
good as a shipyard and dry dock because at high tide a vessel can be brought to land to rest on chocks or can be tied
at a pier with clear access to the machinery on the dock. Joan
watched with wonder as they approached: every cove and bay
in the Gulf of California seemed to be guarded by a sentinel,
a high volcanic peak, here Punta de Machorro. The harbor
was almost too perfect: a true rectangle, all sides proportion-
ate to the narrow entrance, the whole made of rocks and booms.
Once *General Obregón* was tied, its fore and aft lines looped
around large lead bollards, the crew made ready to move their
luggage to a waiting car. Joan stood topside with Turcheff,
alongside the Commandant and his army aides. Alex excused
himself, saying to the captain in Spanish that the excellent fish
had caused an uproar in his bowels. The Commandant per-

mitted himself a small smile. Gringos had weak stomachs and big mouths.

Below, Alex went toward the boatswain lockers, knowing that all the deckhands were topside for the docking. He used a wrench he found on a worktable to break open the armament chest he'd seen earlier in the day, when he had asked, emphasizing his engineering career, for a tour of the cutter. Coaching Turcheff to insist on the tour, he had got the Professor to accompany him and two of the cutter officers. He was not disappointed. Inside were twelve rifles with ammunition and six sidearms, Colt .45s with the modern replaceable cylinders already loaded. He put a .45 in his belt at the back, under the coat he wore—having joked, again in front of the Commandant and others, that if his Russian friend was going to be formal, he must be so as well. Two cylinders he put in his jacket pocket, but then removed one because together they weighted the cloth too visibly. The .45 didn't bulge, he hoped, because the Commandant knew he wore a money belt.

Soon they were ashore and seated in a Cadillac, the three of them in the rear, with one captain in front beside the sergeant driver. Behind them was another Cadillac carrying the Commandant, a second captain, and another sergeant. All the Mexicans except the Commandant carried sidearms. Would they as foreigners be allowed to walk about in the airport inside the United States with weapons? Not under ordinary circumstances, but no doubt Washington had cleared the way. At the airfield northeast of the bay, just beyond Punta de Machorro, there was waiting a Citation 3, a plane that could hold eight passengers, in this instance the three civilians, the Commandant, two captains, two sergeants. It took off against the wind, westward.

"We were not able to make arrangements at Yuma," the Commandant said in Spanish to Alex. "Not enough time. We'll land at Calexico—in the U.S., of course. That should suit you nicely. El Centro is not far, and there you will be on Route 8, the main highway, which can take you either to San Diego or to Phoenix or Tucson. Very convenient."

Alex nodded. He didn't translate for Turcheff and Joan. Nor did he show his skepticism: if his worst fears were realized, he knew that the officials had set up in Calexico yesterday and practiced their routine—they could hardly set up in Yuma on a few hours' notice. It was seven thirty when they took off. Fifty minutes later they put down in Calexico, the light failing fast. They didn't taxi to the small terminal but stayed out on the tarmac.

"Cars will meet us here," the captain told Alex, who now had his answer about the firearms. No tourists in the terminal would see armed soldiers.

This time the cars were not Cadillacs but Fords; again there were two. Turcheff and Joan had said nothing during the flight and remained silent now as their luggage, not including Turcheff's, was transferred from the C-3 to the cars. Now and then they looked at Alex as if waiting for him to give a signal. But he was expressionless, and whatever he said in Spanish sounded to them like small talk. They now sat in the same order as before, as in the Cadillacs. The Fords drove out a gate that opened as they approached. Alex was now uncertain. They were on American soil, approaching Route 5, no more than three or four miles from El Centro. Would the soldiers dare make a move on the highway, near a town? Then he saw the shape of their design. The cars pulled up at the apron in front of a service station. But the station was closed. At nine o'clock in the evening in tourist season, it should have been open. A Nissan was parked nearby—*their* gift of a going-home car, his and Joan's.

On the darkened pavement of the station, everyone emerged from the Fords, stretching their legs. No orders were voiced. Joan and Turcheff stood near *their* captain and sergeant. Alex moved over to the Commandant, where he stood with the other captain and the sergeant.

"Mrs. Dunworth wants to use the restroom, Commandant," Alex said.

He knew the officer would not refuse so normal a request in front of the Professor. It would be suspiciously arbitrary were he to refuse. Now, Alex hoped that he'd gain time and circumstance. If the restroom was open, they had more time. If it was closed, they'd gain still more time and maybe cause inattention if it required opening the station to find the restroom key. He prayed for a foul-up, the restroom closed and some uncertainty how to open the station itself.

Why had the Mexicans chosen this station to arrive at in the night, risking a bureaucratic foul-up? They wanted no onlookers, obviously, no witnesses. If Joan and he were to die, it must be on U.S. soil, victims of an accident of sorts—nothing to do with Mexican authorities.

Alex was certain that the Nissan was wired to explosives, probably on a timer set for a half hour. No, an hour, enough time to get through El Centro even if they stopped to make telephone calls. And time enough for Turcheff to be returned traveling over Mexican airspace.

One captain left Joan and Turcheff and took with him a sergeant. They went over to the restrooms, shook the door handles, and returned to where the Commandant stood. He in turn ordered the two sergeants to force open the station doors.

Now.

Alex pulled out the .45 and shot the Commandant in the

head. He fired at the two captains four times, hitting each in the chest, then replaced the cylinder even though there was one bullet left.

"Get back into the Ford, Joan! Take Viktor with you! No! Don't look at me. Move! Drive away. Keep going north on Five! Don't wait. Do it!"

By now the two soldiers at the station entrance had begun firing. The light was bad and he was not hit. He got into the second Ford, keeping his head low, and charged the engine with his foot hard on the accelerator, driving between the pumps and the entrance, forcing the two men to jump inside, crashing the glass doors of the station. He kept going around the back of the station and then slowed.

Now he put three rounds into the Nissan, hoping to ignite the gelatinite explosive he was certain had been implanted in it. One round went into the engine block. Another hit near the floor pedals, as best as he could gauge while driving and firing out the window, and a third he fired into the rear, hoping at least to hit the gas tank.

It was the second round that proved him right. A huge explosion went up, the force pushing his Ford sideways even as he gunned the car away to mount the highway. Into the air went the windshield, the Nissan doors, parts of the engine, and, amazingly, the front seat intact. A second explosion followed when the gas tank erupted.

In his rearview mirror he saw that the soldiers had stopped firing and were lying on the ground for safety's sake. His last glimpse showed them fleeing the station. No doubt they feared that the underground gasoline tanks would blow soon.

He pulled up alongside Joan, who had slowed, then stopped on hearing the explosion. Her car was on the edge of the four-lane highway leading to El Centro.

Alex rolled down the passenger window and leaned across.

Joan looked at him with wonderment. Turcheff turned, staring back at the huge fires at the station.

"What do you say? It's over. We're safe—all three of us. Let's pick up Scott in Walnut Creek and catch a plane for Moscow."

"Are you sure?" Joan asked, her eyes wide from the lingering fright of a melodrama that was real: you're-dead-if-you-don't-move.

"What if I said I love you?"

"Then I'd be sure."

She managed a smile, turned to Turcheff, and gently brought his head around from its fixation on the skyline a mile back.

"Viktor, we have to do what he says. He's sure of you and me—and he doesn't ask what we think. You get your Protocol with or without Mexico. He gets me."

"Thank God," Viktor said in Russian, addressing Himself.

END

LEE COUNTY LIBRARY
107 Hawkins Ave.
Sanford, N. C. 27330

LEE COUNTY LIBRARY SYSTEM
DISCARD
3 3262 00116 2301

MAY 3 0 1991

JUN 1 7 1991 JUN 0 8 1991

Jovanovich   JUN 2 4 1991
A slow suicide
                         JUN 2 8 1991

LEE COUNTY LIBRARY
107 Hawkins
Sanford, N. C. 27330

DISCARD